This is no dream . . .

He fell, tumbling slowly in the cool air, recalling nightmares of falling into a bottomless pit. In a strange paradox of feeling, the knowledge that it was really happening saved him from the horrid, nightmarish sensation of falling. This turning of reality upside-down made him laugh, and the realization that he had time to laugh made him aware that he was falling a considerable distance. The air was buffeting his face with increasing force as the relentless acceleration of gravity continued to do its work.

This is it, he thought. *The end . . .*

Other AvoNova Books by
Mark Leon

THE GAIA WAR
MIND-SURFER

THE UNIFIED FIELD

MARK LEON

AVONOVA
AVON BOOKS • NEW YORK

THE UNIFIED FIELD is an original publication of Avon Books. This work has never before appeared in book form. This work is a novel. Any similarity to actual persons or events is purely coincidental.

AVON BOOKS
A division of
The Hearst Corporation
1350 Avenue of the Americas
New York, New York 10019

Cover art by Daniel Horne
Published by arrangement with the author
Library of Congress Catalog Card Number: 96-96449
ISBN: 0-380-78651-6

First AvoNova Printing: November 1996

Printed in the U.S.A.

RA 10 9 8 7 6 5 4 3 2 1

This is for Bob and Lee
The Most Excellent of Parents

1

The Biggest Story Ever

Ira Summerset was enjoying the novelty of the brew-pub. Texas law had just changed, allowing beer retailers to produce their own stuff.

He was drinking their latest concoction, a dark amber brew, light on the carbonation and heavy on taste. "What's that stuff?" a tall, lean man with dark hair and eyes asked Ira. The stranger could have been anywhere between thirty-five and a well-preserved fifty. It was dark, and Ira was himself reaching the age when the young look younger, and everyone else just looks more the same.

"Odyssey Ale," Ira said. The stranger ordered a pint and sat down. The owners had spared no expense on the bar; everything was done up in polished wood and brass. Slow-turning ceiling fans, purely for looks since the place was air-conditioned, gleamed in the soft, carefully understated lighting.

"Pretty good," the stranger said, after taking a cautious sip.

"I like it," Ira said, "but I really don't know much about beer."

"Neither do I, but you know they say beer is the reason for civilization." The stranger managed to sound both matter-of-fact and dramatic.

"Oh?" Ira half turned toward him.

"Yeah. Agriculture wasn't originally for making bread. It was to ensure a stable supply of grain for brewing beer. Egypt. Everything started in Africa, *or so they say*." The man laughed.

It was a peculiar laugh. Ira almost thought it bitter, but there was a lighthearted edge to it. It bordered on manic, slightly mad-sounding, yet there was too much awareness and self-control in the way it tailed off into thoughtful silence.

"Interesting," Ira said. "I seem to remember hearing something like that before, but I . . ." He hated to leave sentences dangling. It was a habit Ira found most annoying in others.

"Didn't know whether or not to believe it," the stranger finished the sentence.

"Yeah." Ira took another sip of beer.

"I know the feeling," the man said. "I've seen so many things that I'm not sure I believe anything anymore—or maybe I believe everything."

This statement caught Ira's interest. It wasn't what the man said so much as how he said it. It's the kind of thing you might hear in any bar. But there was a quiet reserve, and, Ira thought, an *authority* that was compelling.

Another thing was that, in spite the man's strange laugh and the *ironic* air that surrounded him, he was curiously lacking in cynicism. Ira knew firsthand about the cynical side of things. It went with his job as a reporter. And, as a reporter, he was supposed to be naturally curious about the strange and unusual. So he forced himself to say, "Really? What have you seen?"

The man laughed again, this time quite softly. He took another, longer, sip and said, "You want the short or long answer?"

"That depends," Ira said.

"On what?"

"How long is the long answer?" Ira said.

"Right, wouldn't want to get bogged down in an epic, would we?"

"Is it an epic?"

"Not really. That's a bit of hyperbole on my part," the stranger said. "A true epic is supposed to contain an entire worldview, a *universe,* if you will. I can't really make such grandiose claims for my own experiences, but they are highly unusual, and possibly significant."

"What's your line of work?" Ira asked, wanting both to keep the conversation going and steer it onto more manageable terrain. To Ira's annoyance the man found this question quite funny and laughed so hard he nearly choked on his beer.

"Sorry," he said. "I don't mean to be rude, it's just that . . ." This time *he* left the sentence dangling.

"What?" Ira said.

"Let's just say that I'm a scientist."

"OK," Ira said warily.

"Alan Fain," the stranger said, turning to face Ira. Ira was struck by the angular, nearly chiseled features of Alan's face. He had seldom seen anyone with such a *well-defined* look. At the same time it wasn't a face that could easily be pegged. Whatever Alan was, Ira was not familiar with it.

"Ira Summerset." Ira stuck out his hand. He noted that Alan's handshake was good, not one of those fashionable, barely perceptible clasps that Ira found so repugnant.

"So what do you do, Ira?"

"I'm a reporter."

"Really?" Alan's right eyebrow went up, indicating an interest that did not seem nearly as forced or feigned as Ira had come to expect.

"Yeah, really," Ira said, and turned back to his beer.

"The *Sun*?"

"Yeah." Ira confirmed that he worked for the city's one major daily newspaper. He neglected to mention that he might not work there much longer.

"Tough for reporters these days?" Alan said.

"Uh, yeah," Ira said, surprised.

"Working on anything interesting?"

"Well, some political stuff, but right now things are kind of slow."

"I might have something for you," Alan said with such calm intensity that Ira turned back to face him. Alan's pint was almost empty.

"Another one?" Ira said.

"No thanks," Alan said. "I try not to overdo it, and besides . . ." He paused, apparently trying to decide what to say. "I'm working on something. I need to get back to it."

"On Saturday night?" Ira said.

"*Every* night," he said. "Do you have a card?"

"Yeah." Ira held out his business card. Alan took it and got up. "What's this story you might have?" Ira said, trying not to show too much interest and failing.

Alan smiled. "This isn't the best time or place, but it could be big, the story of the century. In fact it could be the biggest story ever."

"Damn!" Ira said to himself after Alan left. The curse was for two reasons. He felt foolish for almost believing the stranger might really have something that could save his career, but Ira also regretted not having had the presence of mind to get Alan's phone number, just in case . . .

"Another one?" the pretty bartender said. Ira looked up to see her flip a strand of blond hair from her face as she ran a rag across the bar.

"Sure, why not?" The bitterness of his own voice startled him.

2

Synchronicities

The following Monday was pretty much what Ira expected.

"You know your stuff is good," Drake, the city editor, said.

"Yeah," Ira said, "I *know*. Nearly as good as the stuff Leslie, that new police reporter, churns out. Her copy just *sizzles*. Where did you *find* her anyway?"

"No need to get sarcastic, Ira."

"I'd say this was the perfect moment for sarcasm," Ira

said. "You're about to fire me for all the wrong reasons and . . ."

"You know if it were up to me . . ." Drake said. "I told you, corporate wants us to do *people* stories. You're an issues man. They just don't appreciate that kind of approach."

"Intelligence and good writing is what they don't appreciate," Ira said, "and don't give me that people vs. issues crap. Christ, Drake, I never thought I would be hearing this from you."

"I know," Drake said, "I hate it, but what do you want me to do? I could get myself fired, too, but what good would that do?"

"Give me another week," Ira said.

"A week? What for? They aren't going to change . . ."

"Even if I get them a *people* story? I think I may have just the guy."

"I don't think . . ."

"What if this guy turns out to be the biggest story ever? What then? What if I go freelance and sell it somewhere else? Then it's *your* ass that will be on the line for missing the scoop of the year."

"What are you talking about?" Drake said, looking at Ira with some concern.

"I don't know," Ira said. "Maybe nothing, but I have a feeling about this one."

"Tell me about it."

"No. Give me a week. If I'm right, we will both be happy. Otherwise, I'll quit, move down to Corpus, and open that bait shop."

"You and your *bait* shop."

"I'm serious," Ira said.

"You will never run a bait shop," Drake said. "You can't be anything but a reporter, and you know it."

"Nice of you to notice, after you have fired me," Ira said.

"OK," Drake said. "You have your week. If I were you, I'd use it to send out résumés."

"Thanks. I'll keep you posted."

* * *

Ira tried getting Alan's number, but it was unlisted. So he called in a favor. Ira had done a series on a young computer hacker a few years earlier. The guy had been given an unusually harsh sentence for breaking into the local phone company's system. Ira's articles had helped get him paroled.

"Sure," the kid said, "I can get unlisted numbers, but I don't want to go back to jail. You're talking about a very serious parole violation here."

Ira promised that he would go to bat for him again. In the end it took money, but the kid agreed to do it.

When Ira got back from a long coffee break there were two messages. One was from the hacker. He had Alan's number. The other was from Alan. He said he had something interesting and left his number. "Synchronicity," Ira muttered.

"What?" Leslie of the police beat was walking by and heard him.

"It means two hundred dollars up in smoke," Ira said.

"No it doesn't. It means a coincidence that signifies something." She said this very seriously.

"It was a joke," Ira said, and started to explain.

"There is nothing funny about synchronicities," she interrupted. "They are important clues."

"Clues to what?" Ira said, staring at her. Leslie's humorless intensity baffled him.

"Never mind," she said in a resigned tone of voice, and walked away.

Ira was eager to call Alan and didn't like it, thinking, *How could this strange man have anything that would make a difference to my career?* Ira felt like a man going under, grasping at straws.

He resolved to call him later. It was a statement he was making to himself. Ira was going to play it as cool as possible, no matter how desperate he felt.

It was hot and humid outside. The Texas heat was dragging the city, reluctant and limp, into the dog days of August. Ira headed toward the capitol.

The Speaker of the House was addressing a half-empty chamber, making some sort of impassioned statement about space exploration. Ira asked him afterward what it was all about.

"You know that we have all but abandoned any real commitment to go to Mars," he said.

"Yeah, but what has that got to do with the state budget? That's all federal. You aren't seriously proposing that we start a Texas Space Agency?" Ira said.

"TASA." He tried the acronym out. "I don't like it. It doesn't *suggest* anything. Know what I mean?"

The Speaker, like many before him, had a reputation. Texas House Speakers can get away with a certain kind of crazy. It is expected of them. But this wasn't the right kind of crazy. Shooting at garden hoses that seem to crawl in the dark is OK. Trips to Mars on state time is not. Ira said as much.

"You never know, Ira. This is Texas. Stranger things have happened." Ira started to say, *Like what*?, but the Speaker put his arm around the reporter's shoulder and said, "Let's get some lunch."

"Uh, I . . ."

"Don't tell me that Ira Summerset, the premier political correspondent for the *Texas Sun* is going to turn down a lunch invitation from the Speaker of the House!" he said with mock indignation.

The truth was that Ira wanted to call Alan. He was already worried that he had waited too long. What if Alan had given the story to someone else? Ira was also annoyed with himself for thinking this way, failing to stay cool. After all, he had no real reason to believe there *was* a story.

"I'm working on something right now," Ira said.

"What? Something big?"

"Could be."

"What could be bigger than an expedition to Mars? I'm talking about space, Ira. The *final frontier*." He was grinning. Ira couldn't tell whether or not he was serious. The Speaker had the air that only a seasoned politician gets, making it impossible to tell if anybody is at home behind the handshake and the smile.

"I'll bet you're going over to talk to that dickless,

backstabbing attorney general of ours . . ." the Speaker said.

"Can I quote you on that?"

"Sure! I dare you! It's about time somebody told the truth about that pipsqueak."

"What's the truth?" Ira said.

"Funny you should ask that," the Speaker said, his tone suddenly shifting to the philosophical. They were standing in the big rotunda. He walked slowly to the center of the marble floor and stood in the middle of the five-pointed, lone star. He began whispering something.

Ira went over to him, half-convinced the politician had finally gone nuts. He was repeating the phrase, "What is truth?"

"Put your head next to mine, Ira."

"What?" Ira asked, looking around nervously.

"I'm not going cozy on you. Just do it. You'll see."

Ira did, and found it weird. The acoustics of the big dome caused the Speaker's voice to reverberate back to where they were standing so that the whispered phrase kept coming back in on them, barely audible yet strangely resonant, "What is truth, what is truth, what is truth . . ."

"Wow!" Ira said. A woman gave him a strange look, and he quickly jumped away from the Speaker.

"Damnedest thing, huh?" the Speaker said, laughing. "Most people don't know about it. This dome resonates!" He looked up into the huge, cavernous space. "That's Pilate's question, you know?" he said, looking back at Ira.

"Huh?"

"Pilate's question," he said. " 'What is truth?' That's what Pilate asked Jesus before he had him killed."

"Oh."

"Damn, Ira. Don't you have a philosophical streak in you? You're a fucking reporter, for Christ sakes!"

"Reporters aren't supposed to think," Ira said.

"Really? What's wrong, Ira? Problems at the *Sun*."

"They want more fluff," Ira said. "They want *people* stories. I'm not a people person, I guess. I'm an ideas man, or so Drake tells me."

"Don't tell me they are going to fire you!"

Ira didn't say anything.

"Those damn fools! You're the best political writer we've had in this town since Billy Lee Brammer."

"That's alright, Cliff you don't have to . . ."

"No, man, I *mean* it! Ever since Gannet bought your rag it's been going down the tubes, but I never thought they would be that stupid. Hell, this means you *got* to have lunch with me!"

"Why's that?"

" 'Cause if they want people stuff, man, have I got a person for you!"

"Thanks, Cliff, but I need to get back to this other thing. Drake sort of gave me another week to come up with something."

"Forget it!" the Speaker said. His face was all flushed. He had stepped out of the center of the star and grabbed Ira by the elbow. They were moving toward the exit. "This guy is one of the strangest fellows I've ever met. He's a research scientist too—not with the university. Matter of fact I don't know who he's with, but . . ."

Ira stopped and disengaged myself. "Would this guy's name be Alan by any chance? Alan Fain?"

"How did you know?"

"Synchronicity," Ira said.

"What?"

"Nothing. I'm a reporter remember. I'm *supposed* to know things."

"Oh yeah," the Speaker said without a trace of sarcasm. He sounded like a little kid.

They emerged into the blaze of the Texas sun. As they were descending the capitol steps the Speaker stopped and let out a violent sneeze, which shook his big frame.

"Summer cold?" Ira said.

"Hell no." Cliff laughed. "Photo sneeze reflex."

"What?"

"Light, especially sudden, bright sunlight, triggers the sneeze reflex in some people. I've had it all my life. It's genetic. I enjoy it really."

"I see," Ira said. "So tell me about this Alan Fain."

"I'll let *him* do that," he said. "We're meeting him for lunch."

"Naturally," Ira said.

3

The Eyes of Texas

Alan didn't seem surprised to see Ira show up with Cliff. *Alan Fain would not surprise easily*, Ira thought. Alan projected an extraordinary persona—nothing outrageous—he was neatly dressed and groomed. It was the way he held himself, the the way he looked at you—subtle things, but they added up to a *presence* impossible to ignore.

Ira ordered his favorite dish, shrimp enchiladas.

"Funny scene in here with those things," Alan said.

"What things?" Ira said.

"Your shrimp enchiladas. It was a while back. I was having lunch with a friend, and . . . it's too weird. I'll just say that his food became rather animated."

Ira stared at him, not understanding.

"Never mind," Alan said. "That was another story.[1] It's really all the same story, but there isn't time."

"Does it have anything to do with your research?" Ira asked.

"Always," he said. "The work goes on and on." He smiled a private smile that made Ira all the more curious.

"Tell him about the spaceship," Cliff urged.

"Yeah, I guess now is the time to begin the next chapter of this crazy business," Alan said.

---

[1] *The Gaia War.*

"Spaceship?" Ira said.

"Local scale, aether transport would be a more accurate term," Alan said, "but I think we are stuck with the other term for better or worse."

"So?" Ira said.

"So what?" Alan said.

"Tell me about it." Ira was starting to get depressed. It seemed at that moment that his "big story" was really nothing more than the fantasy of a mad scientist filtered through the distorted ego of a pompous Texas politician. *Bullshit* would be a simpler, more accurate, description.

"You don't believe it," Alan said.

"Frankly, no," Ira said.

"Naturally," Alan said.

"Ira's a good reporter," Cliff said. "It's his job not to believe."

"My job too," Alan said.

"How's that?" Ira said.

"Read Popper on the philosophy of science," Alan said. "I don't wholly agree with him, but he has a point when he says the scientist's job is to *dis*prove rather than prove theories. Humans are passionate believers. The history of philosophy and religion is a grand testament to our will to believe. Scientists just try to inject a little sanity into the whole business, and that often requires a passion *not* to believe."

Cliff, strangely restless, said, "Yeah, but you have the real thing, right, Alan?"

Alan smiled enigmatically. "Maybe," he said. "But Ira here is right to dismiss it all as nonsense."

"But it's not nonsense!" Cliff said. He sounded angry.

"What's the big deal, Cliff?" Ira said, intrigued by the Speaker's sudden show of emotion.

"The big deal is two million dollars of state money!" he said.

"What?" Ira stared at him in astonishment.

"I mean," Cliff stammered, "that we are considering some discretionary funding, and . . ."

"Whoa!" Ira said. Cliff had said more than he intended, and Ira wasn't going to sit quietly while he tried to get the cat back in the bag. "State money! TASA. The Lone Star State finances a trip to Mars. What have you been up to, Mr. Speaker?"

"Keep your voice down!" he said in a violent whisper. "There's some boys from the AG's office in here."

"I see," Ira said. He just stared at the Speaker in amazement for a few moments, feeling light, almost giddy. The Speaker of the House secretly funneling money from the treasury into a backyard space project. *This was a story*!

"I know what you're thinking, Ira," Cliff said, "but you will be making the biggest mistake of your career if you act on it . . ."

"What do you expect me to do, Cliff?" Ira said. "Be reasonable. I'm a reporter! One who is about to lose his job."

"I'm not asking you to give up anything! This business about the money is trivial compared to what Alan has to show you."

"Trivial?" Ira said. "*How did you do it*, Cliff? At least tell me that? I wouldn't have thought it possible."

"There are ways," Cliff said, "and I'll tell you all about them. You don't get to be where I am without learning a few tricks. There are some pretty interesting clauses in our constitution about discretionary use of funds . . ."

"But two million bucks!"

"Think of it like this," Cliff said. "That money stands for something much bigger than you or me . . ."

"Or the law?" Ira said pointedly.

"Even the law," Cliff said. "And there's only one or two things bigger than the law."

"Like what?" Ira said.

"Well, God *maybe*," Cliff said, "but that's not what I'm talking about."

"Yeah?" Ira said, breaking Cliff's dramatic silence.

"*The Eyes of Texas*," Cliff said. "That's what the money stands for. This ain't no common case of embezzlement."

Ira was more impressed than ever with Cliff's abilities. The Speaker's rhetoric made the truth seem almost irrelevant. "OK, I'm along for the ride, but you know if this spaceship deal turns out to be what I think, I will have to shut you down, Cliff."

"Of course, I know," Cliff barked. "But you won't. I chose you because I know you're a man of vision. Like Alan here—and like me."

Ira noted Alan's deadpan expression and could hardly keep from laughing.

"The tab's on me, gentlemen," Alan said, picking up the check, "and then I suggest that we hit the espresso bar. Nothing like a good cup of the black water for the vision thing."

"You into these new coffee bars?" Cliff asked Ira.

"Yeah," Ira said. "And then I want to see this spaceship."

"Spaceships I can relate to," Cliff said, "but tiny, overpriced cups of coffee are a mystery."

4

Going With the Flow

One week later Ira was sitting in San Francisco's Golden Gate Park and shivering. The August fog was sitting on the city like a cold, wet blanket. He was thinking about his last meeting with Drake.

"I can't give you any more time, Ira," the editor said.

"I know," Ira said.

"So level with me. You look like the cat who swallowed the canary."

"You want to know why I'm not begging for my job," Ira said.

"Damn, Ira! We go back a ways. I don't like this any

more than you. If you have something, now is the time to deliver!''

''Sorry, Drake. I'm not ready.''

''Where are you going to go? What are you going to do?'' Drake said.

''I'm going to San Francisco,'' Ira said.

''Why?''

''Put some flowers in my hair,'' Ira said. Drake didn't smile. ''Actually I need to track down another source.''

''And then what?''

''I'm not too worried about that,'' Ira said. ''I think I'll do alright on my own. So long, Drake. I'll miss this place.''

He almost felt bad about it, but there wasn't time to dwell on the past. The future was approaching. Ira recognized him from the photo. His hair was shorter, but there was no mistaking the face. He wore black levis and a maroon T-shirt. There was symbol on the shirt that Ira recognized as a caduceus, serpents wrapped around a staff, the sign that doctors use.

''Ira Summerset?'' He stopped in front of the bench.

''Yeah.'' Ira stood, offered his hand, and noted that the man's grip seemed a little weak.

He instantly sensed Ira's assessment and said, ''I had a bad wrist injury a few years ago and was lucky to regain the use of my hand. It's thrown my tennis game off a little. I only notice it when I play . . . and shake hands.''

Ira saw a serious-looking scar on the other's wrist as he withdrew his hand. ''Wow,'' Ira said. ''That must have hurt.''

''It wasn't so bad. I would have gladly given up the hand if I could have stayed . . .'' His voice trailed off.

''Where?'' Ira prompted. ''Stayed where?''

''No place. That's all in the past. Neither here nor there.''[2] He laughed, and Ira thought the laugh was like Alan's but more emotional, almost poignant.

---

[2]*Mind-Surfer.*

"So you are Mr. Slack," Ira said to break the awkward silence that followed.

"Call me Lew," Lew said, and sat down on the bench.

Ira sat back down beside him.

"So you're a reporter," Lew said.

"Yeah."

"And Alan sent you after me."

"He wanted me to talk to you," Ira said. "He said that you would know about the . . ."

"Spaceship?" Lew said.

"Yes, the spaceship," Ira said.

"Of course. I know more about it than anyone besides Alan, although I haven't seen the full-grown version. How does it look?"

"It's green," Ira said.

"Of course it's green," Lew said. "It's solar powered, just like—" He stopped himself abruptly.

"Just like what, Mr. Sl—I mean Lew?"

"How much did Alan tell you," Lew said. "I mean about what went before?"

"He didn't tell me much, but I have already guessed that it was Alan who was behind last year's havoc in the desert. What did they call it? Oh yeah, the *Genesis Bomb*. And maybe you?"

Lew laughed again. There was nothing vulnerable in the sound this time, and Ira could see that he wasn't going to reveal any more, at least not directly. "OK," Ira said. "Never mind all that. I have seen the ship, and I'm amazed, impressed, and eager to get the rest of the story. Do you know why I'm here?"

"I can guess," Lew said. "Alan wants me to come back to Texas. He thinks he needs me in order to proceed with his plans to fly off into outer space or whatever crazy thing it is this time."

"That's right," Ira said.

"And he sent you because he thinks I will listen to a reporter, an objective third party who can convince me that this is really a fucking fantastic thing, and I should throw my hat once more into the ring—'the game's afoot' and all that sort of thing. Well, Mr. Summerset . . ."

"Call me Ira."

". . . the game may be once more afoot, but I have grown weary of the game. Let me tell you something." He looked at Ira with an intense expression.

"What?" Ira said.

"I am *happy* here. For the first time in my life. I came out here on my own with nothing, not knowing what to expect. I struggled, suffered through more indignities than I care to mention, but now I've got a life. A real *life!* Can you understand that? Do you know what that means?"

Lew's statement caught Ira by surprise. He had not expected such depth of feeling from this man, who had struck him initially as bright, but perhaps a little shallow. In addition what he said hit particularly close to home and Ira's own striving to make a career for himself as a journalist. "Yeah," Ira said, "I think I do."

Lew relaxed and they sat in silence for a few moments. The fog was getting even thicker. Ira had the strange sensation that they were suspended in time, that the moment would last forever, or would somehow slip into a kind of parallel eternity where they would always be there on that bench, lost in themselves but not so very far apart.

"Do you play tennis, Ira?"

"What?" Ira looked up, pulled back to the more familiar sort of time.

"Tennis, do you play?"

"Yeah," Ira said, "a little. I'm not particularly good, but . . ."

"That's OK. Neither am I. It's good for my hand. I need to try and build up the strength. Are you staying close by?"

"Not too far."

"Do you have shoes and shorts?"

"Yeah," Ira said. "I always travel with stuff for running."

"Good, I have spare racket. The courts here in the park are fantastic when they're all fogged in like this. It makes the game seem surreal."

And it did. Lew played with a passionate artistry. His game wasn't all that great. He had a decent forehand, although it was plagued by grip problems caused by the old injury. His backhand, serve, and volley were adequate and reasonably consistent. Ira could have beaten him were it not for the spirit Lew brought to the game. Lew played tennis as though it was all that mattered in the Universe. It was a quiet, self-absorbed energy. Ira sometimes got the feeling Lew was playing himself, and everything else was only incidental, like the trees or the fog.

Ira won the first set. Lew came from a three-game deficit in the second set to take it seven games to five. They were tied at eight games each in the third set and decided to settle it with a tiebreaker. It was the last, decisive point that best exemplified his playing. Ira had him cold. Lew was deep in the add corner of the court, and Ira was at the net. Lew's return was a high one, right to Ira's forehand volley.

Ira's volley was a little too hard, driving the ball deeper than he wanted, but it should have been a winner. Out of the corner of his eye Ira saw Lew flex his knees and leap for the other side of the court. Lew held his racket like a sword. Landing on his stomach he simultaneously twisted his spine in an agonizing effort. He just got his racket face on the ball. It was not well hit. He was way back, and Ira was certain that the ball would fall far short of the net, so he didn't move. Ira would later say that Lew actually willed the ball over. Had Ira not been so stunned, he would have saved the point. But he just watched that impossible arc of the ball as it rose past all reasonable expectation, bounced off the net cord, and fell dead in his court. Ira never forgot the look on Lew's face as he stood up. His elbows were bloody and he had a bad chin scrape, but his eyes were radiant. "Never say die," Lew said with a grin that was frightening in its intensity.

"You should have somebody look at that," Ira said, nodding toward Lew's elbow. They had showered and were drinking coffee in the Haight. Lew's right elbow was still bleeding. Ira thought the gash had nearly hit bone and said so.

"It'll be fine." Lew dismissed it with a shake of his head and sip of coffee.

"Do you always play like that?" Ira said.

"Like what?"

"Like the fate of the world hung in the balance."

"Only since I discovered the truth." Lew laughed.

"And what is that?" Ira said.

"That the fate of the world *does* hang in the balance."

"But it's only a game," Ira said.

"It's all a game," Lew said. "You just have to decide which parts matter most to you."

"And tennis is what matters for you?" Ira said.

Lew thought about this for a while. "It's not that simple," he said finally. "Tennis is just one thing that you can use."

"Use?" Ira said. "For what?"

"For bringing the mystery of life into focus," Lew said, "for renewing yourself. That's all we ever really want or need—a sense of the infinite and a reawakening of self.

"But this isn't what you came all the way from Texas to do—talk philosophy, I mean." He looked at Ira, who was struck by the sense of longing in those eyes. Lew seemed then like a man still infinitely far from his goal but driven by a deep desire to bridge the gap between dreams and reality.

"Alan told me . . ." Ira began.

"That he couldn't proceed without me," Lew said. "I know. Listen, I don't mean to be rude. I have to go, but I want you to come see the show tonight."

"Show?" Ira said.

"Yeah, my band, The Resonators. We're playing at the Mojo Palace. I'll make sure your name gets on the guest list. Maybe after you see the show you'll understand better why I don't want to go back.

Ira did. The inside of San Francisco's "historic" Mojo Palace theater is like the interior of a giant brain. Everything from the chandeliers in the domed ceiling down to the texture of the wood carvings on the walls suggests this. When The Resonators started playing the effect was enhanced.

Lew's guitar playing was like his tennis game. Technically it was merely adequate, but the energy he brought gave the music a unique, meandering, yet rhythmic sound that brought the kids to their feet. The result was a mass of individual cells all squirming to the same music, like a big brain. It was music which sustained a peculiar balance of spontaneity and structure. To be sure, *all* music does this to some extent—Lew's just did it in a way that sounded new.

Ira was surprised at the youth of the crowd. The Resonators' fans were mostly under twenty-five. The unique blend of traditional rock and roll, San Francisco psychedelic sound, and otherworldly modulations appealed to the kids.

Ira liked it, too. After the show, backstage, he said, "That was great. You guys ought to make a record."

"We're negotiating with a major label now," Lew said. "This is Tana, by the way."

"Hi." Tana extended her hand. She was not so young, at least mid-thirties. She had long, straight black hair. Her body was petite, and she projected a controlled sensuality.

"Tana writes for a local magazine," Lew said. "You two are in the same business."

"Do you write?" Tana said.

"I'm a reporter," Ira said.

"Wow," she said. "A real reporter." Ira couldn't tell whether or not she was being sarcastic.

"Ira's here to take me back to Texas," Lew said.

"Back to *Texas*." Tana said "Texas" like it was a disease. "Why?"

"Shades of the past," Lew said. He put his arm around Tana. She pressed into him and wrapped her arm around his waist.

"Interesting shades," Ira said. "And they're knocking on reality's door."

"Wow," Tana said. She wrapped her arms around Lew and kissed him. Lew opened one eye and looked at Ira as if to say, *See what I mean?*

* * *

"Did you give him the letter?" Alan said. They were sitting in his living room.

"Yeah,"

"Well?"

"He didn't read it," Ira said.

"I don't understand," Alan said. "He announced he was leaving one day last year. Just like that. I mean, it's not that Lew owes me anything. We're just friends, but he has been in on this since the beginning, and now when we are finally starting to get somewhere . . ."

"He thinks that this is just another road to nowhere," Ira said.

"Road to nowhere!" Alan said. "Finally mankind is ready to break free from the planet! Do you realize that the earth is really a huge gravity well? And we are stuck at the bottom! Our rockets really can't free us—they're too costly, too primitive. But with the levity drive we are finally free, *really* free.

"I know what Lew thinks. He thinks this will be like the other adventures. I have to admit that those didn't take us very far in the long run. Maybe they *were* dead ends, but this is something else—this is the real thing."

"You don't have to convince me," Ira said.

"What's he doing out there in San Francisco?" Alan said, almost whining.

"Playing tennis, and he has a band—The Resonators. I saw them perform. Pretty good actually."

"Tennis and rock and roll! That's nothing!"

"He would disagree, I think," Ira said, "but that's not all."

"I *see*." Alan smiled. "What's her name?"

"Tana," Ira said, "and she does seem kind of worth it."

"Don't they *all?*" Alan said. "Well, we can't come between true love, *can* we?"

Ira found the sarcasm in Alan's voice disturbing, but had little time to think about it, because the next thing Alan said was, "Want to go for another ride?"

* * *

It was like gliding except you weren't at the mercy of the wind. Alan said that he grew the ship, and Ira half believed him. The sleek craft consisted of an advanced, organic polymer shell around a light, metal alloy, carbon composite frame. But what made it seem alive was the feeling that the ship had senses of its own. Alan had to fly it—he used a sphere set in the panel in front of him, but the ship made little adjustments of its own when Alan's hands weren't on the controls. The result was an incredibly smooth ride. They almost never felt the bumps of unruly air currents.

The drive system enhanced the sensation of floating. According to Alan they *were* floating—this was the fantasy made real, antigravity. When Ira asked him how it worked, Alan said, "It simply recognizes gravity for what it is."

"What's that?" Ira said.

"Gravity is grave, serious. The ship uses a levity drive," Alan said.

"You mean we are flying because the ship has a sense of humor?" Ira said.

"Something like that." Alan smiled.

When Ira pressed for details Alan was so skillfully evasive that Ira decided a better explanation would have to wait.

Ira's first flight had been brief, a quick circle of the city, but this time they were much higher, and the lights of the city were receding. They were rapidly gaining speed and altitude. "Where are we headed?" Ira said.

"San Francisco," Alan said.

"But, why?"

"I need to talk to him," Alan said.

"Why did you send me?" Ira asked.

"I knew that Lew wouldn't listen to me," Alan said, "so I thought you could explain things to him in a way that would seem less provocative. But I should have known it wouldn't work."

"What makes you think he will listen to you now?" Ira asked. Alan just shrugged. "Another thing I don't get," Ira said.

"What's that?" Alan said.

"Why do you need him? You're the scientist. Why can't we just take this thing to the stars ourselves?"

"Now that is a very good question," Alan said, volunteering nothing in the way of an answer.

They continued to accelerate. With a shock Ira realized that they were out of the atmosphere. He could plainly see the curve of the earth's horizon and the thin little film of air that lies between terrestrial life and oblivion.

"What!" Ira exclaimed. He felt suddenly short of breath.

"We have our own pressurized air," Alan said calmly. "This is a spaceship, remember?"

"Yeah, but how . . ."

"We're solar powered. Every square inch of surface area uses an advanced form of photosynthesis. The energy pressurizes and filters our air, among other things. This thing is incredibly efficient. We have enough power right now to sustain us for several more hours in the deepest void. And if we were to run low, all I would have to do is aim for the sunny side and we could recharge."

"But . . ." Ira gazed out the clear polymer windshield, feeling something between awe and terror.

"Breathtaking, isn't it?" Alan said.

It was. They were only outside the biosphere for a few minutes. Their descent was rapid, and Ira wondered at the heat resistance of the vehicle. Even the most advanced synthetic materials would have burned away, but the hull remained intact, and the temperature inside stayed comfortably cool.

"You really *grew* this thing?" Ira said.

"Yeah," Alan said. The lights of the San Francisco Bay Area were already visible.

"Where are we going to land?" Ira asked.

"The park."

"The park? Which park?"

"Golden Gate Park, where else?"

"But . . ."

"Don't worry," Alan said. "It's night, and I know a

good spot just behind the conservatory. We'll be walking distance from Lew's place, too."

"What makes you think he will want to see you?" Ira said.

"The nuance of the moment," Alan said.

They touched down in a grove of trees behind the big glass palace that houses the tropical solarium. The descent was completely silent and, since they were running no lights, undetected. Alan skillfully brought the ship to rest in a particularly secluded place. It was extremely unlikely that anyone would stumble upon it in the dark.

"Where are we going?" Ira said, noting Alan's determined pace.

"The Haight," Alan said.

They walked into a coffeehouse that was jammed with students, aging hippies, poets, and tripsters. Ira could hardly believe the song that was playing on the radio. It was that old, shlocky Scott Mackenzie ballad about going to San Francisco. Alan looked around and smiled as if he had known that he would be there at just that moment.

"Hey!" somebody yelled. "Turn that crap off! Put on some music!"

The pretty, young coffee girl started to comply, but stopped abruptly when Alan yelled, "No!" All eyes in the place turned to where he and Ira stood. Alan spoke with serene authority. "Let it play," he said.

And they did. It was strangely quiet while they ordered coffee drinks. "I particularly like this part," Alan said as they sat down. Mackenzie was droning on about new vibrations.

Alan's infatuation with the melody and the lyrics was so infectious that Ira almost fell under its spell, but the sound of his name broke the momentary magic. "Ira, I thought you had gone back to Texas." Ira realized that he was staring at Lew, who had just walked in the door with Tana.

"Uh, yeah," Ira said, "I did but . . ." Alan turned around to face Lew, and Lew's eyes grew suddenly wide.

"Hi, Lew," Alan said.

"Oh man!" Lew said. "What are *you* doing here?"

"Going with the flow," Alan said.

"Yeah," Lew said. "I guess we are."

5

A Question of Evil

''Ira tells me your band is really something,'' Alan said. They were back at Lew's apartment. ''What do you call yourselves?''

''The Resonators,'' Lew said, ''Initially it was going to be The Resonators of Truth, but . . .''

''Yeah,'' Alan said, ''I know.''

Lew put on a tape. It was The Resonators, and Alan was impressed. ''I can see why you're happy here,'' Alan said. He carefully avoided looking at Tana, but she was staring at him, and the look in her eye was not friendly.

''Tell me about the spaceship,'' she said.

This caught Alan off guard. He looked first at Lew and then at Tana. She was smiling, but there was an edge to it. ''Uh . . . well it's not really . . .''

''I don't think Alan wants to talk about it right now,'' Lew said, trying to ease the tension.

''So you write?'' Ira said, looking at Tana.

''Yeah, sort of. I do music reviews for some of the local magazines. Its no big deal really,'' she said.

''Not much money in that, is there?'' Alan said, rather sharply.

''No,'' she said, looking at Alan with calm appraisal, ''but I get by.''

''I'm sure,'' Alan said.

The situation remained tense until Tana finally left. She claimed she had a deadline. Lew obviously didn't want her to go. ''Why did you have to be so rude?'' he said to Alan after she left.

"Rude? You told her about the project! I don't believe it! A stranger," Alan said.

"She's not a stranger to me," Lew said. "You have to understand, Alan, I have a new life out here. Tana is part of it. I'm hoping to marry her."

Alan snorted derisively. Lew ignored it and said, "Anyway I don't see what the big confidentiality deal is. After all, you brought Ira here in on it."

"That's different," Alan said. "Ira's a reporter. This is strictly business. We can't keep this secret forever, and when the time comes we'll need someone we can trust to break the story in a professional manner."

"Tana's trustworthy," Lew said.

"You're not going to like what I have to say," Alan said.

"Go on," Lew said.

"Tana may not be quite what she appears."

"What do you mean?" Lew said.

"Just that," Alan said. "There are forces involved here that you don't understand. *I* don't understand. I sensed something about her. It may be nothing, but . . ."

"But what!" Lew said, glaring at Alan. "You think you can just casually analyze the most personal details of my life? That's arrogant, Alan."

"Well, I'm arrogant then," Alan said. "I admit it. But use your head. Think! The arrogant are sometimes right, that's often what makes them arrogant."

Lew was so angry he couldn't speak. "Maybe we should go for a walk," Ira said.

"Yeah," Alan said. "I'm sorry, Lew. Despite appearances, I really don't want to be telling you how to run your life. Just come with us down to the park. You haven't seen the ship since the early stages. I think you'll be impressed."

Lew got up slowly. He put his jacket on, looked at Alan, and finally nodded, "OK," he said. "I can't deny that I'd like to see how she turned out. Let's go."

They walked in silence through the park. The fog was settling in, and Ira again had the impression that they were outside of ordinary space-time.

"I love the conservatory," Lew said, as they circled

around behind it. "During the day it's steamy and tropical inside. You can smell the lush jungles of the world. It reminds me of . . ."

"Yeah, I know," Alan said. "Me too. I'm telling you, Lew, you should come with us. There are Edens and Paradises beyond your wildest dreams up there." Alan pointed to the stars.

"I've already been beyond my wildest dreams, remember?" Lew said. "That's why I'm trying reality for a change."

"What is real?" Alan said.

"Nothing is real when you start to talk that way—" Lew began, but he was interrupted.

"No!" Alan said. "I don't believe it." He ran around, looking behind other nearby trees to make sure.

"What?" Lew said.

"It's gone! Stolen, hijacked!" Alan wailed.

"Impossible," Lew said. "Who would have known? And even if someone found it, they wouldn't have been able to . . ."

"Tana!" Alan said.

"What do you mean?" Lew said.

"I suspected," he said. "And now I know."

"Know what?" Lew's voice was tinged with fear.

"She's one of *them!*" Alan said.

"Who? What do you mean? Who are *they*?" Lew said.

"We're trapped!" Alan screamed.

Alan was uncharacteristically on the verge of hysterics, but he managed to get a grip. "What do you mean 'trapped'?" Ira asked him when Alan was again coherent.

"I told you," he said, looking at Ira with tears glistening in his eyes.

"What? Told me what?" Ira said.

"The gravity well," he said. "Earth is a gravity well. We have been stuck down here at the bottom for the entire history of human culture. In fact the story of humanity is really the story of our struggle with gravity. As long as we remain stuck to the finite surface of a sphere we are competing for limited resources."

"But," Ira said, "how can you say we are trapped when we are just where we have always been?"

"Exactly," he said, and hung his head dejectedly. "Exactly."

"Years ago, when I went to India and Tibet," Alan said, "I thought that the Universe was an absolute unity."

"What are you talking about?" Ira said. They were back in Lew's apartment.

"I'm talking about one of the oldest questions in the book," Alan said. "Are there any distinctions to be made in reality, or do all distinctions ultimately fade away into unity?"

"Oh," Ira said.

"Yeah," Lew said. Unlike Ira, Lew was warming to the topic. "The mystics of the East generally say that all duality is really illusion. I thought so, too, back in the days when life was simple." He said this with a trace of sarcasm.

"Well," Alan said, "whatever you decide is important because it colors the way you see the world. I won't go into all of it, but there is one thing in particular which is very important. You can't avoid it. You either come down on one side or the other."

"What's that?" Ira said.

"The problem of evil," Alan said. "If you reject all notions of duality, then you must also reject the concept of evil. Evil is that which is opposed to good. If evil just disappears into the absolute unity along with everything else, then there is really no difference between good and evil. A lot of the so-called New Age philosophies subscribe to this view."

"What view?" Ira said.

"The view that evil does not really exist, that all things are one."

"But you don't buy it anymore?" Lew said.

"No," Alan said. "I regret to say that I don't. I wish I could, but life is a teacher, isn't it? I would be a bad pupil if I insisted that the truth is what I want to believe. I want to believe that there is no such thing as evil, but I don't know how to account for my own experience, let alone all of human history, without admitting that there is some wicked stuff at play in the system."

Lew got up and walked over to the bay window. He stared out into the fog. Then he picked up the telephone and punched a preprogrammed number. He listened once more to the empty rings. When he came back and sat down he looked tired and heavy.

"Still no answer?" Alan said.

Lew shook his head. Finally he spoke, "What did you mean, Alan? One of *them*."

"It's what I'm trying to tell you," Alan said. "There are forces working against us. There always have been! The New Age mystics who try to deny this are deceiving themselves. Normally these forces keep a low profile. Sometimes we may suspect their existence, but they rarely show their hand directly. By developing the levity drive, we have forced them to become more active than they ordinarily like . . ."

"Are you talking about the devils and demons?" Ira said, incredulous. Ira was once again beginning to wonder about Alan Fain. A spaceship was fantastic enough, but now Alan was spouting occult, metaphysical nonsense.

"Call them what you like," Alan said. "They exist. To call them devils and demons is perhaps just what they want. It makes them sound preposterous, absurd. And it reinforces the idea that if we ever met a demon, we would recognize it. The reality is far more familiar, and, therefore, more dangerous. I don't know if they are demons and devils. But they are enemies. They want to keep us trapped here on earth while they help to turn the planet into a garbage dump."

"But why?" Ira said.

"You *are* a good reporter, Ira," Alan said. "You ask the tough questions. I'm not sure why. I'm not sure there is a why, or if there is I'm not sure they know it. Evil doesn't have to make sense. That's one way of recognizing it. The essence of our enemy may be nonsense, but that doesn't make the struggle any less real."

"So these forces, these *people* . . ." Ira said.

"Walk among us," Alan said, "and they always have."

"But Tana!" Lew said. "I can't believe it!"

"What made you suspect her?" Ira said.

"She had that look," Alan said.

"What look?" Lew said.

"Like she had been around for a long time," Alan said.

"How long?" Lew said.

"You don't want to know," Alan said quietly.

"How long!" Lew said. His fists were clenched.

Alan got up and began rummaging around in Lew's record collection. He found an old, vinyl album and put it on the turntable. "This thing still work?" he said.

"Of course," Lew muttered.

The thing sputtered to life and the track started out with pops and clicks, but, after a few seconds, the sound was remarkably clear. It was the Rolling Stones' "Sympathy for the Devil."

"Oh man!" Lew said.

"Yes," Alan said, "something like the song says." They listened to the music and watched the fog roll in. It *was* beautiful.

6

Another Story

When Ira got back to Austin things looked bleak. Without a real spaceship, his story was gone. He didn't bother to call Drake. Alan wasn't too happy either.

But Cliff was the most dramatically despondent. They were sitting in Cliff's big office. Alan was suffering the standard reaction to the painting on the wall behind Cliff's desk—interest, amusement, disbelief, and finally admiration for the personality that could so casually display such a ridiculous monument to the ego.

The painting was huge, 10' × 12'. The motif was aerial, almost aethereal. It featured Cliff at the center. It was a Cliff who looked twenty years younger. He was wearing form-fitting jeans and a denim jacket. He wore the jacket open with no shirt underneath. His chest was bulging with muscles which the Speaker had probably never possessed. Cliff, tan and wearing a Stetson hat, was flying, ascending through the fluffy clouds to the heavens with a burnt orange Texas sunset in the background.

Alan stared at the picture, waiting for Cliff to say something about it, but he was disappointed. Ira had never heard Cliff mention the thing. Finally Alan took his eyes from the wall and briefed the Speaker on the latest turn of events.

"What do you mean stolen?" Cliff said. His face drained of color, and there was raw fear in his eyes.

"I mean it's gone," Alan said.

"But . . ." Cliff couldn't even get the words out. Ira wasn't telepathic, but he knew what was on the Speaker's mind: the State Ethics Commission, the House Ethics Committee, the Travis County Grand Jury, and $2 million dollars of state funds with the Speaker's fingerprints on each bill.

"I'm sorry, Cliff," Alan said. "It's my fault. I should have been more careful. I should have known."

"You're sure it was the woman?" Cliff said, finally regaining some composure.

"Well, she's gone, too. Lew doesn't want to believe it. He's still hoping she just went on a sudden vacation, and it's a coincidence, but I know. I could tell."

"I *see,*" Cliff said. "They why the hell didn't you do something!" He slammed his fist down on the table, scaring Ira and Alan with his sudden fit. "She just did a ballet step up to you and stole my career away, is that right? I don't suppose you asked for a receipt! You should run for state treasurer, man! The agency accountants would *love* to do business with you boys!"

There was an awkward silence, during which Cliff stared out the window. "I guess it all makes sense, though," he said finally, in a new tone of voice, as if he had come to understand something. "Alright, what's done is done. Let's get on with it. We're not beaten yet."

"I still don't get it," Ira said to Alan. "You say you could tell about Tana, that she is somehow older than she looks, but how?"

"It was in her eyes," Alan said. "I've seen it before."

"Where?" Ira said.

"That was a long time ago," Alan said, as if it were unimportant.

"She is of the shadows then," Cliff said solemnly.

"What are you talking about, Cliff?" Ira said, annoyed. It was disconcerting to hear this Texas politico talking occult mumbo jumbo. It threatened the reporter's whole worldview.

"Cliff belongs to the Church of the Golden Grail," Alan said.

"What the hell is that!" Ira couldn't keep his voice down.

"If I tell you, Ira," Cliff said, "it is strictly off the record. OK?"

"Sure," Ira said.

"We are an ancient order, going back at least as far as the Knights Templar. I personally believe our lineage stretches back to the pre-Christian era, even to the ancient Greek Mystery Cults, but that's not really so important. The crucial thing is our central, binding belief—tenet, dogma—whatever you want to call it."

"Yeah?" Ira said.

"We belive that our destiny is there." He pointed up. "Humans were never meant to stay bound to the surface of planet earth. We were supposed to begin the migration to outer space thousands of years ago. But something went wrong. There was a glitch in the evolution of human intelligence. We got stuck to the planet, forgot our true destiny, and the rest, as they say, is history."

"Oh man," Ira said. "I don't believe I'm hearing this."

"Believe it," Cliff said, "because it's the truth."

"What do you think about all this?" Ira turned to Alan.

"Well," Alan said, "I'm not a member of Cliff's

church, but, as you already know, I do share some of their beliefs. Where I draw the line is in the theological interpretations. I am, after all, a scientist."

Cliff snorted. "Science! You scientists can't see the forest for the trees. Where do you think all your theoretical structures and forces come from?"

Alan shrugged and looked back at the mural.

"What's this Golden Grail?" Ira said.

"It's symbolic . . ." Alan began.

"Symbolic hell!" Cliff said. "It won't be no goddamn symbol when you find yourself standing in front of it! It's the *goal*. Once we are liberated from terrestrial space we will make the cosmic pilgrimage to the source of all life. Even the scientists will tell you that life began in the stars. That's where the heavier elements like carbon were formed. Without the tetrahedral carbon bond there wouldn't be any organic molecules. Hence no possibility of DNA or any of the other structures essential to life."

"Maybe so, maybe so," Alan said. "In the meantime we need to get our spaceship back."

"How?" Ira said. "She could be anywhere. She could be halfway to Mars by now."

"No," Alan said, "that's not possible. Not yet anyway."

"Why not?" Ira said.

"It won't fly beyond the orbit of the moon yet. I know—I've tried," Alan said.

"Why not?" Ira said.

"I wouldn't want to speculate yet," Alan said, "but I think the moon harbors a secret."

The room became silent, as if momentarily filled by that secret. Then Cliff, sounding like a schoolboy, said, "What do we do now?"

"I have a tracking device," Alan said. "I think I can locate her."

"What are we waiting for!" Cliff said.

"Take it easy," Alan said. "Finding her will be fairly easy. In fact, I have a pretty good idea where she is. It's regaining control of the ship that will be difficult.'' With that, Alan excused himself, explaining that he was going back to his lab to try to locate the craft. ''I'll call you as soon as I know something definite,'' he said to Cliff. ''I promise.''

''Ira,'' Cliff began after Alan left.

''You know my situation, Cliff,'' Ira said.

''I know! But you're in on this thing now! You can't just treat it like another story.''

''I don't want to ruin your career, Cliff,'' Ira said, ''but how long can you hide the misappropriation of funds? It's bound to come out sooner or later, and it is a story that could save *my* career.''

''First of all, it wasn't a misappropriation,'' Cliff said. ''This isn't embezzlement, and you know it.''

''I know nothing of the sort,'' Ira said. ''Look at the facts . . .''

''Facts! What are *facts*!'' Cliff said. ''Jesus, Ira! Get off that reporter mode! We are talking about something that goes far beyond the petty concerns of state government here.''

''I would have thought that the Speaker of the House might give those concerns a rather high priority,'' Ira said.

''Yeah, yeah. You saw it! You flew in it! What more do I need to say?''

''OK, Cliff,'' Ira said. ''Here's what I can do. I can hold off as long as you can keep the lid on this thing. But I see no reason to let someone else scoop me on it. What good would that do? We both suffer. If you're going to go down anyway, why shouldn't I get something out of it?''

''I'm not going down, Ira. I'm on top of this thing. So far there is no chance that anyone else is going to get even a whiff of this story. I promise you that if it does start to break, I'll give you the green light to go ahead and blow me out of the water.''

''I'm counting on that promise,'' Ira said. ''It's all that's keeping this grand adventure from becoming just another story.''

7

Reality Check

That night Ira had a particularly vivid dream. It was a falling dream, which started out in the usual way; an awful fear gripped him in the pit of the stomach before the bottom dropped out. But this time, instead of falling, he found himself being drawn toward a radiant, fiery golden sphere. He was pulled by a golden cord that penetrated and merged with all his nerves and blood vessels. As he got closer an all-consuming ecstasy began to possess him.

The phone rang and his body snapped awake so violently that he jerked an inch off the bed. He fell back into reality and grabbed the phone with a sense of deep loss. He was also a little pissed off. "Hello."

"Ira," the voice was familiar in a disturbing way.

"Yeah."

"I'm sorry to call you at such a bad time, but I've got to talk to you." Ira recognized Leslie's voice, the recently hired police reporter.

"Oh?"

"Yeah, this could be really big, I've found some . . ."

"You know I don't work for the paper anymore," Ira said.

"Yeah," she said with an amazing lack of emotion. *Where do they find these kids*? Ira wondered. "I know it's late," she continued. It was 3:00 A.M. "But since I now have your job . . ."

"What!" Ira said. "They put *you* on the political beat?"

"I thought you knew," she said, quite unabashed. "And why shouldn't I be on the political beat?"

"No reason," Ira said, having no desire to go into all the valid reasons. "So what's going on?"

"I've been looking at the discretionary budget for the next fiscal year," she began.

Her words brought Ira fully awake. Two things were racing through his mind. The first was that his big scoop, his ace in the hole was gone, and the second was that he had underestimated her abilities. Maybe she *did*, unfortunately, belong on the political beat. "Run that by again," Ira said, having missed her last few rapid-fire sentences.

"There are some major discrepancies. Money that hasn't even been certified by the comptroller has apparently already been spent."

"Have you been able to track any of it?" Ira asked, forcing a neutral, objective tone of voice. After doggedly pursuing lying, manipulative state officials for years, Ira was, for the first time, getting a taste of what it felt like to be on the other end of things.

"Not yet. That's where I need your help."

"You know I was fired, Leslie," Ira said.

"Fired?" She sounded surprised, but Ira detected a false ring to it. "I thought you had taken a job in Washington or something."

"Not exactly. But the point is why should I help you? What's in it for me?"

"Uh." Again she sounded genuinely surprised at Ira's question. "You mean you'll want to share my byline?"

"At the very least," Ira said.

"What can you tell me about these discretionary funds? Who has access to account numbers?" she said quickly.

"Leslie," Ira said, "first thing first."

"Oh, well," she said, "I've got some other sources. I'll see what I can dig up there. I'll get back to you." She hung up.

"Bitch!" Ira said, slamming the phone down and staring at the ungodly hour beaming forth in that ghoulish green. He picked up the phone and called Cliff. There was no answer. The moment he set the phone down it rang.

It was Alan. "Can you come over?" he said. "It's important."

Alan answered the door looking fresh and relaxed. He was dressed casually, faded jeans, beat-up running shoes, and a black T-shirt. "Follow me," he said.

He went through his bedroom and into a closet, where a door opened onto a staircase leading down to a basement. Basements were a rarity in central Texas, and when Ira remarked on this Alan said, "I had it built a few years ago."

It was a sophisticated underground laboratory. It was also quite comfortable. There were two stuffed chairs and a sofa at the far end of the room. These were arranged around a beautiful coffee table of bird's-eye maple with rosewood inlay. There was a thick Persian carpet underneath. Cliff sat in one of the chairs. Ira took the sofa. Alan sat in the remaining chair and poured some coffee from a thermos on the table.

The coffee was particularly delicious. "What is this?" Ira said.

"A blend of beans you aren't likely to find around here," Alan said.

"Here? You mean the city?"

"I mean the planet," Alan said.

"Really?" Ira said, staring hard at Alan.

"Really," Alan said casually. "I'm sorry to get you out of bed, Ira, but I think I have located the ship."

"We have another problem," Ira said.

"What's that?" Cliff spoke sensing trouble.

"There is an enterprising police reporter, young woman named *Leslie*"—Ira pronounced the name with some distaste—"who is on to Cliff's financial adventures with the state treasury."

"Me!" Cliff said. "How did she . . ."

"Actually I don't think she has traced it to you yet," Ira said, "but it's only a matter of time, and not much time if I know anything about these things."

"Doesn't matter," Cliff said bitterly. "Political games, nothing more."

"I thought you would see it differently," Ira said. "Political games are your life."

"Means to the end!" Cliff said. "That's all politics is, all it ever was."

"What end?" Ira said.

"The Golden Grail," Cliff said, "the ultimate truth, the final goal."

"Oh," Ira said, sorry he had asked.

"Things are never exactly what they seem, Ira," Alan said, as if sensing the reporter's thoughts. "They may be completely different from what they seem, for that matter. But, believe me, you can get used to it."

"Used to it!" Ira said. "But surely we need something to believe in!" Ira had never been particularly religious or philosophical, so he was surprised at his own words.

Alan smiled. "Now that is a very good question. Do we, in fact, need something to believe in? If so, what? And why?"

"Dammit!" Cliff said. "My whole career is about to go down the toilet, and you two are talking a lot of horseshit!"

"I thought you didn't care about your political career," Ira said.

"You see," Alan said. "Apparent contradictions are all around, and still we have no choice but to play the game as it unfolds. It would be imprudent and arrogant to do otherwise. And most contradictions vanish when seen from the larger perspective."

"And what is that?" Ira said.

"That is what we are reaching for," Alan said. "The larger view. Now let's get down to work."

The story Alan proceeded to tell was more fantastic than anything Ira had yet heard. As he listened he also analyzed with the objective sense of discrimination that all good reporters are supposed to have. It told him that none of it could possibly be true, but experience told him otherwise, and so he tried to understand.

When Alan finished Ira tried to summarize the gist of what he had heard. "So," Ira said, "you tracked the ship through the cosmic aether. This *aether*, which the ancient

Greeks first postulated, is real and it fills the empty space inside the atom as well as the spaces between the stars?''

''Yes,'' Alan said.

''Thought travels on the aether in the form of nouons, which are particles of thought. The aether is, in some mysterious way, both associated with truth and the secret of gravity. All humans have the latent ability to modulate the gravitational field and fly, but this requires a concentration beyond the reach of ordinary humans. In prehistoric times there were such people who could fly.''

''I *think* so,'' Alan said.

''And this secret of gravity is a *subjective* thing, which is why scientists, who are only concerned with objective phenomena, haven't found it. You, however, have discovered how to design a ship that can levitate. Levity requires a special kind of *resonance*, which is really the same thing as *truth*, and it all relates to having a sense of humor?''

''A very deep sense of humor,'' Alan said solemnly.

''You have used the term 'ordinary human,' '' Ira said. ''What do you mean?''

''You remember the *Genesis Bomb*?''[3]

''Of course.''

''And the person who called herself Miranda?''

''Yeah, she monopolized the entire planetary communications network and gave one of the most bizarre speeches I have ever heard,'' Ira said.

''Well,'' Alan said, ''Miranda is human in form. I suppose she is actually human, but she is not ordinary. She is not hampered by the mental occlusion that infects the rest of us on the planet. She has the ability to fly, and other powers as well.

''It is not widely known what happened to the *Genesis Bomb*. The government was able to cover up the details. They claimed it disappeared as quickly as it appeared. That is correct, but what they are not eager to reveal is where it went.''

''Where?''

''It is now a city in orbit around the sun, a self-

---

[3]*The Gaia War.*

contained biosphere, a floating paradise, free of terrestrial space."

"How do you know this?" Ira said.

"For one thing, I saw it lift out of the desert in White Sands, New Mexico, and ascend to the sky. I also have been in communication with Miranda via a channel on the Asklepian band."

"And?" Ira said.

"She needs our help, but won't admit it," Alan said.

"Help? Why?" Ira said.

Cliff interjected himself forcefully at this point. "Her colony is small. They cannot hope to defend themselves."

"Defend themselves?" Ira said. "Against what?"

"There are others out there," Cliff said, looking up.

"You recall all the UFO reports during the *Genesis Bomb* incident?" Alan said.

"Yeah, and I also recall UFS reports, Unidentified Flying *Subjects*, or flying people."

"Those reports were real," Alan said. "There is an ancient colony much bigger than Miranda's little Arlandia."

"*Arlandia*?"

"That's what they've named it," Alan said. "It's tiny compared to the other one."

"Other one?"

"Yes," Alan said. "They came back to earth to check us out at the beginning of the *Genesis Bomb* incident. They were worried that we had unlocked the ancient secrets. They soon learned that it was just an aberration, and humanity remains safely chained to the planet.

"But now that Miranda has taken her little city to the skies, there are political problems brewing. She doesn't understand the seriousness of the situation. They are much larger and more powerful that she."

"Wait a minute," Ira said. "Who are *they*, this other vast power floating out there in space?"

"You've heard of Atlantis?" Cliff said.

"Atlantis?" Ira felt that the whole thing was slipping away. Were there no limits to the outrageous absurdity of it? "Atlantis," Ira said weakly, "is a *myth* based on some obscure reference in one of the Platonic dialogues."

"The *Critias*," Alan said. "Most scholars place it among Plato's final works. The myth of Atlantis figures into Plato's discussion of the ideal society."

"And just because something is a myth doesn't mean it isn't true," Cliff said.

What is truth? Ira wondered. "OK," he said, "suppose Atlantis does exist outside of myth. I thought it sank beneath the waves thousands of years ago."

"That's the part of the myth that isn't true," Alan said. "That's what they want you to believe, the cover story. Atlantis was a continent about the size of present-day India in the middle of the ancient Atlantic ocean. It did not sink. It went the other way. They saw what was happening down here and had the good sense to levitate."

"So what is the deal with the ship?" Ira said, feeling very tired. "Did Tana take it to Atlantis?"

"No," Alan said. "She can't. Not yet. But she has gone as far as she can go at this point."

"Where is that?"

"The dark side of the moon," Alan said.

"Why?" Ira said.

"Why don't you ask her yourself?" Alan said. "I'm about to open a channel. Now that she's beginning to realize how stuck she is, maybe she'll want to talk. It will be an exclusive interview."

"Yeah," Ira said. "The *New York Times* will go nuts over it. Can't you just see it? *Reporter Talks to Alien Vixen on Dark Side of Moon*!"

"You might be surprised at the things people will believe," Alan said, "especially when they are true."

"Yeah," Ira said, "I might. On the other hand, I feel like I'm overdue for a reality check."

"Ah, but don't you see?" Alan said.

"What?"

"That's what this is all about. You mistake the mundane and the everyday for the real. This whole fantastic adventure, Ira, this seemingly absurd plot, this *is* the reality check!"

8

The Resonator

"Can't we go after her?" Cliff spoke up.

"How?" Alan said.

"Well you grew one spaceship, why can't you grow another one?"

"That would take a great deal more time and money," Alan said.

"You mean it's all gone, all spent?" Cliff said.

"Most of it" Alan said.

"On what?"

"Some of the equipment you see here in this lab," Alan said, "and, as I already explained, I had to compromise on the materials. The ship is not one hundred percent organic. In order to do the job right we would first need to begin the process in a zero-gravity environment. And, frankly, I simply lack the knowledge and skill. I did the best I could. That meant that the skeletal structure of the ship required aluminum and titanium. I also had to use sophisticated carbon composites in places where the organic polymers would not bond properly to metal surfaces. Those kinds of materials are very expensive.

"So yes, in theory I could grow another ship, but I lack the means. And even if we could get the money it would take at least a year. We may only have a few days."

"Days?" Ira said. "Why, what's going to . . ."

Ira was interrupted by a soft, low-pitched beeping sound coming from a dull gray, metallic box on a nearby lab bench. "What's that thing?" Ira said. Alan was already up and walking toward the machine.

"It's a nouancer," Alan said.

"A what?" Ira said.

"*Nouancer*. A very crude one," Alan said. "You can think of a nouancer as a radio capable of receiving and broadcasting on the Asklepian bands of the cosmic aether. This one can only operate over a very limited range of frequencies. We had one a few years ago that could actually receive the most rarefied and subtle vibrations yet discovered."

"What are those?" Ira asked.

"Thought waves," Alan said. "There may be even finer more fantastic frequencies and spaces accessible through the aether, but they are as yet unknown, perhaps even *unknowable*. Thought, the pulse of consciousness itself, marks the present limits of understanding where these matters are concerned. We had a device, for a short time, that could probe those limits.[4] My little machine, however"—he gestured toward the nouancer which was beeping with an increasing insistency—"is hardly more than a toy in comparison."

Alan sat down in front of the nouancer. "This will be, I hope, the call I've been waiting for." Cliff and Ira were standing behind him. The machine had an antenna of concentric circles, reminiscent of an old, 1930s radio set. Alan fiddled with a large dial on the front panel. It crackled, and then the sound came alive. It was curiously full, more immediate-sounding than anything one normally hears over conventional electronic media. Alan explained that the dynamic range was vastly superior to the best FM technology.

"This is Alan Fain"—Alan held a large, square microphone mounted on a circular stand—"transmitting on the Asklepian wave. Is there anyone there?"

"Mr. Fain?" It was Tana. "Good of you to answer. This is Tana Vane. I suppose I should apologize for appropriating your transport, but it was rather necessary."

"I think the word is 'steal,' " Alan said, "but let's not argue over semantics."

"No," she said, "let's not. There are more important things at stake here."

---

[4]*Mind-Surfer*.

"I'm sure," Alan said drily.

"I didn't expect that you would believe me," she said. "You people are so shortsighted. Well, that hardly matters. The truth is the same no matter what you imagine or desire. Right now the truth concerns someone else who wants to talk with you."

"Hello, Alan." There was no mistaking the voice. It was Lew.

"Lew!" Alan said. "She's kidnapped you!"

"Afraid not," Lew said. "I came willingly."

"But why?"

"Tana is not who you think, Alan," Lew said. "There may be a way for us to work together."

"How's that?" Alan said, dully.

"She wants to take us to Arlandia," Lew said. "Miranda's colony. That's where you wanted to go anyway, isn't it?"

"Don't listen to her, Lew," Alan said. "She can't be trusted."

"Tell me how to program the ship," Tana interrupted, "so we can get to Arlandia."

"You can't," Alan said. "Additional technology, which only I can provide, is necessary. You won't get any farther on your own."

"I don't believe you," she said. "There must be a disinhibiting code that will free the navigational net."

"Believe it or not," Alan said, "it's the truth. Let me talk to Lew again."

"I'm right here," Lew said.

"Are you alright, Lew?" Alan said.

"Yeah, it's beautiful up here. I can almost believe the stars are alive."

"They are!" It was Cliff. He grabbed the microphone. "This is Cliff Sanders, son," Cliff said in his best Texas, good ole boy voice.

"The *Speaker of the Texas House*?" Lew said, incredulous.

"That's me. There are powers involved here that you probably know nothing about. But don't give in to fear.

I want you to know that the eyes of Texas are watching and no matter what happens . . ."

"What the *hell* is he talking about!" Lew interrupted.

Alan took the microphone from Cliff. "Nothing," Alan said. "Cliff is just helping me a little. Don't worry about it."

"I'll give you ten hours"—it was Tana again—"to transmit the disinhibiting code."

"And then what?" Alan said.

"I can't be responsible for what may or may not happen." She lowered her voice to a near whisper. "Lew is not exactly equipped to survive out here on his own." Then the connection went dead.

"Bitch!" Alan slammed his fist on the hard metal surface, causing the microphone to jump.

"Who's telling the truth?" Ira asked.

"What do you mean?" Alan said.

"I mean about the ship. Does it really require additional hardware or is it just a matter of reprogramming like she says?"

"Not exactly," Alan said.

"That doesn't answer my question," Ira said.

"It isn't that simple," Alan said. "The ship *is* complete. On the other hand, there is one more piece of technology that I need to install. Without it, I'm not sure what will happen if she attempts to fly into extraterrestrial space. Right now the ship relies on the strong gravitational field of the earth to calibrate all its navigational functions. As you move away from the earth the gravitational force varies inversely to the square of the distance. If she attempts to travel any significant distance past the moon, that force will quickly become negligible, and then I'm afraid the ship will essentially lose all its navigational functions. They could be hopelessly adrift, at the mercy of whatever gravitational field happens to be the most powerful. They could crash into the sun, get snagged by Jupiter, or go flying off into interstellar space."

"What's this other piece of technology you mentioned?" Ira said. "The one you still need to install."

Alan got up and walked to the end of the lab bench.

He opened a heavy wood box. A wild, musty smell came from its interior. "*This* is also alive," he said, reaching into the box. "It consists entirely of neurons. They're not human, so it's not really a brain. It doesn't *think*." He held a gray, textured sphere. It was shiny, slightly moist, and seemed to pulsate gently.

"It doesn't think?" Ira said.

"No."

"Then what does it do?"

"It *resonates*." Alan smiled. "It's a *resonator*."

"A resonator? To what does it resonate?"

"Truth." Alan was now grinning, and the effect was disturbing. "It's a *truth* resonator."

9

The Shield

Lew Slack, an amateur tennis player whose main ambition in life was to make a record, was fifty feet beneath the surface of the dark side of the moon. Alan's ship remained inside the outer chamber of an air lock on the surface.

Lew did not share Alan's conviction that Tana represented the forces of evil, but he was suspicious. "I can't answer you now, Lew," she said in response to his many questions. "You have to trust me."

"You lied to me," Lew said. "You claimed we were going to Texas to see Alan. This is hardly Texas."

"But you have to admit it's more interesting than Texas," she said.

"Is it?" he said. "What is this place, Tana? Why are we here?"

"This is an ancient place," she said. "Look around."

Lew noted the rough-hewn walls and the solid wood

doors that sealed off their chamber. She was seated in large, overstuffed armchair. Lew occupied the corner of a wide couch. Tana had given him a drink, and he cautiously sipped it. It tasted of wild mushrooms and honey, with a hint of alcohol. It was very strange and good.

"My people built this place," she said, "a very long time ago."

"Your people? Who are they?"

"They are the stuff of legend now. But things are changing rapidly. The millennium approaches. Legends come back to life." She took a sip of her drink and gazed at Lew while licking her lips. He was lost in her big brown eyes.

She approached him, slowly undulating. Lew's gaze went from her eyes to her hips. She wore a thin skirt, and in the soft luminescence of the place Lew could see through the fabric. She stood still for a few moments, then began to unbutton her blouse. Her small, inviting breasts seemed to glow with their own pale moonlight. She touched one nipple. The resolution of visual detail in that soft light was unexpected and extremely sensual.

She untied her skirt. It fell slowly to the floor, making the lesser gravity of the moon erotic. Physics, the science of matter in motion, was suddenly *physical* and sexual.

When Lew woke up a few hours later he was alone and naked. He stretched out on the couch. His limbs felt relaxed, yet taut. *Must be the gravity,* he thought. He sat up and hugged himself. The air was cool and slightly damp, but it felt good on his skin. He walked to an adjacent wall and noted that while the stone was rough, the room did not appear, as he had first imagined, to have been blasted out. Rather, he thought he could see evidence of hand carving in the surface. He stepped back and was sure of it. There were patterns cut into the stone. They were hard to categorize aesthetically, seeming both primitive and sophisticated. The designs also played with the shadows from the eerie light that had, as far as Lew could tell, no source. The same area looked radically different when viewed from a slightly different angle.

There was no sign of Tana. Lew's clothes lay on the

floor where they had been hastily shed in the passion that was now only a memory. He dressed slowly, savoring the details of it. There was a coldness in Tana's sexuality that Lew found irresistible.

His attire consisted of a pair of faded black jeans, well-used running shoes, and a gray cotton sweater. It was perfect for the temperature and humidity. *Like San Francisco without the fog*, Lew thought.

It wasn't long before he was hungry and thirsty. He went to the recessed cabinet and opened the carved wooden door. It was a finely crafted piece, fitting snugly in the stone. Lew found a bottle of the drink Tana had served him but no food. He poured himself another glass and set out to retrace the path to the surface.

It was a simple matter to open the door, another beautiful piece of carpentry, it swung out smoothly without a sound. A stone staircase led to the air lock. Lew went flying and bouncing up the steps. A painful collision with the wall on his left reminded him that flesh and bone were still vulnerable in reduced gravity. The air lock door at the top of the steps was made of a green metal. There was a glass portal at eye level. He could see into the inner chamber and through a similar portal in the opposite door to the outer chamber. The ship was gone.

Alone on the moon! The thought both thrilled and terrified him. *Why did she bring me here*? he wondered. Lew still could not believe that Tana was evil, but he could no longer pretend that she was benign. Another thought, all too familiar to Lew, was quickly supplanting all his other questions. *Why me?* He wondered whether or not the question really made any sense. After all, he thought, *In the final analysis isn't it always me?*

He took a sip of his drink. The stuff did not seem to be intoxicating, but it was refreshing and soothing. More than anything he felt the need to act, if only to direct his mind outward, away from the questions that had no answers. *That way lies madness*, he thought.

He returned to the chamber and began examining the walls more closely. Some of the patterns he had seen earlier almost looked like writing. But it was tricky to see it.

You had to look at just the right spot from just the right angle. The more he looked, the more admiration he felt for the artist. The work was multifaceted, taking on totally different modes of expression depending on the viewer's perspective, the ambience of light and shadow.

Walking down one wall, he came to a place where he was sure he saw legible writing. He had to step back and adjust his position laterally before he could read it. The writing was carved calligraphy, very expressive in execution. He began to read.

Always the same question, "Why?" Why indeed? I, Tantalyes, no longer ask. Our greatest wisdom says the answer is in what we do, not what we think or say. So we have done it. What else could we do?

It is sad to leave the mother planet. Sadder still that such a thing is necessary. But we had no choice. It was as clear as if it had already happened. The future, like the past, is present to my eyes. I wouldn't know the names of individuals or the exact places and times, but of the events themselves I would be deadly accurate. Wars, wars, and more terrible wars. Feeble progress in scientific knowledge that will do more harm than good. Terrible weapons of destruction. Callous disregard for the interlocking web of life that sustains us all. Population growth that begins to look like a cancer choking out all other forms of life even while the air gets more foul and the waters become polluted sewers.

We had to leave. And we had to protect ourselves. Our earthbound brothers and sisters will someday develop the ability to leave the planet. Probably their technology will consist of force-thrusting machines, crude compared to the elegance of the levity drive. But they will come and will surely find us. So we have learned to use the alien resonator *deep inside the moon. How fitting that Luna should be our protector from earthly man, the rational animal gone mad. The moon is our* shield.

That was all Lew could make out. He tried to find another position where he could read more. He only succeeded in losing his perspective on what he had just read and could in no way find it again. Frustrated, he continued to follow the wall but found nothing more which he could decipher.

He came to another door at the far end of the room. It did not open so easily. The latch clicked, but the door wouldn't budge. Assuming that it was stuck from years of disuse, Lew threw his weight against it. It gave a little. Again he heaved his shoulder into it, and it opened with a whoosh of air that swept him across the threshold. The air in this new chamber was slightly thinner. It was this pressure difference that had sucked him in. It was also much darker—Lew could hardly see his hand in front of his face. None of this mattered much to Lew at the time, because he was falling, and gravity, even lunar gravity, is always serious.

10

A Dangerous Game

Tana did not want to admit it, but she was afraid. *Fear is a wave which I must ride through to the other side, where there is peace and clarity of purpose,* she told herself. It was an old mantra from one of her favorite childhood books. But that was a very long time ago for Tana, and she no longer believed the stories and lessons of youth.

The little craft was pushing the limits of the lunar gravitational field. The moon showed itself as a small, pale disc when Tana looked behind her. She had not believed Alan, preferring to trust her own instincts, which told her the craft could make the plunge into extraterrestrial space.

But she also knew about the field resonator—it was also part of her cultural legacy. The moon was supposed to protect her people, keep the beast of earth in his cage, until such time as the beast learned to be truly human.

But Tana doubted that story as well. She was beginning to suspect that her own people were neither more nor less human than their planetbound counterparts. They had the key to life extension, possibly immortality, and had mastered the force of gravity, but what did these things really signify? There were signs of rot in the place she called home. She had heard things she did not want to believe.

That was why she had, for the first time, acted alone in her capacity as terrestrial agent. *I've got to do something*, she thought, *before the planet is destroyed*. What, exactly, she would or could do was not clear.

That bastard! she thought, recalling her last conversation with Tantalyes.

"You need not fear for your own safety," the man had said. "It's all been carefully planned."

"A planetwide evacuation of terrestrial agents you mean?" Tana had responded. "Before the holocaust?"

"Your term is distasteful—unfair really."

"What would *you* call it?"

"Certainly not a *holocaust*. It would be far more accurate to describe it as a cleansing, regrettable but necessary. Surely you don't doubt the wisdom of the council in such matters?" There had been an ominous undertone, artfully ambiguous but unmistakable, to his question.

"Of course not." Tana also recalled the not-so-artful sarcasm in her reply.

Her reflections were interrupted by a shudder that went through the ship. It was slight, barely detectable, but impossible to dismiss as imagination. "Tana." It was Tantalyes. He had opened a channel on her nouancer. She did not respond.

Suddenly the ship pitched wildly to port and began a crazy tumble that defied all the natural laws of motion—it seemingly had no inertia, and no force field known to physics could have caused such wild fluctuations of trajectory. It stopped as suddenly as it had started.

"Tana," Tantalyes said again. "Do I now have your attention?"

"Yeah," she said, voice shaking.

"Good. Now listen to me. I know you think you are acting from some sense of higher purpose. Perhaps we left you unsupervised for too long. These things happen. You begin to identify with your subject, to see things from the alien perspective."

"*Alien* perspective?" Tana said. "Aren't we, after all, human too?"

"Yes," Tantalyes said, "and *no*. It is better to think of human as a type rather than a species. There is no denying the type. That much we share with the creatures of earth, but the same *species*?" He said this with obvious revulsion. "I hardly think so. Maybe once, but no longer.

"In any case," he continued, "you need to consider your situation. I don't think you have any choice now but to return to Luna."

"What will happen to me then?" she said. "Maybe I'll be better off out here."

"You will surely die if you persist in your folly. I will have no choice but to activate the resonator again. You will either careen into the sun, or, if you are lucky, become trapped in a long elliptical orbit. Maybe you could become a comet—comet *Tana*." He laughed.

There was nothing malicious in his laugh. This display of wholesome good humor struck Tana as particularly perverse. It made her cold and fearful. "But what happens to *me* if I return?" she asked again.

"You know our law, Tana," Tantalyes said. "The matter will be turned over to the council. Emotions are running high now."

"The holistics?"

"Yes, their numbers continue to grow. Personally I don't think they are anything more than a passing fad. Political and social movements come with a fanfare and usually go without a whimper. My view is that the council is overreacting. Still, there is the rare exception. Revolutions are not impossible—they do happen."

"But surely—I mean I'm not a holistic. This has nothing to do with—"

"Don't be naive, Tana! Maybe you are and maybe you aren't. *I* believe you, but your unauthorized actions as a terrestrial agent showing earth sympathies put you under suspicion. The holistics would love to know what you know and would pay dearly to recruit you to their cause."

"You don't give me much incentive to turn this little ship around," Tana said.

"I'll do what I can with the council," Tantalyes said. "I can't promise you leniency or even a fair trial, but I do still have influence. They haven't quite forgotten me back home although many would like to. In any case, you really have no choice if you want to live, and I think that you do."

For a brief moment Tana wasn't sure. She imagined spiraling out of control into the fiery heat of the sun, merging with the primordial energy dance that fueled all life in the solar system—a wave of white-hot bliss washed over her. It was terrifying in its intensity.

Tantalyes seemed to sense her wild flirtation with death. "Yes," he said, "I know how tempting it is. But the source of life is deadly for our faint flames. There are cults on earth that nourish such crazy dreams. The Golden Grail they call it. But I don't think you really want to die."

No, dammit! she thought. *I don't.* She moved her slender fingers across the silver ball on the panel in front of her. The ship responded with the nimble, fluid grace of a racing yacht. The arc of the wheeling vessel had an aesthetic component that seemed deliberate. Beauty was, at that moment, not a random accident, nor was it artificial; it was the essential, unifying force in nature.

Tantalyes was waiting for her, seated in one of the stuffed chairs. He didn't get up when she came down the steps and walked to the opposite chair. "Alright," she said, sitting down, "I surrender."

"You need not take it that way," he said. "In fact, I wish you wouldn't. Think of it as an expedient survival strategy. A compromise, if you like, although I loathe that word. In a few years it will all be forgotten.''

''A few years in lunar isolation seems like an eternity,'' she said.

''But what is eternity to one who is virtually immortal?'' he said.

''Immortal?'' She laughed. ''Don't try that one on me. I may be centuries younger than you, but I have already figured out that stuff about immorality is a lie. We may last a long time, but we aren't any more immortal than our earthly cousins.''

''Maybe not,'' he said, ''but you have many centuries, possibly millennia ahead of you. It's long enough to make youthful indiscretions vanish into insignificance.''

''Is that what this is?'' She laughed.

''I don't care what you think!'' he said, his sudden forcefulness silencing her. ''I'm trying to help you. It's your best chance. There are members of the council, Monica, for one, who are concerned about the increasingly conservative political climate. These are precisely the members with whom I have the most influence. If you play your cards right, I have good reason to believe that things will not go too badly for you. We may even be able to negotiate a suspended sentence.''

''Thank you, counselor,'' she said.

''Such juvenile sarcasm doesn't suit you,'' he said.

''What have you done with him?'' she said.

''Who?''

''You know very well who.''

''Ah, the *boyfriend.* He's gone.''

''Gone? Where?''

''When I arrived from my office, which is, as you know, a considerable distance, the other door was open and there was no sign of the earthling.''

''Oh no!'' she said, getting up and running to the door at the opposite end of the chamber.

''Don't bother,'' he said, ''I've already checked. And you know he wouldn't last ten minutes down there.''

Tana managed to get the door open. ''Lew!'' she screamed, ''Lew, answer me!''

"I'm sorry, Tana," Tantalyes said. He was standing behind her and put an arm around her shoulder. He closed the door and led her to the sofa. "You know, the scientists of earth are busily searching for the holy grail of physics. They call it the *unified field*. They think all the fundamental forces of the universe can be resolved into one elegant set of equations, and that will be it. All living things, all matter and energy, will then be understood as a unity. *All* things will be *one* thing—the field.

"This is a noble effort. I, in fact, envy them their innocence. Such naïveté is poignant. But it is, I'm afraid, a fiction. The field will never be unified. It is hopelessly fragmented. The resonator proves that.

"He was not one of us, Tana, nor could he ever be. That was your mistake, thinking that there was a unity of kind and purpose between his world and ours. That's what is so upsetting to you. You'll get over it. Trust me."

The look in her moist eyes held little trust.

"Forget the earth, Tana! Our culture is founded on that one commandment. *You* are playing a dangerous game."

"And Lew?" she said.

"Got *caught* in a dangerous game."

11

Such a Bitch

I could have written it myself, Ira thought, as he read the front-page, lead story in the *Texas Sun*. "House Speaker embezzles discretionary funds, ex–*Sun* reporter implicated in scandal." Ira sipped his morning coffee and tried to smile. It was a damn good story. *Too good*, he thought. *How did she do it*?

Leslie hadn't even interviewed Ira, yet she had most of the story right. She had magnified his role in the thing, indicating that he had received some of the money, but, as a reporter, Ira could forgive her for that. It would have appeared that way to an outsider gathering information. As a human being Ira could not. "Damn!" He slapped the paper down with enough force to splash some coffee onto his robe. It was an off-white, long staple Indian cotton robe, the one relic from his marriage that was worth keeping. Now it would probably be stained for life, which seemed perversely appropriate.

Ira called Cliff, both at his home and office, and was not surprised to get a recorded message to the effect that he would be away for a few weeks. Then he called Alan.

"Hello," he answered immediately.

"Have you seen the paper?"

"Yeah, too bad, Ira. I'm sorry."

This really irritated him. The one thing Leslie did not uncover was Alan. Instead she had speculated that some secret, corporate lab was behind the research. Alan had got off scot-free. So far.

"I guess that's it then," Ira said. "The money's gone, and so is the ship. My career is over and . . ."

"It's never over, Ira!" Alan was suddenly angry. "The work goes on, understand! Never say die!"

"That's what Lew told me on the tennis court," Ira said.

"So Lew's quite the tennis player these days, is he?" Alan said with inexplicable irony.

"Well, he's alright, I mean he beat me, not by much but . . ."

"But he won! Don't you see? That's what matters . . ."

"I thought it was how you play the game," Ira said.

"Don't be a chump, Ira," Alan said. "We have work to do. Meet me over here as soon as you can, and make sure no one is following you. No telling who might be on your tail now." He hung up.

"Weirdo!" Ira said after he put the phone down. But he felt better. Alan's passion was infectious, and Ira needed something for his sagging spirits.

Ira took a circuitous route, but wasn't too worried about

being followed. He figured that most reporters would initially try to get to Cliff, the major player.

Alan met him at the door, looking quickly up and down the street. Ira followed him down to the lab, where he poured coffee.

"Thanks," Ira said, taking the cup and sitting down on the sofa. The place had a relaxing effect on him, as if it were somehow outside the ordinary flow of time. Ira found himself getting lost in the beautiful patterns on the Persian carpet.

"Things are kind of a mess right now," Alan said.

"Any word from Tana?" Ira asked, popping back to ordinary reality.

"No, I can't raise her. Either she is ignoring me, or something has happened."

"Is it really true," Ira said, "that she can't fly beyond terrestrial space without your . . . ah, thing . . ."

"Resonator?" Alan said.

"Yeah, the resonator."

"It's true," Alan said. "Exactly why is still not totally clear to me. Either there is a natural flux in the gravitational field just beyond the orbit of the moon, or it is caused by an artificial device. In either case, my levity drive by itself can't maintain stability. That's where the resonator comes in."

"Artificial?" Ira said. "Who has the technology to jam a gravitational field?"

"I don't know—Tana's people maybe. But it's all speculation at this point. We need to focus on what we know, not what we don't know," Alan said, leaning back in his chair. "Can you get hold of Cliff?"

"I can try," Ira said. "I'm almost certain he's beaten a retreat to his ranch."

"Where's that?" Alan said.

"Pedernales," Ira said, pronouncing it as the locals do, Perd *'nal*eez. "LBJ country. He has a ranch out there. It's his little Eden. He goes there to shoot quail, ride, and unwind. I have his unlisted number."

"Try it," Alan said, indicating the phone on the end table.

Ira got a recording and left a message. "If I know Cliff, he'll call us back within the hour," Ira said.

Alan's doorbell rang and he sat bolt upright, spilling his coffee. *More nervous than he looks*, Ira thought.

"Follow me," Alan said, getting up and heading for the stairs.

At the front door Alan whispered, "Stand just inside the door there to the left, in case I need some backup."

Reluctantly Ira obeyed, and Alan opened the door. Alan's eyes opened wide, and he fell back a step, as if something had knocked all the wind out of him.

"Hello, Alan." Ira heard a female voice. "May I come in?"

"Sure," he said breathlessly.

The woman crossed the threshold. She wore a long-sleeved cotton dress, a wide-brimmed hat, and wraparound sunglasses. The dress flattered her narrow waist and long legs. "How are you?" she said.

"Uh, OK," Alan said. He seemed either afraid or in awe of this person, whose face Ira still could not see.

"Good," she said, sounding sincere. "We have to talk."

The woman turned to face Ira and removed her shades. The sight of her face made Ira gasp. It was beautiful, and her eyes shone with an aethereal radiance. She removed her hat and waves of black hair tumbled down to her shoulders. But the most unnerving thing was her skin—it was a deep, luminous green.

"Hello," she said, extending her hand, "I'm Miranda."

"Ira," the reporter said, taking her hand. "Pleased to meet you."

"I'm sure," she said, without a trace of sarcasm. "You must be the journalist."

"That's right."

"Any coffee?" she said to Alan.

"Downstairs," he said.

"Ah yes." She sounded wistful. "The lab. You may not believe it, but I have fond memories of my womb, the place of my creation. Not exactly a real mother, but then mothers can be such a bitch."

12

The Strangest Places

Over yet more coffee, Alan explained that spaceships were not all he grew. Miranda had sprung full-blown from the very same lab in the not-so-distant past.

In this strange story,[5] Miranda was Alan's creation, and she did show her creator a curious respect. There was something of the daughter in the way she spoke to Alan.

But Alan was less like a father than a queen's subject. He was deferential, and there was a hint of anxiety bordering on fear in the way he responded to her questions.

"Is the resonator ready?" she said.

"Almost," Alan said. "It's only a matter of days, possibly hours."

"And Lew?" she said.

"I don't know." Alan sighed. "We've lost all contact with the ship."

"Alan," Miranda said, "why couldn't you have left him out of this? He was finally beginning to find himself, and now . . ." Her voice trailed off.

"Now he is lost on the dark side of the moon," Alan said. "I know. What can we do?" His voice took on a pleading tone. He was looking to her for answers.

Before she could give any the phone rang. Alan motioned for Ira to get it. It was Cliff.

"I'm sorry, Ira," Cliff said. "I guess now both of us are in it pretty deep. I don't know how she did it. There's

---

[5]*The Gaia War.*

no way she could have traced the money that quickly unless she had help. We have enemies out there. *Unseen* enemies!''

''Don't start getting paranoid on me, Cliff,'' Ira said. ''It's just possible that Leslie is a damn good reporter—''

''Hell, Ira!'' Cliff interrupted. ''I know what I'm talking about. I may be finished in politics, but this ol' dog still hunts. They're onto us.''

Ira didn't bother to ask who *they* were. ''OK,'' he said. ''Are you alright?''

''I'll be a hell of a lot better if we get that spaceship back. Any word?''

''No,'' Ira said. ''Alan wants to talk with you.'' Ira handed the phone to Alan.

They waited until night. Miranda was reluctant at first. She hadn't known about Cliff and regarded it as an unnecessary complication, but finally agreed to take the three of them to his ranch. Her vehicle was hidden so well in Waterloo Park that it would have been hard to notice in broad daylight. The thing just disappeared in the flora that grew in a small cypress grove on the banks of Waller Creek.

Alan's craft had an artificial skeleton. The alloys and carbon composites that went into the frame had used up a good deal of Cliff's embezzled Texas money. Miranda's ship was completely organic. It had the same green luster, but the thing just pulsated with life. On entering it, Ira felt as if he were climbing into the chamber of a large heart. The smells were warm and rich, slightly sharp and pungent.

She took the helm and expertly maneuvered through the tree branches. Then they shot up thousands of feet, with an acceleration that was simply impossible. They should have been killed by the G forces, but there were none.

Alan silently examined the control panel. It consisted of a soft, blue-green shelf just below the seam where the transparent polymer dome grew from the body. There were subtle indentations where Miranda placed her hands. She guided the ship with hand motions.

"Is this a sensory interface?" Alan asked in awe.

"Yes," she said. "The ship's nervous system connects with mine through my fingers and palms."

"So you actually navigate by thought?"

"Thought mediated by sensation."

They were descending, and the Texas hill country, illuminated by the waning moonlight, came into view. They settled down on a plateau of limestone and climbed out among the cedar and juniper trees.

Cliff found them before long. "Welcome to Texas, ma'am," he said to Miranda. He removed his hat in a gesture of deference to the lady.

Miranda laughed. "I'm charmed," she said, and held out her hand.

"The Angel of Arlandia," Cliff said, taking her hand.

"I suppose so," she said.

"Come on," Cliff said.

They walked the half mile back to Cliff's ranch house. He got beers for Ira and Alan and poured himself a whiskey. Miranda asked for wine and Cliff, clearly embarrassed, confessed he had none, so she drank water.

Cliff was like a little kid. He couldn't wait to show Miranda his library. It was stocked with arcane books on prehistory, strange metaphysics, and stuff that was plain occult nonsense. Some of the books dealt with legends of Atlantis. Miranda took more than a passing interest in those.

There was one book he pressed on her with a force that was nothing short of rude. He just could not help himself. "*You*," he said, "of all people, will be able to appreciate this! It's my prized possession. Go ahead, sit down, have a look!" He practically pushed her into his personal reading chair. He turned on the light and placed the heavy tome in her lap.

It was an old volume, bound in heavy, maroon cloth. In a faded, yellow-gold script, which was probably garishly bright at one time, the title read, *Secrets of the Golden Grail.*

"I'm told it dates to the seventeenth century at least," Cliff said, "and it was translated from an older, Latin text. No doubt that was also a translation."

"No doubt," Miranda said drily.

Cliff, oblivious to her sarcasm continued. "The original language was probably the universal language of man. The tongue we all spoke before the Tower of Babel—"

"Cliff," Ira gently interrupted, "I'm not sure Miranda . . ."

"It's OK," she said. "I'll have a look."

"The Golden Grail is to the life of the spirit as is the sun to earthly life." She read this solemnly from the title page. Looking over her shoulder, Ira could see the image of a grail that radiated light just underneath the inscription. "Hmm," she said, turning the page. Then she got very quiet and began reading with concentration.

Ira took a seat on Cliff's cowhide sofa. Alan and Cliff sat in two chairs opposite the sofa. They set their drinks on the ridiculous coffee table. The thing had a polished, laminated cedar surface, and the legs were genuine Texas longhorn cattle horns. The silence was awkward, but Ira was grateful for it, and he began to appreciate Cliff's taste. It was the worst sort of Texas gaudy, but it was sincere, almost childlike in its innocence. Cliff's intense passion for his quest for the Golden Grail invested the library with an incongruous sense of the sacred.

We find peace in the strangest places, Ira thought as he reached for his beer.

13

Over the Edge

He fell, tumbling slowly in the cool air. *This is no dream*, Lew thought, recalling nightmares of falling into a bottomless pit. In a strange paradox of feeling, the knowledge that it was really happening saved him from the horrid, nightmarish sensation of falling. This turning of reality upside down made him laugh, and the realization that he had time to laugh made him aware that he was falling a considerable distance. The air was buffeting his face with increasing force as the relentless acceleration of gravity continued to do its work.

This is it, he thought. *The end.* With that thought his feet slammed into something hard and cold. A white-hot pain went through his body with the impact. His arms shot out in an instinctive move to brace himself. He was still going down, but very slowly. He opened his eyes to an eerie underwater underwater panorama. There were fantastic coral formations in all directions. The reefs were luminescent. They radiated soft pastel light in shades of yellow and green. The underwater currents, combined with the subtle variations in texture and intensity, produced a twinkling effect. He looked up and could discern no surface from his depth. He was suspended about ten feet from the bottom.

He kicked and rose a little, but his soaked sweater and jeans were a significant drag. Desperate for air, he pulled off his running shoes and unbuttoned his pants. He began swimming in earnest, pulling for his life to get to the still-invisible surface. He interrupted his breaststrokes just long enough to pull his pants off. His black jeans and red briefs settled slowly to the bottom of the sublunar coral garden. Then he jerked his sweater over his head. He knew it was only a matter of seconds before he ran out of oxygen. Naked, he felt suddenly free. The water caressed his every pore, and he spread his legs wide, kicking like a newborn amphibian. He had always been an excellent swimmer. In college he had once tied the school record for the thousand meter. He forced himself to remember that race, the feel of his body sliding wet as his arms pulled him through the water.

He detected a subtle change in the light just above and pulled hard with what he knew would be his last stroke. Then his head broke the surface and water was sputtering from his mouth and nostrils as he sucked air into his lungs with heaving gasps.

When he was able to breathe normally again, and his heart was no longer trying to burst from his chest, Lew began to look around. He was in the middle of an underground lake. The soft light from the coral filtered up through the clear water, partially illuminating the underground vault. Cavern, Lew decided, was too modest a term for it. Looking up he could not find the place from where he had fallen, nor could he see any roof. And in all directions he saw only water.

A disturbing series of thoughts began to creep through his mind. *I could be in the middle of a vast lunar ocean. The moon is a place of nightmares. This is where I finally come face-to-face with the dark side!*

These fears and others took his breath away, and he began flailing as he struggled to keep himself afloat. He recalled the two most terrifying dreams from his childhood in vivid detail. The first was a classic dream of falling. The other was finding himself in the middle of a limitless ocean, where unknown creatures, leviathans of the deep, swam beneath him.

Lew flung himself backwards and spread his arms. *This is ridiculous, I'm about to drown of fear.* That thought helped to calm him. It wasn't that he was no longer afraid, but the thought of drowning from fear was too embarrassing. He rolled over and began swimming freestyle.

The rhythmic strokes and regular breathing brought him back to himself and the need for action.

Several minutes later he stopped to look around. There was still no sign of a shoreline. As far as he could tell he was still in the middle. Worse, there were no visible landmarks by which he could gauge his direction—he could end up swimming in circles. He knew, in fact, that, no matter how hard he tried, he would eventually make a large circle. Without lanes to guide him, Lew's right-hand stroke, slightly more powerful, would dominate.

He rested on his back for a while, and noticed two things. The water was cold, he guessed about sixty-eight degrees Fahrenheit. His arms and legs were not yet numb, but he knew they soon would be. Before long he would succumb to hypothermia and sink to a watery lunar grave. The other thing he noticed was a slight current.

He begin to swim in the direction of the current, reasoning that it must lead to a narrowing of the water's boundaries. The flow was subtle at first. He had to stop every few moments to regain his sense of it. Soon, however, it was carrying him, so that when he floated on his back there was no mistaking the drift.

Constantly scanning in both directions perpendicular to his motion he finally thought he detected something to his left. He began swimming that way, noting that his arms and legs felt ominously heavy. He pulled harder and was sure of a shoreline.

The current was now stronger than he would have liked, pulling him away from his goal. He adjusted his stroke accordingly. He saw a rocky shelf jutting into the water. The surface was luminescent, giving off a textured, golden glow.

Finally he was close enough to reach for a purchase. His fingers were numb, and it was difficult to hold on to anything. His task was made harder by the slippery vegetation and the current, which was now quite strong.

He managed to close his fingers around a protruding piece of rock, which would have been jagged were it not for the mossy growth covering its surface. He stopped himself, trying to marshal enough strength to pull his body out. He could only move his legs with a great deal of effort and concentration, and the cold was moving in, closer to his viscera.

Lew glanced over his shoulder in the direction of the current and gasped. The channel was still very wide, but he could just make out the other side. Of real concern, however, were the rapids a short distance downstream. The lake was now a wide river, and, judging from the sounds, there was white water up ahead.

He gripped with a last heroic effort and began to pull. He could still barely kick, and it was enough to get his chest out of the water. He was able to grab another protrusion with his other hand.

The drama of the struggle that ensued would not have been immediately evident to a casual observer. One would have seen Lew's naked body, looking extremely pale in the eerie half-light, upper torso out of the water, pulling to rise an inch or so more onto the slippery rock ledge. A long pause would ensue with some rapid shallow breathing, and then the effort would be repeated, with perhaps another inch or so of progress.

In the lunar gravity, if the cold had not robbed him of most of his strength, he could have leapt onto the shore. As it was, he was fighting for his life. *How could it come down to this?* he wondered. *Nothing I have learned or experienced matters at this moment, except my ability to concentrate, grab, and pull.*

And this he did. He needed just one more inch before he could wriggle the rest of the way out. With his right hand he grabbed for another slippery hold. His fingers closed around the mossy rock, and he began to pull. Then the old injury to his wrist, no doubt aggravated by the cold, caused the tendons and nerves to fail. It was only a split second, and then the whole intricate system of forearm, wrist, hand, and fingers was back on-line. It was the sort of thing that might have cost him a volley in a tennis game or caused him to miss a lead guitar riff.

In this case, however, the consequences were more serious. His left hand was holding tight to a thick clump of the mossy growth. When he lost the other grip the added strain cause the vegetation suddenly to tear free from the rock. His chest and pelvis, denied support, slid swiftly back down into the water.

He tried to swim, but it was useless. In his weakened condition he was no longer a match for the swift current. Within moments he was being swept into the raging torrent. It was all he could do occasionally to thrust his head above the spray and steal a few gulps of air.

The sound he had heard became a roar. The channel was narrow only relative to the dimensions of the lake. It was still several hundred yards from shore to shore. It was coming, however, to an abrupt end. Lew had a sense of it, and got one momentary glimpse. The falls were gargantuan, on the scale of Niagara, a wide whitewater river suddenly become vertical. The awesome sight laced his terror with a tinge of euphoria as he was swept over the edge.

14

A Serious Game

Monica sat alone in the Palace of the Sun. Her privileged seat as one of the ten Guardians was at the far end of the hall atop the steps that ascended ten feet off the marble floor. The steps were wide, extending along the entire curved wall at the rear of the palace.

She gazed out over the hardwood judicial bench into the vast expanse of the building's interior. It was said that the palace was built before the ascension, but Monica, a student of history as well as the law, knew better. It was less than fifteen hundred years old.

Years are measured on Atlantis exactly as they are on earth, by one revolution around the sun. Atlantean years are of precisely the same duration as terrestrial years because the ancient Guardians purposely positioned the lost continent in an orbit exactly opposite that of earth's. Atlantis is invisible to earth, always on the other side of the sun, always the same distance from the golden giant that rules the solar system. This hid the continent from view and the giant resonator buried deep underneath the palace masked any gravitational evidence of its existence.

Monica's century of tenure as a Guardian would be up at the year's end, only a few months off. For many years she had looked forward to relinquishing her responsibilities, but now, as she looked up at the giant domed skylight, her mind was troubled.

The "problem of earth" had never much concerned Monica. She had given the necessary lip service to the policy of monitoring that kept agents on their ancient home. She had carefully avoided ideological clashes with Jistane, her most conservative colleague, on the issue.

This personal policy of accommodation had been an uncomfortable compromise. She was convinced that all the espionage and secret "contingency" plans were a waste of valuable resources. It was expensive, the necessary transports and monitoring systems were a constant drain on the treasury. Young citizens were forced to waste years in the mandatory tour of duty as terrestrial agents, and youth was an ever more precious commodity on Atlantis. And the obsession with earth carried a psychological cost that was even harder to measure.

While she seldom admitted it, even to herself, Monica dreamt of a unified field. She had a vision of a universe in which life existed in the stars and the nucleus of the atom. She hoped, along with a core of other visionaries, that humanity was destined to explore these regions. The key would be the final theory that unified all the known forces of nature. *Actually,* Monica thought, *it won't be a final theory at all, only a new beginning.*

But she saw her people, her culture, looking more and more to the past, to earth as a threat, a problem to be solved. Certainly earth was at a crossroads. The teeming mass of earthbound humanity would either come to grips with looming ecological and social crises and rise to the challenge of exploring new macro and nano frontiers, possibly joining with Atlantis, or they would destroy themselves.

It was a situation worth monitoring, and, if possible, Atlantis should help to guide their primitive ancestors, but earth was not, in Monica's opinion, a threat, and certainly not a problem that demanded such a large redirection of valuable resources. Political realities had, for several decades, dictated that Monica keep publicly silent about these views. Ever since the earthlings had unlocked the secret of atomic energy, the mood had grown uglier.

Now she was beginning to wish she had not been so reticent. She had assumed that the militant attitude toward earth was a passing fad, nothing to risk valuable political capital over. But things were slipping out of control and soon she would be just another citizen, unable to do much about it. She was the most senior of the liberal Guardians. After she was gone Jistane would have his way.

She knew he was just biding his time. And she also knew that he was acutely aware of her moderating influence, how she had subtly rewritten decrees so as not to challenge him directly, but having the effect of disarming his most radical policy initiatives. He could have chosen to confront her more directly, but he, too, understood the value of political capital. Why spend it when time was on his side?

She looked again at the brief before her. The seal, which she had broken that morning, was bright green, indicating top secret. There were only ten copies, one for each Guardian.

She loved the view from behind the bench. The palace was built from the classical paradigm that predated and guided the architects of ancient Greece and Rome. The greatest buildings of those earthly civilizations placed beside the palace would be seen as imitations, good imitations but copies just the same.

It was some hundred yards long and thirty yards wide. Monica looked down the length of the great aisle that led to the entrance at the other end, where she could see the magnificent gold-and-nickel-plated doors. The domed skylight was a full fifty yards above the marble floor. It occupied the center of the palace's vaulted roof and was fifty feet in diameter.

The great aisle went through an atrium in the center of the palace. The atrium was filled with a vast array of antediluvian plants. Giant ferns and orchids of astounding beauty reached for the sunlight that constantly filtered through the dome.

Behind her and along both sides of the interior were Doric columns. The overall effect was one of great power united with breathtaking beauty. It was the image that all empires strove to create. As such it was an ideal never perfectly achieved. Monica had, until recently, believed in the ideal as something her culture would always strive for.

But when she again opened the brief she could no longer entertain that optimism. She read again, with disbelief, the title:

EARTH, THE FINAL RESOLUTION,
THE FRACTURING OF TERRESTRIAL FIELD RESONANCE
USING A NEW AND REVOLUTIONARY APPLICATION
OF THE LUNAR RESONATOR

Then she turned the page and reread the first paragraph,

> Whether or not any humans survive the field dissonance is irrelevant. Any that do can easily be controlled or eradicated. The main problem will be solved. A dangerous and renegade culture that threatens the peace, stability, and very life of the solar system will be gone. Any humans that survive will do so in a primitive state—*there will be no more threat.* Whether or not we make use of the earth as a natural resource or merely choose to continue monitoring the planet is a political matter not relevant to this report.

"Contemplating a life free from all this?"

Monica, startled at the voice, turned to face Jistane.

"Sorry, Monica," he said. "I don't deliberately sneak up

on people. It's just my nature to move quietly. I forgot my notes for the speech I'm giving this afternoon."

"What speech is that?" Monica said, closing the brief and trying to appear casual about it.

"The Academy of Gnosis. They want me to talk about the population 'crisis.' The students are agitating again for renewed research. All the usual stuff. But now some of the faculty have joined in. They are clamoring for more funds to investigate the supposed drop in fertility rates."

"It is a fairly well established fact," Monica said.

"If you believe statistics," he said.

"Can we afford to ignore the data?" she said.

"These sorts of fluctuations happen. I don't doubt the analysis. But the data only go back five hundred years. I'm sure that if we had a more complete set, the bigger picture would not predict anything so dire as . . ."

"The death of our race?" Monica smiled.

"Exactly. This is all troublemaking for political leverage. Nothing more. The liberals want to change our policy of mandatory conscription for the young and ease up on terrestrial operations. But soon the point will be moot." Jistane returned the smile. The tension was palpable. "Can we count on your vote, Monica? It's probably the last major issue that will arise before your term is up. I should think you would want to go on record with the majority."

"Do you have a majority?" she said.

"Most certainly, but we would like to have you on board. Your support will give us the unassailable authority we need in order to . . ." his voice trailed off.

"In order to what, Jistane? Don't tell me you're having second thoughts? You, the rock of resolve, the pillar of conviction. After I'm gone you should easily dominate. You have no peers among us." She smiled again.

"I'm going to miss you, Monica," he said, sounding sincere.

"I'm sure," she said.

"But I meant what I said, we need your support. We're at a crossroads. The time to deal with earth has come. We can't put it off any longer, and a unanimous decision will give us the decisive mandate we need for such bold action," he said.

"*Bold*," she said, "is not quite the word I would have chosen. I'll give the report due consideration."

"Fair enough," he said, retrieving his notes from the drawer in front of his big, padded chair. "It really is time, Monica," he continued, straightening up and looking at her with a peculiar intensity, "for a *final solution*."

"Maybe it is," she said. "But in my experience final resolutions are far more final in theory than practice. They have a capricious way of changing into new beginnings."

His expression got very dark. "I'll see you," he said, struggling to smooth the creases on his brow, "later." Clutching his notes, he quickly walked down the steps, and strode down the long aisle. Monica noted the filtered sunlight that struck his head, giving his jet black hair a halolike shine.

Handsome man, she thought. *He must be close to a thousand years old.* She remembered that he had been something of a sportsman and wondered if he still had time for recreation now that he was consumed by such a serious game.

15

The Fate of the Earth

"We have compelling reasons," Ira said. "I need the story, and Cliff needs to get away until this thing cools down."

"But Alan is the only one *I* need," Miranda said.

"It's true I'm the only one who knows the details of the ship's structure," Alan said, "but wouldn't it be useful to have this story documented? Ira's the ideal person."

"Why?" Miranda said.

"You can't just let something like this go down without any record for posterity!" Cliff said.

"And having that documentation just might save your political career as well?" Miranda said pointedly.

"Hell yes!" Cliff said.

"I want to make sure, Ira," Miranda said, "that you won't turn your report into a tabloid piece. If you do it, write it straight."

"Ira's the best," Cliff said. "Old school. He won't tell it if it ain't true."

"I won't need to exaggerate anything in this story," Ira said.

"I suppose not," Miranda said. "We'll need to leave immediately. You realize we could all be killed."

"How's that?" Ira said.

"There are ominous signs that the lunar field resonator has more power than anyone realized and can act as a *dissonator*."

"What does that mean?" Alan said.

"No one knows who installed the lunar resonator," Miranda said, "but the Atlanteans have been using it as a shield for many thousands of years. The resonator had a limited range, but it was powerful enough to cloak the planet in an impenetrable barrier."

"What about all the space probes we have launched over the last twenty years?" Ira said. "They haven't been knocked off course or cast back into the atmosphere."

"No," Miranda said. "There was no need. Those things were never any serious threat. Mere toys, and quite primitive ones. It would have been foolish for them to reveal their presence just to knock an impulse drive rocket off course. The same goes for the lunar landings. NASA was too timid to send any explorers to the dark side of the moon, and even if they had, they would never have found the base. Those astronauts hit a few golf balls and fell back to earth never to return. It was a joke, kind of pathetic really. But Alan's levity drive is something else."

"What about you?" Ira asked. "If I'm to believe what I'm hearing, you ascended with an entire city, the so-called *Genesis Bomb*, the place you now call 'Arlandia,' past the moon into your own orbit around the sun. Why didn't they stop you?"

"They couldn't," Miranda said. "Alan has designed and grown his own resonator, an organic neural net that can resolve the powerful field-fracturing force of the lunar one. Without it, his ship could never utilize the levity drive to get past the moon's orbit. But I don't need a resonator."

"Why not?" Ira said.

"Because," she smiled, "I'm my own resonator. It's latent in your genes as well, but you are a long way from activating it. The human nervous system is designed to resolve the force of gravity into levity. With that power, the human brain acts as a powerful resonator, like the one Alan has grown."

"And the Atlanteans?" Ira asked.

"Many thousands of years ago, they discovered the technology that Alan has so recently utilized. They were also able to manipulate their DNA to greatly increase their longevity. Beyond that, however, their evolutionary progress is as blocked as yours is. Except for their long life spans, they are no different from terrestrial humans.

"They built a powerful resonator that enabled them to raise their entire continent into its own solar orbit. But they still have not unlocked the levitating potential in their own nervous systems, nor the photosynthetic power latent in their skin."

"And how are these things done?" Alan asked, eyeing her suspiciously. "You've said all this before—that we have the code in our DNA that will enable us to fly. And you claim that we can also develop superphotosynthetic molecules in our skins so that we can get our energy directly from the sun, freeing us from the necessity of producing our food. But I've been probing into the so-called 'silent strands' of human DNA, and have found nothing that makes any sense."

"It makes no sense," Miranda said, somewhat sharply, "because your biochemistry is too primitive. What I am is what you can become. You have the potential. But these more advanced characteristics won't just become active by themselves. As long as the human race remains obsessed with money and territory, and petty little career ambitions, you'll stay stuck.

"The next step in human evolution requires *active participation* on your part. It no longer suffices for you to play the old game of 'survival of the fittest.' Nature is waiting, waiting for you to rise to the occasion. It's a self-protective, self-regulating mechanism. Nature, the entire *cosmos,* is the ultimate cybernetic system. The latent powers to reverse the pull of gravity and tap directly into the energy of the sun won't become active while you still function at, or below, the level of selfish, vicious beasts."

"She's right," Cliff said. He was holding the book, *Secrets of the Golden Grail.* "It says as much in here. 'To look upon the Golden Grail we must first cleanse ourselves of the spiritual grime that keeps us bound.' "

A smile like that of the Mona Lisa stole across Miranda's face, but she remained silent.

"None of this tells me much as a *scientist,*" Alan said, annoyed. "Unproven theories of evolution and occult mumbo-jumbo aren't particularly useful in the lab."

"Have you *read* the book?" Cliff said, suddenly angry. He pounded his fist on the cover of the thick volume. It made a resounding thump.

"I've read enough of it to know that it's all been said before," Alan said. "I spent twenty years meditating and studying in Tibet and India. I am no stranger to secret doctrines. They have their place. In my experience, however, that sort of thing promises more than it can deliver, which is why I've turned to science."

"You think you will find the *truth* in science?" Cliff said.

"I don't think science is particularly concerned with truth," Alan said. "That's a popular misconception, that scientists discover the truth about things. Science is what works, and to that extent it may further our understanding, but as far as truth is concerned—who knows?"

Ira spoke up. "Miranda claims that she is somehow the next step in human evolution, but something sort of mysterious has to take place before we can become like her. Is that it?''

''Nothing that mysterious about it, really,'' Miranda said, ''but more or less that's right.''

''And so far, you are the only one?'' Ira said.

''With my abilities to fly and take nourishment directly from the sun?''

''Yeah.''

''No, I'm not. There is another in my colony of Arlandia. She, like me, is something of an anomaly. The circumstances that conspired to make us possible are no longer operative, nor are they likely to be again. But there are others as well. At first I thought they made their homes in our solar system, perhaps in other orbiting biospheres, like Arlandia. But now I suspect they have migrated farther out, possibly living in the spaces between the stars.''

''But nothing could survive in that void,'' Ira said.

''Evolution goes on,'' Miranda said. ''These creatures, I suspect, have developed energy systems so efficient that they can survive for long periods on starlight. They may occasionally need to return to the field of the sun or even the earth. I think that those visits are what account for the various sightings of UFOs and UFSs that have so captured our earthly imaginations.''

''UFS, Unidentified Flying Subjects,'' Ira said, ''the stuff of tabloid journalism.''

''Just because it's in the papers doesn't mean it isn't true,'' Miranda said. ''*Even* those papers.''

''Have you come in contact yet with any of these more advanced creatures?'' Ira said. ''Up there, I mean, in Arlandia?''

''No,'' Miranda said. She sounded slightly disappointed, anxious even.

''The Atlanteans?'' Ira said.

''Not directly,'' she said, ''but they know about us, and we know about them.''

''And what about Lew? Why did Tana kidnap him, and what the hell are they doing on the moon?'' Ira was in his element, questions spawning more questions.

''I'm concerned about Lew,'' Miranda said. ''We have

a special bond.'' She didn't elaborate on this. ''But I'm afraid Lew's fate may be inextricably bound up with a much larger issue.''

''What's that?'' Ira shot back.

''The fate of the earth,'' Miranda said.

16

The Golden Grail

Lew was turning around slowly as the lyrics to an old Neil Young song spun through his mind. There were sparkles in front of him. He blinked and took a breath.

Immediately he was sputtering and choking, flopping and flailing. He had been floating facedown in a little pool, spinning to the eddy. *Why didn't I drown*? he wondered, realizing that he had been floating facedown and unconscious. That he was still alive was remarkable. He could only imagine that some deep-seated survival instinct had kept his head bobbing enough so that he could steal sufficient air to ward off death.

''Alright,'' he muttered, and felt a smooth bottom with his feet. The pool was shallow. He stood up and hugged himself. The air was about the same cool seventy degrees. Wet and naked he began to shiver. He fell back into the water and breathed a deep sigh of satisfaction.

The pool was warm. Lew remembered the numbing cold of the lake and being swept over the falls. He realized how lucky he had been. If he hadn't been drawn into warm, spring-fed pool, he would most certainly be dead from hypothermia.

He floated on his back, soaking up the delicious warmth. The cavern in which he found himself was smaller than the huge chamber with the lake that fed into the massive waterfall. Lew shuddered at the image of that precipitous wall of water.

The walls and ceiling, about fifty feet high, were lined with the mossy, luminescent growth. His eyes were growing more accustomed to the strange light. Curiously, one could make out more, rather than less, detail. Since the light came from all directions, shadows were virtually eliminated. This gave the scene an odd flatness. The colors of the growth in the smaller chamber were brighter and more varied. The overall effect was cartoonlike. Lew had the bizarre, somewhat pleasant, feeling that he was inside one of the classic animated Warner Brothers or King Features cartoons that had so captured his imagination as a child.

The lunar landscape below the surface was the exact opposite of the barren, colorless terrain visible from earth. Water sounds dominated the acoustic landscape. The rushing, babbling, and dripping noises blended into an alien harmony that Lew found especially relaxing after his ordeal.

As he continued to float and slowly turn, he thought, *I can't stay here forever*. He was already beginning to feel the pangs of hunger and thirst. He cautiously sipped some of the warm springwater and realized it was foolish to be so conservative. He had already swallowed large gulps in his struggle with the rapids and falls, and, in any case, he would die without water.

Thirst sated, he stood up and stepped out of the pool. The contrast in temperature caused him to cry out. Yelling, projecting forcefully from his diaphragm, seemed to help. The echoes reverberated for several seconds, which gave the brief illusion that he was not so alone. He began jogging in place. The soft moss was less slippery away from the water and made the action surprisingly easy on his feet.

Several minutes of this took the edge off the bitter chill. He was almost dry, and, while not warm, he felt that he could survive. His hunger, however, had grown far more insistent. His body needed fuel.

He walked to the bank of the river. The channel was

about thirty feet across. There were patches of white water, but the fury of the water was much abated. He saw that he had been lucky indeed. A large boulder broke the flow upstream. He had been swept to the side where the current wound its way into the little spring-fed pool. If he had gone the other way, he most certainly would not have found so safe a haven. *I would be dead*, he thought, looking at the dark turbulent waters on the far side of the rock.

"One could always be dead," he muttered to himself. Then, with startling clarity, he thought, *Dead's easy, life's a little more complex.*

Afraid of getting lost in the labyrinth of his own mind he gazed upstream, searching for the falls. He could hear them clearly, and they sounded relatively close. But the underground lunar light, while it gave a surprising vividness to objects close by, made distances impenetrable.

With nothing more than a desire to sustain his life, Lew began to work his way along the shore back upstream in search of food. At first the peculiar lack of depth and soft pastel illumination made the going difficult. When he looked more than a few feet in front he became unsteady, and he tripped over his own feet more than once. He learned to focus only on his immediate surroundings.

The rewards were delightful. What was flat and disorienting at a distance became sharp and detailed up close. By relaxing his eyes he could see things in astonishing detail. He stopped at one point to stare at a rock. It seemed alive, so intricate were the colors and forms. *This is a place of jewels,* he thought. He imagined Sinbad the sailor and Odysseus the wanderer—their separate adventures in the treasure cave of the Cyclops where rubies, emeralds, and gold sparkled in every corner.

He blinked, and the image vanished, but the reality was actually more impressive. Lew got down on his hands and knees to examine the rock more closely. It was mostly covered with mossy growth that varied in color. There were patches of forest green, deep blues, and sunset pinks. All this light came from a living source and, consequently, shimmered slightly. The light from the walls was slightly more intense, and the river itself sparkled from the growth that lined its bottom.

Lew scratched the moss on the rock's surface, and it gave off a pungent smell, slightly sweet but sharp. He tore a small piece and cautiously nibbled it. The taste was shocking in its intensity. While not a connoisseur of mushrooms, Lew assumed it was something like the taste of exotic wild fungus only much stronger.

He let the sensations on his taste buds subside. He decided that, for all its alien harshness, the stuff did taste like food. He tore a larger piece and ate it very slowly.

Hunger somewhat satisfied, Lew resumed working his way upstream. He felt the spray before he got to it. The roar of the falls dominated all other sounds, but because of the lunar gravity, it was more mellow than comparable cascades on earth. The water, accelerating more slowly in its descent, hummed more than boomed.

The sight was something earthly tourists would pay dearly to see. Lew estimated the width of the falls at more than half a mile, and the height at several hundred feet. At its base the water formed a lake, much smaller than the one above. This emptied into the river that had carried Lew about a mile downstream.

He followed the rim of the lake as far as he could, trying to get as close to the falls as possible. He stopped where it was too steep and rugged to proceed with ease. He knew that he could climb faces that would have stopped him on earth, but without the protection of shoes and clothing, he felt more vulnerable on the jagged and slippery stuff.

He hugged himself. The spray striking his bare skin made the lunar chill more immediate. He was standing on a ledge looking into a particularly calm part of the lake. The water was crystal clear, and he could see to the bottom. It looked to be about twenty feet deep. There were colored plants and strange-looking fish swimming in it.

Something flashed on the bottom, catching his attention. It was a shimmery golden gleam, oddly stationary in the incessant motion of the aquatic life. Knowing how chilly the water was, his action was foolish, a little crazy.

He leapt, executed a passable dive, and knifed into clear, cool depths. The shock was exhilarating. He came up for air and went back down.

His ears gave him a sharp pain, and he ran out of breath before he could get to it. He surfaced and floated on his back, getting his breath. He could already feel the cold begin to penetrate his limbs, but he had to make one more dive.

This time his ears cleared and he got to the bottom. His long, wavy brown hair flew about in all directions as he frantically searched for the source of the flash. He saw something just as he knew his air was all but gone. He was surprised at how easily it yielded to his wild grasp. Again he raced madly for the surface, and broke through just as he felt a nauseating blackness begin to take hold.

He swam a few dozen yards to a place where the shoreline rose only a few feet above the water. Even so it was not easy getting out. Lew clung to his prize with one hand and struggled with his other, but finally flopped up onto the soft, moss-covered rock.

That was stupid, he thought. But he immediately changed his mind when he looked at the object he had retrieved. It was a golden cup with two handles. The thing was elaborately worked without being ornate. It was an elegant piece of art. Lew looked inside and saw an inscription. It was in script that reminded him of both Sanskrit and Arabic. *Maybe Alan could decipher this*, he thought.

He was sure it was significant. He recalled another object that had seemed to carry a special significance from the moment he saw it. That had been the beginning of a series of adventures that he still did not understand.[6] Staring at the Golden Grail that he now held in his hands made him shiver with a chill that went deeper than the cold of the icy waters and the lunar air.

[6]*Mind-Surfer.*

17

Something Like a Philosopher

Miranda's green disc settled gently on the lunar surface over the air lock entrance to the Atlantean outpost.

"Is there any reason why you designed this thing to look like a flying saucer?" Ira asked.

Miranda took her hands from the recessed controls, looked at Ira, and smiled. "No special reason," she said.

Ira was beginning to appreciate the subtleties of this strange creature. Her response convinced him that it was a wry gesture of humor on her part to make her vessel the image of 1950s science fiction fantasy and phobia.

"The green color *is* functional," Miranda said, as if reading Ira's thoughts. "The skin of my ship is a high-performance version of my own skin, able to generate power directly from sunlight."

She opened an iris-shaped hatch in the floor by passing her hand over the center of it. The thing responded by dilating, and they descended into the air lock.

"What if they don't want company?" Cliff said.

"They've got it," was Miranda's only reply.

But the chamber was empty. There was no sign of Lew, Tana, or Alan's spaceship. They wandered about for a few minutes taking it all in.

"What *is* this place?" Ira said, finally.

"I don't know," Miranda said, "but I suspect it is only the tip of the iceberg."

"What do you mean?" Alan had found the cabinet and was sniffing the bottle that contained some of the drink Lew and Tana had so recently enjoyed.

"I mean," she said, "that this is only a reception chamber. The resonator is most likely hidden somewhere else, along with other mysteries."

"Yes, of course," Cliff said, almost to himself.

"Of course what?" Ira said.

"The Golden Grail. The book says that it may be found in the bowels of the great cosmic shield, the shield of *secrets*. The moon, as Miranda already explained, functions as a shield. The resonator shields the rest of the solar system from the barbarous earthlings. The moon is also a place of secrets. One of those secrets may be what I am searching for."

"The Golden Grail you mean." Alan failed to conceal the sarcasm he felt. He took a swig from the bottle, as if to make up for the barb.

"You should be careful what you drink in a place like this," Cliff said.

"It's alright," Alan said. "I have some experience in these matters. This is a harmless fungal extract. It may even be quite nutritious, possibly intelligence enhancing as well." He offered the bottle all around. There were no takers.

"So how do we proceed?" Cliff said.

"Proceed where?" Ira said.

"To find the greater mysteries of this place," Cliff said.

Miranda was already examining the door at the far end of the chamber. Tantalyes had secured it, so that even with her great strength she could not budge the thing. "I suspect this is the way down and in," she said.

"So we are stuck at the surface of things," Alan said, "as *usual*." He had taken the bottle and was sitting on the sofa. "Maybe that's the key to life, after all." He said this with bitterness. "Just be content to live at the surface, never try to get to the *bottom* of anything. With the possible exception of the *ladies*, naturally." Miranda gave him a hostile look. He took another drink.

"I'd be careful with that stuff, Alan," she said. "It could be quite potent." Her eyes were fiery. Ira was stunned at the sudden ferocity there.

"Where are the Atlanteans?" Ira said. "I mean, if this

is their base, shouldn't someone be here—minding the store or something?''

''Some of the time,'' Miranda said. ''But I don't think Lew and Tana are here any longer.''

''Then where?'' Ira said, equally surprised at how quickly she had regained her composure.

''They couldn't have gone anywhere in the ship, without Alan's resonator,'' Miranda said, ''unless . . .''

''Unless what?''

''Unless they were kidnapped. Either someone from Atlantis temporarily shut down the resonator, or, what seems more likely, escorted them away.''

''Captives!'' Alan said loudly. He was grinning, brandishing the bottle. He had drunk about half the contents. ''Prisoners of the lost continent on the other side of the sun! What a story, Ira! You finally got it, the scoop of the century! If you can just get someone to believe it.'' He began laughing so hard that he doubled over on the couch, clutching his belly with one hand.

Before the bottle could slip from his other hand, Miranda deftly removed it, corked it, and put it back in the cabinet. Alan didn't seem to notice. When his fit subsided he got very quiet and continued to lie in the fetal position.

''Will he be alright?'' Cliff asked.

''An overdose,'' Miranda said, ''I'm pretty sure the stuff contains some novel organic compounds that mimic the action of certain neural transmitters. One or two cups probably act as a mild stimulant or even a gentle euphoric, but Alan downed half the bottle, and now his brain is busy trying to metabolize it all. He'll be OK in a few hours.''

''In the meantime?'' Ira said.

''I don't suppose I have any choice,'' Miranda said. ''I'll go to Atlantis and try to find Lew.''

''Is that wise?'' Ira said. ''I mean what kind of reception are you likely to get?''

''I don't know,'' Miranda said, ''I'm not an enemy—yet.''

''What about us?'' Ira said.

''I'll have to drop you off in Arlandia. You'll be safe there, unless . . .''

"What?"

"Unless things escalate. Atlantis has taken a neutral, observer attitude toward our little colony. But I suppose that could change."

"War!" Cliff spoke up.

"Possibly," Miranda said.

"But," Ira said, "you couldn't stand against them. You're just a small city. Atlantis is an entire continent. They must have weapons of incredible destructive power. And you . . ."

"It may not come to that," Miranda said. "And if it does, we may have some surprises for them."

"I'm staying here!" Cliff said.

"Are you crazy?" Ira said. "You can't . . ."

"The grail is down there!" Cliff pointed to the door. "And I'm going to find it! I have waited all my life for this. I may never get here again, and I'm not about to—"

"Be reasonable, Cliff," Miranda said. "I doubt if you can get that door open, and even if you could, what makes you think the conditions down there are anything but inimical to human life?"

"I'll find a way!" Cliff said.

"How will you survive?" Miranda said. "The only evidence of food or drink is that stuff that Alan drank. Do you want to lie around like that, waiting—until something just *happens*?"

They all looked at Alan. He was now lying on his back, eyes closed, but it was clear he was not sleeping. His whole body had a tension that signified rapt attention to something that none of them could see.

Cliff looked quickly away. "OK," he said. "You're right! It doesn't make sense for me to stay here." He walked over to Miranda and stood very close, looking deep into her eyes. "You must take me with you!" He whispered so forcefully that they all heard.

"I can't—" she began.

"You must!" he shouted. "Don't you see? Only in Atlantis can I find what I need to know, how to get down there, how to get to the Grail!"

"You don't understand, Cliff. These people are highly sophisticated. They have not lived on earth for millennia. Your quest will seem trivial to them. I don't want you to get hurt."

"You are not my savior," Cliff said solemnly. "It's my life, and I will risk it as I choose in the pursuit of the one thing that is worthy. It's wrong of you to gainsay it!"

Miranda blinked and looked away. Ira noted it was the first time she appeared unsure of herself. "We'll see," she said softly, "but right now we have to get to Arlandia. Help me with Alan."

They carried him back through the air lock and into the ship. His body was strangely pliant yet totally inert. His breathing was slow and regular.

"Is he going to be alright?" Ira asked, as they ascended, and the scarred, other face of the moon rapidly receded.

"I hope so," Miranda said, sounding more doubtful about her maker's prognosis.

"He has gone to the flip side," Cliff said.

"What?" Ira said, but Cliff said no more. He just stared back at the moon, then turned to look out into the vast deep. The solar rays that bathed one side of his face gave him an odd dignity that Ira had never seen in the man.

He looks like Aristotle or something, Ira thought. But soon he, himself, was caught up in the awesome beauty of the solar system beyond the terrestrial field. At that moment Ira looked something like a philosopher himself.

18

Mistress of Riddles

Lew was too scientific minded to believe the grail had any magical powers. But, after finding it, he felt like exploring, following the waters downstream. He dismissed the subtle change in attitude as psychological—*whatever that means*, he thought.

There was no tracking of time in the ordinary sense. He ate the mossy stuff when he was hungry, drank from the cool waters when thirsty, and slept when tired. With clothing, the temperature would have been ideal, but Lew was naked and cold. The vegetation was nourishing, if monotonous, and Lew sensed that it had a mild stimulating, possibly euphoric, effect.

The going was fairly easy. There were some steep descents, but the lunar gravity helped. And, in spite of the conditions, Lew felt that he was getting stronger. He wondered if the strange diet was responsible. He normally kept himself in pretty decent shape, but he could actually see the muscles in his arms and legs filling out. His chest felt bigger, and, while he had no way to measure it, he was sure his endurance was increasing.

After what felt like a week, Lew thought he detected the beginnings of a trail. With the slow duration that passed for time, he became certain. Others had walked this route although, by the looks of it, not for a very long time. The path was about two meters wide. It was most conspicuous because it was the only place that the moss did not grow. The surface consisted of a thin layer of light brown dust. Lew wondered at that since he had not seen dust anywhere else. Almost certainly the path had been laid and the dirt brought in. It made for a comfortable walking surface. Occasionally Lew thought he detected footprints. But when he knelt to inspect them it was impossible to be sure. They were too faint. If they were footprints, they were old, probably ancient. The air was almost still, but there were subtle currents. Those and the damp air could obscure any tracks, but it would take a long time.

The river was about a hundred meters wide. The cavern extended another hundred meters or so on either side and was at least that high. The dimensions of the place gave it an aura of majesty. His feelings were so new and different that introspection was baffling, so he stopped analyzing. He was not lonely and, while his sense of his former life was vivid and clear, he did not think of escape or rescue.

He did wonder, *How far does it go? To the center of the moon? Or could it go on forever?* He found that prospect strangely exhilarating.

Then he reached the end. For some time he sensed a different quality to the light, a brightness ahead. Then he was surprised to see the path flanked by trees. They were small, not more than ten feet high, and their leaves were a rainbow of different colors, all of them in the soft, pastel hues of the mossy growth.

The path diverged from the river, and for the first time in his journey Lew was ascending. He could just make out something white and round in the distance. As he got closer it took on the contours of a dome. It had a marbled look—the surface was really an off-white streaked with thin lines of gray and brown. The dome was the top of a rectangular building that was supported by columns.

The path ended at the base of a hill. The domed structure sat at the top, and leading up to it was the most impressive entryway Lew had ever seen. Two flights of stone steps snaked symmetrically up the hill. There was a lush green landscape between them. At the top where the two flights of steps met was an ornate, carved stone structure that reminded Lew of a giant keyhole. Trees flanked the entrance on both the right and left. These trees were large with smooth bark. The leaves were long and pointed, not quite green, almost blue.

Lew looked at the grail and back at the beautiful entrance. He was sure the two had a common origin. The contours of the cup suggested the curvature of the two stairways and vice versa. Lew had an immediate sense of the art of a culture, a people. It gave the scene an identity. For an instant he saw people ascending and descending—tall, elegant beings with noble bearing—and then it was gone, a figment of his imagination.

He started up the steps on the right. The stone was worn where many feet had gone before. It felt good on his naked soles. He could have easily taken the steps three or four at time, but he was enjoying the feel, his feet savoring each new surface. At the top he walked through the narrow, keyhole opening and stood before the building.

There was a large fountain in front. The water from it caught the colors of the cavern as it fell back into the pool. More of the large trees flanked the fountain on both sides. They were planted in hyperbolic arcs that made the area leading to the wide steps of the building look bigger than it was. The illusion had a pleasing effect on Lew. The space felt both personal and universal. He filled the grail with some of the cool water from the pool and drank. Then he approached the domed structure.

The words above the entrance were in the same script as the writing on the grail. Lew stared for a moment with the absurd feeling that he should be able to read it, that he recognized the language. Then the characters resolved back into an alien script. *Trick of the light*, he thought.

He walked up the steps and past the columns. The entrance to the building was a rectangular opening framed in carved stone. There was no door. Inside, in the center underneath the dome, was a circular marble table. A sphere, about one meter in diameter sat on a pedestal on the table. It gave off a pale white light. On reflection the glow revealed a subtle shade of yellow. It was particularly eerie in that the light did not fade in direct proportion to the square of the distance from the source. This was the glow Lew had seen in the distance, and it did not appear to obey natural law.

Consequently the interior of the building was illuminated with a remarkably even intensity. Everywhere one looked, objects were shown in the same soft tones, giving a *filmed* sense to the scene. Lew could almost convince himself that he was watching a movie in which he just happened to be one of the actors.

He approached the light. The interior was sparsely elegant. There were no statues, no paintings; the place was its own work of art. A terrifying figure suddenly shattered the sense of powerful beauty. Lew froze, the muscles in his legs tightened, his heart began pumping more forcefully, and his adrenal glands pulsated, flooding his system with the juice of action. Naked, his body taut, he looked like an ancient warrior, from a time when battle was purely a matter of flesh and blood.

He felt like a rat in the jaws of a hungry cat. Before him was the sphinx, beast of legend. The legend was seven feet high. Her human face and head merged perfectly with the body of a huge lioness. She sat in the classic posture of the cat, regal and powerful. Her expression was suitably inscrutable for the mistress of riddles.

He backed away and stepped to his right. Her eyes and then her head followed him; the hint of smile teased at her lips. She spoke. Lew couldn't understand, but as before, with the alien script, he felt that he *should* understand that he was on the verge of understanding.

By her expression, Lew did understand that her speech was a question. As the seconds passed with no answer she began to scowl. She shrieked and raised a massive paw. Lew jumped back, and the cat's claws sliced through a few millimeters of skin. He turned and fled. He ran out the entrance and past the fountain. All restraint gone, he fairly flew down the steps of the entryway, colliding with the stone post at the bottom. This sent him sprawling into the soft dirt of the path. He lay there breathing heavily for a few moments, a cloud of dust settling around him.

Then, remembering the terrible creature, he jerked himself up and around, but there was no sign of her. His left shoulder ached from his collision, and he was afraid it was dislocated. Cautiously raising it, he found it more or less intact. "The sphinx!" he said, and stood. He peered up the steps and saw only the wonderful light streaming through the big keyhole at the top.

Recalling the sudden appearance of the creature, Lew thought it could not have been real—perhaps a sophisticated hologram. Then he looked down at his chest to see the claw marks. He traced one of the crimson tracks with his finger and raised it his mouth. The sight and salty taste of his own blood convinced him she was no illusion.

Lew checked his pulse and found his heart striving to slow itself back to a more civilized pace. His mouth was very dry, and he walked to the river to drink. Thirst satiated, he went for a swim, which served to calm him further.

He thought of fleeing the scene, but found the prospect of turning back utterly depressing. Where would he go? There was nothing back the way he had come. And there was the grail. In his panic he had dropped it inside the domed structure.

He thought about his encounter with the sphinx, trying to separate his fear and analyze it rationally. She had only become violent when he had not responded to her question. *Perhaps if I can answer her*, he thought. But how to answer someone you don't understand?

He wanted to retrieve the grail and something more. In spite of the terrifying beast of legend, there was something attractive about the place. Lew knew that he could not leave without at least trying to find out what it was that drew him.

He ate some more of the mossy stuff, again surprised at how satisfying it was. Weary from his journey and fearful encounter, he lay down on a smooth flat rock. He listened to the soothing sound of the water for a few moments and fell into a deep sleep.

When he awoke he was amazed to see that there was no trace of the claw marks. His shoulder still hurt, so his fearful flight and tumble must surely have been real. But what had happened inside the building?

He slowly ascended. Each sight and sound seemed ominously significant. The splashing fountain spray whispered danger as he approached the open doorway. He stood outside, looking at the globe on the big table. Again the light drew him with a cool excitement.

So tense that he felt ready to leap up through the big dome, he entered and approached the table. He bent to retrieve the grail. Picking it up he looked again at the inscription inside. He was so surprised by what he saw that he nearly dropped it again. He looked up quickly, but there was no sign of the monster.

He looked back at the grail and could hardly believe his eyes. He could now read the inscription. At least that's what he thought at first. The characters were now familiar. He recognized words and grammatical structure, but just as he was on the verge of understanding the whole of it would slip away.

He thought he was about to get it when he heard her voice again. He looked up into the deep black eyes of the sphinx. Her hair, also black, tumbled thickly down to her feline shoulders. "Who are you?" he said, surprised at the strength of his voice. Fear was again taking hold.

She questioned him again. The sound of her voice was the audio equivalent to Lew's experience in trying to decipher the inscription on the grail. This time he recognized the words, but could not quite grasp the meaning of her query. She repeated it, more insistently. She rose up a little on her haunches. Lew could see her long tail twitching. He knew that twitch from watching his pet cat hunt. It was not a good sign.

But he held his ground and met her stare with his own deep brown eyes. He recalled someone telling him that his eyes had an unusual intensity. Real or imagined, he tried to summon that intensity to life. Again she spoke. This time he was sure that he understood, but the meaning played with his mind, teasing from some place just beyond his conscious grasp. He saw that she was about to strike again, and this time he was too close to escape the full force of those claws.

Suddenly he understood her question. She had repeated his question, "Who are you?" He said it back to her, amazed to hear himself speaking in her alien tongue. The words were suddenly part of his mind, as natural-sounding as English, yet clearly a new vocabulary and syntax.

She relaxed back on her haunches and her tail stopped its jerking. She smiled. It was not a reassuring smile, but at least her paws were again safely tucked beneath her. "Ah," she said, "we understand. Good. Understanding is important. Don't you think?"

"Uh, yeah," Lew said. He began to back away slowly.

She sprang up with terrifying speed and advanced so that her face was only inches from his. "Where are you going?" she said. Her fetid breath washed over him.

"Nowhere." He choked on the words, feeling quite nauseous.

"Nowhere to go?" she said. "Why don't you stay with me a while?"

"OK," Lew said thickly.

19

Axis of Creation

Alan was convinced that he was finally home. "After all these years," he said softly. He was newly awake, examining his room. He lay on a low bed with crisp white sheets. A beautiful hardwood wardrobe stood a few feet beyond the foot of the bed. All was light. The room was a small, transparent dome constructed of the same living polymer that formed the giant dome protecting Arlandia from the cold vacuum of space.

He sat up, still staring at the luscious green outside. He walked to the sliding door and opened it. Inhaling was delicious, so many scents of fresh new life. He reached down to pluck a blade of grass. It was more defined, more truly *a blade of grass*, than any he had chewed as a kid. *Hold infinity in the palm of your hand*, he thought, recalling the words of Blake, his favorite poet. He put it between his lips and bit, the acrid green taste sending a wave of pleasure through his mouth.

I always thought it would be like this, Alan thought. "Death!" he said out loud. "What a joke! This is life everlasting!" He skipped out onto the soft, green-blue turf, threw out his arms, and danced a little twirling jig, laughing all the while.

"Hello, Alan." The voice stopped him cold. He let his arms fall and turned to see a beautiful, green-skinned woman, not Miranda.

Alan realized he knew her, and the recognition forced him to admit that he was not yet in everlasting paradise. The woman was Raya, daughter of Arlandia, and he was on the tiny colony in orbit between earth and Mars. She had been born in Arlandia's genesis back on earth.[7] She was a truly synthetic woman, but to Alan she had always seemed perfectly natural.

"Are you alright?" she said.

"I think so," he said, an uncharacteristic expression of bafflement on his face.

"You were out for a long time. We were worried."

"How long?" he said.

"Two days."

"This place is different," Alan said.

"Yes," she said. "More civilized, don't you think?"

Alan remembered an uncultivated tangle of wildly differentiated flora. The diversity was still there, but Arlandia was more cultivated, more like a garden.

"You have houses now," Alan said, looking back at his little dome.

---

[7]*The Gaia War.*

"A few," she said. "We don't need them really, but they are cozy, don't you think?"

"Yeah," Alan said, "cozy." He rubbed his eyes and shook his head.

"You should rest. You need nourishment." Raya led him back to his room. He sat down on the bed. She opened a cabinet and poured him a ruby-toned, clear liquid. It went down like nectar, and Alan began to gulp.

"Drink it slowly," she said, putting her hand on the glass. "In a few hours we will eat."

"What happened to me?" Alan said.

"You drank too much of the mundi juice."

"The what?"

"Concentrated extract of mundis fungus," she said. "A little makes for a nice bit of euphoric stimulation, but the amount you took is dangerous. Your synapses were overloaded . . ."

"I had a vision!" Alan said, remembering suddenly.

"I'm sure you did," Raya said. "You can tell me about it later. But now you should rest."

But Alan could not rest. His face was flushed with the memory of his vision. "That's why I thought this was it!" he said, jumping to his feet. "The final resolution of all conflict, the ultimate harmonious state of being. Because I saw it! I *was* there."

"Please, try to calm down," she said. "You need to rest, and eat—"

"There is no time!" Alan suddenly stopped, thinking about what he had just said. He began to laugh so long and loud that Raya became worried. "I mean there is all the time in the world!" he said when his laughing fit ended. "Time is really an illusion, you know. I saw this. I experienced it directly. That's why I thought I had finally stepped outside of time for good when I woke up. But, alas, it appears I'm back."

"Welcome back," Raya said, eyeing him carefully.

"Ah, yes, I am back," he said, ignoring her. "But now I know what I have to do."

"What, Alan? What do you have to do?"

"I'll tell you about it later, when I know I can trust you," he said.

"Alright."

"Where are the others?" Alan said.

"Miranda is on her way to Atlantis. She took the journalist with her. He is to 'tell the story,' I think."

"And Cliff?"

Raya smiled, as if this were a joke. "Your friend Cliff is here . . . somewhere."

"I'll bet he was pissed. He wanted to go find the golden heart of the universe or something."

"On the contrary," Raya said. "He is actively engaged in searching for it here."

"We all have our little obsessions," Alan said, sitting back down. "You are right as usual, Raya. I do need to rest. Why don't you have a nap with me before dinner?" He smiled and patted the bed.

"I don't think that would be wise," Raya said. She affected a serious tone, but was secretly pleased that he seemed more like the Alan she remembered.

"Why not?"

"We shouldn't get involved. That's all. Things are complicated enough as it is, without . . . that . . ."

"And what, pray tell, is *that*?"

"You, sir," she said, getting up, "are an incorrigible bastard. I'll see you in a few hours."

Alan watched her leave, wondering if he preferred her with or without clothes. She had taken to wearing Indian-style clothes, loose-fitting white pajama pants and long navy blue tunic top. The garments enhanced her graceful movements, he decided, even as he remembered the lovely form underneath.

Raya's place was a bower with vines hanging from tree branches as walls and leaves and leafy canopy for a roof. But the vegetation in Arlandia all grew to a purpose. "This is what they were looking for in the last century," he said as he sat down on the grassy mound.

"What?" Raya said. She set a variety of fruits, vegetables, and herbs on the table before him. The table was a living thing, a tree that twisted out of the ground so as to present a large flat surface with part of its trunk. The bark was conveniently smooth. At the end of the table the tree straightened itself out, its branches providing a canopy for the diners.

"Evolution," Alan said. "The theory. You have heard of it?"

"I know about it," she said.

"There were those who opposed Darwin simply because they thought the whole idea of evolution threatened the orthodox religious view. Those same nuts are running around today, the fundamentalists.

"But there were others, scientists, who were uneasy—not about evolution, but about natural selection as the sole mechanism for it. Some thought it failed to account for the aesthetic in nature, the sublime patterns that run throughout creation. Others found natural selection simply inadequate to account for such diversity in so short a time."

"But we are talking about billions of years, Alan," she said.

"I know. That *is* a long time. I don't know, but when I look around me here it is plain that life is guided by more than a blind urge to survive and procreate. Arlandia is an ecosystem actively structuring itself to be a beautiful garden, a garden for us! Doesn't that tell you something?"

"Maybe," she said. "But what?"

"There is a purpose. There is a destiny. Each one of us plays a part, and I have discovered my part!" He picked up a hard, orange fruit and bit into it. The juice was mildly sweet with complex undertones of flavor that fired more than his taste buds.

Raya did not like the drift of the conversation. "What is it like on the moon?" she said.

As if he didn't hear he said, "All my life I have been searching for my place, my role. That's why I went to India and Tibet. I studied with the greatest masters but failed to find it. So I came back. These last few years have been frustrating, but now finally I've got it! It's glorious beyond words, and I'm part of it, no, more than part of it! I'm the axis of creation!"

"What do you mean? What are you talking about, Alan?" Raya was pouring a lightly fermented nectar. She offered it to Alan.

He took the cup and sipped, "Ah, what's this?"

"It's made from the prism berry. A very relaxing drink."

"You think I need to relax?" He smiled.

"It's a pleasant drink. Very mild."

"It's good." He drained the cup, and she refilled it.

"I am talking about my vision," Alan said. He did seem slightly less wound up. "That fungal extract is the key—the mundis juice. You see it opened a doorway, and I went through. Now I am prepared to lead others."

"What others?" Raya was beginning to wonder if the effects of the mundis had worn off, or worse. *Such a large dose on an ordinary human nervous system, the effects could be permanent*, she thought.

"You think I'm mad," Alan said. "No, don't deny it. I can see it in your eyes, plain as day. I don't hold it against you. I understand."

"You did have an awfully large dose of a powerful drug," she said.

"And it did change me," he said. "For the better. I'm going to save the earth. I know something about the *Genesis* process, you may recall. It shouldn't be too difficult for me to synthesize the active ingredient of the mundis.

"But I can do more. I know how to design fungal DNA that can infect most seed-bearing plants. The stuff is benign, a harmless fungus that would go virtually unnoticed. But once I have the molecular structure of the mundycin drug, it should be a relatively simple matter to splice a DNA sequence specific to the production of that molecule. In short, all grain and most fruit and vegetables will be factories for the stuff."

"And then?" Raya was growing more alarmed. Alan was more in control of himself—the sedative had done its work—but this only made his wild talk more disturbing.

"Then all the people of earth will be able to share in my vision!"

"But, Alan," Raya said, "the effects of the drug are

highly personal. Others will react differently.''

''Exactly! That's why the newly awakened minds of earth will need a leader.''

''And you think you're the one?'' she said.

''You think it sounds crazy. I don't blame you. But I know! I've *seen* it. This is all part of the cosmic plan. I don't have any illusions to grandeur. I'm not God. I'm just the particular instrument of the moment. I'm the temporary . . .''

''Axis of creation,'' she said.

''Yeah.''

''How will you get back to earth, to carry out this bold plan, I mean?''

''I don't need to go back just yet. Right now I need to design the fungal spores. Then we can send them in a little package, special delivery, a small organic missile. It should be easy to design. And I even have a guidance system ready-made. I've still got my resonator.''

''What's this 'we' business?'' Raya said.

''I'm counting on your help.''

''But this is crazy, Alan.''

''You think it's crazy now, but wait a few days, think about it. I'm talking about initiating a revolution in consciousness on earth that will save the planet, usher in a new era of harmony. Like here—in Arlandia.''

Raya did not want to admit it to herself, but as mad as Alan sounded she was beginning to suspect there was a divine method to it.

''You see this proves me right,'' Cliff said. The Speaker was sitting with his back to a giant tree. He still wore his jeans. His cowboy boots rested on massive roots. He chewed a long grass stem between his teeth, and his hat was pushed back. Alan had been looking for him for several days. Arlandia was never in darkness, but Miranda had set the colony in an axial rotation that produced shades of light and dark on an earthly twenty-four-hour cycle. It helped regulate the temperature of the giant terrarium and also gave the humans a familiar reference.

''What do you mean?'' Alan said.

"The *Secrets of the Golden Grail,* man! What do you think I'm talking about?" Cliff thumped the book. It was propped on a root next to him. "There is a whole chapter here on the Celestial Arcadia. It's the last stopping point before you penetrate the final mysteries . . ."

"Whoa, Cliff," Alan said. "This isn't some mystical Arcadia, the pastoral paradise of legend. This is a new world. I should know, I sowed the seeds that became Arlandia back on earth. In White Sands, New Mexico."

"What does that matter?" Cliff said. "Who cares how? We are all instruments in the plan."

"So what's next, Cliff?" Alan said.

"I wait."

"For what?"

"I wait for the Golden Grail to come to me. I no longer doubt that it will. I've broken the bonds of earth. Now it's only a matter of time."

"And then?"

"Then we will see," Cliff said. "The book is hard to understand at that point. The prophecy is unclear. But I have faith that all will become plain when I hold the cup in my hands.

"In the meantime I have all this. The clear sky, the radiance of the stars, and the intensity of the sun." He leaned his head back against the tree, causing his hat to tip forward, brim shading his eyes.

The polymer dome that enclosed Arlandia was a living part of the miniature biosphere. It shielded the life within from deadly solar spectra, and also gave the upper reaches of the atmosphere a slight blue tint. But it was no earthly sky. Looking up one saw the blackness of space and a dazzling display of starlight. Depending on the axial rotation cycle one could also see the majestic king of the solar system. Sol appeared as a brilliant yellow disc. Earth was a bright blue star.

Alan explained to Cliff that Miranda had installed a gravity resonator so that there was an effective three-quarter-G gravitational field throughout the colony. Cliff didn't seem to care.

"So you see," he said from under his hat, "everything

is as it was foretold. Long time ago. Son o' the Lone Star gonna see it through, too. The Eyes of Texas are watchin'."

"Yeah," Alan said, "the eyes of Texas." *Except*, Alan thought, *now those eyes are on me.*

20

Don't Fall on Me

Tana felt the familiar thrill as Atlantis loomed large. It was tempered by the realization that home was now almost certainly her prison—but it was still home.

Tantalyes guided Alan's ship into one of the port's many air locks. He shared Tana's conflicting feelings. Glad to be home, he was not eager to turn the woman over to the arcane Atlantean judicial system. As the inexplicable decline in birthrates continued, the Guardians were asking more of the young. *Too much*, Tantalyes thought.

They emerged into the customs station of Port Eidon. Tantalyes made all the proper declarations. The agent eyed Tana with a lascivious contempt. "I'll have to search the prisoner," he said.

"That won't be necessary," Tantalyes said. "She's my responsibility."

"And mine," the agent said, reaching for Tana's hips. He started to slide his hands around and down, squeezing her flesh through the silk pajama pants.

Tantalyes put his hand on the man's shoulder. The agent growled, "I can have you arrested."

"And I you," Tantalyes said, holding his shield in his palm in front of the agent's face. The badge was a small, gold-and-nickel-plated disk. The stylized sphinx engraved in its center identified him as a former Guardian and special envoy to the current council of ten.

The agent reluctantly released his hold on Tana and waved them on with a dark look.

Eidon was a city of approximately half a million on what was called the eastern side of the continent. Atlantis, like Arlandia, rotated around an axis through its center. The twenty-four-hour rotation was at a thirty-degree angle to the axis, so while it was never dark, there was a terrestrial, diurnal rhythm to the flow of time.

It was dawn, which meant that Eidon was beginning to slip down to its angle of maximum exposure to the sun. A few people were moving about the port in typical morning preparation for a day's work. Eidon was a busy port. Most of the traffic consisted of cruise ships. The rings of Saturn were an increasingly popular destination. Some mining ships put in there. But their cargos were small, consisting of precious gems and rare minerals valuable for their aesthetic appeal. Eidon was not an industrial city. The big shipments of ore and ice came in on the other side of the continent at Criton, a sprawling industrial center with ten times the population of Eidon.

Atlantis was roughly the size of the Indian subcontinent, about one million two hundred thousand square miles. Its shape was also similar. The northern side was the widest, and it tapered to a narrow point at the southern end. The directions, north, south, east, and west reflected the continent's former position in the Atlantic Ocean. They were the old terrestrial points of reference, and were retained out of convenience. Its position, relative to the sun, is the thirty-degree planar tilt that, together with its rotation gives Atlantis its days. Up was toward the massive polymer dome, and down pointed to the underside of the continent, where nothing lived since it was naked to the void of space. The underside of the continent housed an ancient gravity resonator which produced an effective force of approximately one G for the inhabitants.

Tana would have enjoyed the trip across the coastal mountain range, but the knowledge that she would soon be facing the Guardians in the Palace of the Sun made it impossible to relax. "Not the most pleasant homecoming," Tantalyes said. They were almost out of the foothills, nearing the high mountain pass.

"So the holistics are making a fuss," Tana said, referring to the demonstration outside the port.

"Eidon has always been a hotbed for liberal activity," Tantalyes said. "You should know. It's you hometown."

"I was always a good girl. I never got involved in any of that stuff. From what I hear the demonstrations are not confined to Eidon," Tana said.

"No, they are not." He didn't offer any more information on the subject. He was looking out the window of the coach at the subtropical greenery. The big ferns and spectacular orchids would soon yield to the more sparse, alpine forest.

Their transport was a horse-drawn coach. Atlantis held firmly to a philosophy of integrated technology. This meant that they never discarded anything from the past that might be of use. Horse conveyances were relatively nonpolluting, and with advanced suspension systems and nanotechnology applied to the wheel bearings, they were very comfortable and efficient. Solar-powered rail linked the manufacturing centers, but most citizens found the coaches a more genteel way to travel. In any case, the difficulty of maintaining a highway or rail line through the thirty-thousand-foot Poseidon Pass would have challenged even the most advanced engineers of Atlantis. Tana and Tantalyes could see the snowy peak of Mount Poseidon in the distance. Legend had it that one day the giant would shake, destroying the city of Eidon for its sins. It was an ancient piece of mythology, from before the ascension, and no one believed it anymore, although some wanted to.

The coach pulled into a long U-shaped drive. It was lined with palm trees. They were met by the inn's proprietor, a short man whose accent identified him as coming from somewhere in the central region.

"I'm sorry to hear you will be staying only one night," he said, as Tantalyes registered. "There is so much spectacular scenery—the Falls of Ino, the Cercian Gorge . . ."

"It's a pity," Tantalyes said.

"What's the hurry?"

"Pressing business in Telamon," Tantalyes said.

"May I inquire as to the nature of your business?"

"No." Tantalyes picked up their bags and ushered Tana to their room, without looking back.

"Sorry for the lack of privacy," he said, as they surveyed the space. "It's rather necessary, I'm afraid."

That night, while Tana was sleeping, Tantalyes retrieved his handheld nouancer from his bag and punched in a special code that linked him to a high security channel.

"Monica?" he said.

"Yes, it's me. How are you?" she said.

"Fine. Has the ship arrived?" Tantalyes had been required to turn Alan's craft over to the Guardians on arrival. He was forbidden to fly it in Atlantean airspace.

"Yes, it arrived this afternoon. Jistane is elated. He's convinced that this is the last bit of evidence he needs to sway a majority to his side. The man is positively glowing about the prospects of destroying terrestrial humanity."

"What do you think?" Tantalyes said.

"I don't know. It's going to be close. Very close, and now that we have absolute proof that the earthlings have levity drive . . ."

"But they don't," Tantalyes said. "Not really. This is an anomaly—the work of one rogue inventor who has no standing in the accepted circles of terrestrial science. If he is neutralized, the problem is solved. The circumstances that enabled Alan Fain to utilize levity could never happen again."

"How do you know?" Monica said.

"Tana, my agent prisoner. Her recent lapse in judgment aside, she has been an extraordinary agent. Fain and a guy named Slack chanced upon the Asklepian field a few years back. No one on earth would believe either of them, and it could never happen again."

"And you trust Tana?"

"About the information concerning the ship I do. Her mistake was in getting too close to one of her subjects."

"Who?"

"The Slack character."

"Where is he now?"

"Dead . . . an unfortunate accident. He accidentally fell into Lake Artema."

"Then he's taken care of. What about this Fain?"

"I'm not sure, but I suspect he may be in Arlandia," Tantalyes said.

"That's not good. Arlandia is another one of Jistane's arguing points."

"But that little space garden! How can that possibly be a threat?"

"You don't need to convince me," Monica said. She paused, considering her words carefully. "Tantalyes, I need to know where you stand. You have been off world for so long—I don't think you understand the seriousness of the situation. We are on the verge of terrestrial apocalypse. I don't want to see that."

"I'm not on the side of the holistics," Tantalyes said.

"Nor am I. They're a symptom of the problem. Some of them are sincere, but I suspect that Jistane and his agents have infiltrated the group. That kind of agitation is just what they need."

"You mean some of these demonstrations are actually the work of the other side, Jistane and his faction?"

"I can't prove it, but it makes sense."

"Unfortunately it does make sense," Tantalyes said. "The situation here is worse than I thought."

"That's why I need to know where you stand," Monica said.

"I'm a loyal citizen," Tantalyes said. "I'm no friend of earth. Terrestrial culture is humanity gone mad. They are on the verge of destroying the planet's ecosystem."

"I know," Monica said. "But do you really think it's our place to destroy most of humanity? We both agree that the self-defense argument is nonsense."

"We'll talk more when I arrive," Tantalyes said. "We should be there tomorrow evening. I'm going to hop a train when we get to Criton."

"A train?" Monica said. There was a teasing tone to

her voice."That's rather out of character for you, the hopeless romantic."

He laughed. "Not completely hopeless—not yet. Listen, Monica. Tana is in way over her head. She did far too many tours without any relief. It's no wonder she got too close. I've been warning terrestrial security for years about just this sort of thing. Is there anything you can do for her?"

"Her offense is serious," Monica said.

"I know that! Dammit, have a heart! What would you have done if you had been posted down there for that long?"

"I'll have to talk with her," Monica said. "I can't promise anything."

It was difficult to hear since Tantalyes kept his voice down, but Tana understood enough to know she was in more trouble than she had thought. When she heard Tantalyes's slow, deep breathing she got up and peered out through the night shade. Mount Poseidon was more beautiful than she had remembered. *Fall mountain, just don't fall on me*, she thought.

21

Any Good Thing

After Tantalyes delivered his prisoner he took a high-speed train to Criton. He tried to forget the expression on Jistane's face as he handed Tana over. The Guardian had looked at Tana with an expression full of triumph. There was something unseemly, almost lascivious, about it that made Tantalyes want to get away as quickly as possible.

Tantalyes looked out at the fertile plain. The golden wheat and barley fields were almost ready for harvest. He missed the rural life of these farms where he had grown up. He recalled riding in the horse-drawn combine. Another blend of ancient and advanced technology, the machines were both pastoral and highly efficient.

Those days are gone, he thought. His last conversation with Monica was not reassuring. "I told you it is going to be close, and there is no way Tana is going to escape a prison sentence—probably lunar isolation. The only question is how long," she said.

Tantalyes showed his badge at the port, and the officer led him to his ship. *Lunar isolation,* Tantalyes thought, *is not so bad.* But he was used to it, and his station had some amenities, access to some of the mysterious ancient fields underground. Tana's lot would be different—a crushing isolation in a barren chamber for a minimum of two years. It could be longer.

Miranda and Ira were headed for the other side of the sun. Ira, looking out, was surprised to see the terrestrial field drawing near. "I thought we were going to Atlantis?" he said.

"We are, but first a short stop on Luna. I haven't given up on Lew."

The nouancer gave a soft hum, and Miranda picked up the handset. It was Raya. "I thought you should know that Alan has recovered consciousness," she said.

"That's good. How is he?" Miranda said.

"He's fine except . . ."

"What?"

"He says that he's had a vision, that he is the new axis of creation or something."

"Not again," Miranda said.

"And he has a plan. He wants to synthesize the essence of the mundis juice and send a missile to earth. He thinks he he can design a fungal spore to infect all seed-bearing plants on earth. The fungus will have a gene to produce mundycin, the active ingredient of the mundis juice. He plans to launch an organic missile, using his resonator—"

"Sounds like a plan," Miranda interrupted. She

sounded weary. "I can't come back now. You have to stop him."

"But how?"

"I'm sure you can think of something," Miranda said, and hung up.

"What was all that about?" Ira said. After Miranda explained he said, "Another big story."

"Except this one isn't going to happen," Miranda said, an uncharacteristic tension in her voice.

"What if Alan's right?" Ira said.

"Right?"

"The situation on earth is pretty bad. It really does look like we are on the eve of global catastrophe. It may not happen for ten–twenty years or more, but overpopulation, deforestation, toxic waste buildup—it's inevitable unless we change our ways. Maybe humanity needs some sort of radical shake-up."

"Do you really think a mass market, artificially induced vision is the answer?" Miranda said.

"I suppose not," Ira said, looking at the big blue marble that was his home as it loomed large behind the moon. "I guess that's really the history of mankind when you get right down to it, a series of artificial vision quests, some more well intentioned than others, but all ultimately failures." An all-consuming resignation swept over Ira. He was visibly shaken by it, and slumped in his seat.

"Don't give up," Miranda said. "It's not nearly so hopeless as that. Just because Alan Fain's mad scheme is not the answer doesn't mean there isn't any. And I wouldn't go so far as to say all your striving, religion, philosophy, science, and art are ultimately futile."

"What then?" Ira said. "Look at the evidence! How many more millennia must we go on like this?"

"Not many," Miranda said.

"How do you know that?"

"I don't. Not really. But as crazy as Alan's plan is, I do believe he is part of a building awareness that it can't go on much longer. Change is on the way."

They docked at the Lunar port. Ira immediately noted the second ship. It was a sleek craft with a metallic gleam, very different from Miranda's green saucer. "We have company," she said.

Ira immediately saw Tantalyes's resemblance to Tana. It wasn't his physical build—he was a tall, strongly built man, not petite in any sense. It was the color of his hair and eyes, and something more subtle, the look in his eyes, the way he carried himself. He now saw what Alan had seen in Tana, something unearthly and alien.

"You must be Miranda," Tantalyes said.

"This is Ira," Miranda said. "He's a journalist."

"I'm an admirer of your work, Mr. Summerset," Tantalyes said. "The *Texas Sun* is a noteworthy journal—highly underrated."

"Texas, you know," Ira said. "Nobody takes it very seriously."

"A big mistake," Tantalyes said, sitting down on the sofa. Ira and Miranda sat in two of the stuffed chairs. "I've followed the Lone Star since the beginning. I am reminded of that passage from the Gospels—Who was it that said, 'Can there any good thing come out of Nazareth?' "

"Nathanael, John 1:46," Miranda said.

"Yes," Tantalyes said. "Anyway I have always thought the same about Austin—that something good from there may surprise us all one day."

"You know about Austin?" Ira said.

"I'm not like most of my people," Tantalyes said. "I take a keen interest in earth that goes beyond the usual smug superiority. I could retire to a quiet, pastoral life in my native continent—you should taste the bock beer we brew in my home village—but circumstances now call me to a higher purpose."

"And what might that be?" Miranda said.

"Don't worry," Tantalyes said. "I'm not eager to see it all come to an end. You have made a terrible mess of things down there, but it's not my place to pass judgment. We chose to leave a long time ago. A wise choice, I think, but one that is also tinged with sadness."

"The mess to which you refer is not mine," Miranda said.

"Of course. You are truly something new"—Tantalyes stared at Miranda—"neither of this world nor that—a true child of the Universe."

"And no less human for it either," she said. "Come on, let's cut all the bullshit . . ."

"Forgive me, I'm a hopeless romantic. Too much time on my hands for too long. I've become a dreamer, and you are quite right, this is no time for dreams." Tantalyes got up. "Can I offer you something to drink?"

"This drink has further complicated things," Miranda said, sipping the mundis cocktail that he handed her a moment later.

"Oh?" Tantalyes cocked an eyebrow.

"Alan Fain—he's the one who—"

"I know about Mr. Fain," Tantalyes said. "What is he up to now?"

"He is quite mad from an overdose of this stuff," Miranda said. She proceeded to explain Alan's plan to intoxicate the earth and return as the new world savior.

Tantalyes laughed. Even Miranda was surprised at the spontaneity of it and smiled in spite of herself. "Sorry," he said, catching his breath. "Not really so funny, is it?"

"Not if he can actually carry it out," Ira said.

"I would not underestimate Alan Fain," Tantalyes said. "Nor, I think, would Miranda." He looked into her eyes.

Miranda actually blushed. It turned her face a more vibrant green. "No," she said, "I would not."

What must she feel for Alan, her maker? Ira wondered.

Tantalyes did not at first think it a good idea for Miranda to go to Atlantis. "Things are unstable now," he said.

"Partly because of me," she said. "I need to convince your people that Arlandia is no threat."

"It's not that simple," Tantalyes said. "No one in Atlantis sees your little world as a threat. It's more subtle than that, a symbol. You did, on a much smaller scale, what we did in ancient times. There is an element of wounded pride there—irrational—but there it is. I don't know what kind of reception you will get."

"Nor do I," she said, "but I have to try."

In the end he admitted that she might be able to accomplish something by showing herself. ''If you show yourself to the Guardians, it might serve to *humanize* the issue,'' he said with more than a trace of irony. ''In any case, I can't stop you.''

''There is one more thing,'' Miranda said.

Tantalyes finished his drink and set it on the table. He was beginning to like this strange woman. *We have something in common*, he thought, *in that neither one of us quite knows what to make of our humanity.*

''What happened to Lew, the earthling who was lost here?''

Tantalyes led them to the door and opened it with a key. They stiffened at the inward rush of air. Miranda peered into the darkness for a long time. ''What's down there?'' she said.

''There is a vast body of water that feeds into a river,'' Tantalyes said.

''I know Lew is an excellent swimmer,'' Miranda said.

''No one could survive it,'' Tantalyes said. ''It is a long way down, even by lunar standards. And even if the impact did not render him unconscious, the water is cold. He would be dead of hypothermia in a matter of minutes.''

''He is alive,'' she said.

Tantalyes was taken aback by her fierce tone. ''I know that's what you want to believe, but—''

''He is alive! You have to find him! What's wrong with you people, have you no sense of honor? Lew Slack was kidnapped by one of your own and left alone in this alien world. Don't you feel any responsibility?''

''It's not a question of—''

''What's down there?'' she interrupted. ''Besides the lake, I mean.''

''There is a huge waterfall, that feeds into an underground river.''

''You have been down there?''

''Many years ago—the landscape is largely unexplored.''

''Unexplored? Surely this is all artificial; it was created.

Are you telling me that your race had nothing to do with it?''

Tantalyes said nothing.

``Then who? Where did it all come from?''

``That is something of a mystery,'' he said. Clearly he did not like to admit it.

``You will go after him,'' Miranda said.

``Alright,'' Tantalyes said, surprised. ``I will.''

``He is alive, and you will find him,'' she said.

22

Alethis: Temple of Truth

Lew was afraid as he faced the beast of ancient legend, but there was an unfamiliar dimension to his fear. He had faced what he thought would be death and come through it before. That lent a peculiar stoicism to his situation.

``Are you afraid of me?'' she said, showing her sharp claws.

``Yeah.''

``But you don't run. I can see your heart pounding, but you don't collapse from fear.''

``I have felt fear before,'' he said.

``Good, you are learning to deal with it. What is a man?''

``I don't know,'' he said.

She raised a giant paw and slapped him to the hard marble floor. The force of the blow sent the grail spinning into a corner and would have killed him had her claws been extended. His instincts told him to run, but he knew she could easily catch him, so he lay very still, trying to breathe even as he felt his lungs freeze and his pulse race.

``Not an acceptable answer,'' she said, crouching so

that her head was next to his ear. "Don't try to be clever. Now, I ask you Mr. *Slack,* what is a *man*?"

"A rational animal," Lew said.

"So sayeth the philosopher," she said, relaxing a little. "What do *you* say?"

"I am a mystery," he said, "a riddle." Lew rolled over and sat up. He looked her in the eye. For an instant he thought he saw the riddle of human existence in those eyes, and more—the answer. He laughed and could not stop. It was so funny, so absolutely hilarious, that all of human history, striving, suffering, defeat, and victory could be . . . and then he lost it.

"What's so funny?" She was now lying down, her feline body stretched out behind her. This put her face only a few inches above his.

"Nothing," he gasped, catching his breath. His side ached from the force of the laughter. "I mean, I saw—or thought I saw—"

"The answer." She smiled, the enigmatic smile of all the ages—Lew saw the face of the Mona Lisa as she might appear in a thousand different places and times in the smile of the sphinx.

"Who are you?" he said.

"I ask the questions, and that's my favorite. You did not answer, if I recall."

"Are you going to hit me again?" he said.

"Why don't you try answering me?" she countered, eyes flashing with menace.

"I'm a man," he said, "and I already told you what little I know about that."

"That's better. Are you going to die?"

"I suppose so," he said. "Eventually."

"Eventually, so why not now?" She smiled again, but this smile was not enigmatic.

"I don't know. All I can say is that I would prefer not to."

"Ah, Lew," she said. "Ah, humanity!"

"What's the significance of the grail?" he said.

This time it was her turn to laugh. She rolled over on

her back, her big, padded paws lazily slapping at the air. "How long?" she said.

"How long what?"

"Will you search for grails, golden fleeces, and the philosophers' stone?" She continued to lie on her back, looking ridiculous.

Lew could not keep himself from smiling.

"Are you laughing at me?" she said.

"Not exactly," he said.

"Because," she said, "I wonder which one of us is actually the more ridiculous."

"Actually?"

"You know," she said, "objectively, in *reality.*"

This set them both off. They laughed together, until Lew thought he would die from lack of oxygen.

He was still gasping for air when she rolled over and sat up, again assuming her classic pose. "Hilarious," she said. "Nothing is real?" The sounds of the Beatles' song, "Strawberry Fields," suddenly filled the chamber with music from Lew's past.

"What?" he said, looking around, trying to locate the source of the music, but it was already gone.

"Not so simple as the beautiful music suggests to your weary mind," she said, "not so simple as that. But here is a clue. Remember it." She paused and drew herself up a little higher. In a lyrical voice she said, "The real is *seeming*, bright as any *sun.*"

Lew couldn't describe what happened next. "Vanish" or "Disappear" would not suffice. But she was gone, leaving him with the cryptic phrase running through his mind.

He stood up and looked around. He went to fetch the grail and found he could easily read the inscription on the inside. The curved writing repeated the curious phrase of the sphinx. He went back to the table and set the grail next to the globe. The light played with the golden hues of the cup, making it appear radiant in its own right.

He went outside and descended the ten wide stone steps beneath the columns and turned to look at the building. He was not surprised to see that the inscription at the top of the columns again proclaimed the same message. "So," he said, 'the real is seeming, bright as any sun.' I guess that's it."

Because the expression raised more questions than it answered, he decided it was, for all practical purposes, meaningless. But the sphinx, real or not, could not be ignored. *Maybe that's what reality boils down to,* he thought, *that which we cannot ignore.*

He went back inside to explore. At first he was relieved to be alone, but he soon felt a desire to confront the sphinx again. Her riddles were infectious. He found a staircase at the far end of the room and followed it down to a smaller, dimly lit chamber. He was drawn to an armchair in the center of the room. It felt luxurious after his wanderings to let real furniture support him. He drifted off to sleep.

He awoke with a jerk that brought him bolt upright. He was staring into the eyes of the sphinx, and he realized it was the sound and feel of her breath that had awakened him.

"Don't you have any questions?" she said.

"I thought *you* were the interrogator," he said.

"Does thinking make it so?" she said.

"No—I mean I don't know. I really just don't know anymore."

"Ask the obvious," she said.

"Who—or what are you?" he said.

Her expression immediately changed from benign to threatening.

"Alright!" he said. "Wrong question. Where am I? What is this place?"

"You are in the Temple of Alethis," she said.

"Alethis?" he said.

"Truth," she said. "You may call it truth."

"But what is truth?"

"Truth," she said, "is resonance."

"Resonance?"

"If you would just look within yourself, you will see this," she said. "The dance of the senses is a series of vibrations from the subatomic to the neurochemical."

"But that can't be all there is to truth!" he said. "You

can take drugs that alter those vibrations, and . . ."

"You're right," she said. "That's not all there is to it. There are vibrations that lie beyond your comprehension. The point is that when these all *resonate,* you get *truth*, which is quite simply the right representation of reality."

"Who built this place?"

"I don't know," she said.

"How old is it?"

"Old, *very* old."

"Why?"

"Why what?"

"Why is it here? On the moon? An underground . . ."

"They came here long ago," she said. "Had they not come, you would not be as you are."

"What do you mean?" he said.

"Do you really think that the mechanism of natural selection in organic evolution is sufficient explanation for culture? Why art, why science?"

"I don't know. Why?"

"You would still be swinging from the trees, the mystery of life nothing more than a drink of water or a piece of fruit."

"Are you real?" he said.

She rose and put her paws on the arms of the chair, trapping him. Her furry chest brushed his. Looking down at him she said, "I could kill you—right now. How real is that?"

"Real enough," he said.

"Now I have a question for you," she said. "What are you doing here?"

Something in her tone roused Lew's anger. It also caused him to reflect on the circumstances that had brought him to this place. "I did not choose this!" he said. "If it were up to me, I'd be back in San Francisco making a record and playing tennis. But it appears that I am not master of my destiny."

"No," she said, amused, "you are not. The sooner you realize that, the better." She backed off and sat down.

"Why is it that I can now understand you and read the alien script?" he said.

“It probably has something to do with your diet,” she said.

“The moss?”

“Is most likely infected with the mundis fungus, which contains certain alkaloids that act as lexical disinhibitors. All human language is based on the same semantic archetype. Meaning exists in nouspace on the Asklepian wave . . .”

“I get the picture!” Lew said.

“Did I strike a *nerve?* she said. Lew wondered at her smile and tone of voice. *Can she read my mind; Does she know?*

“I know enough,” she said, “and I can see a little of what is in your mind. For example, you have experienced something of this before, haven't you?”

“Yeah,” he said, “but that was—different. It makes sense—about the lexical akaloids, I mean. But I want to know what this place is, *why* it is.”

“Why you?” she said.

“I don't want to get into that,” he said.

“You should.”

“We agreed that I'm not master of my fate, didn't we?” he reminded her. “So what's the point of probing any farther into it?”

“Just because you are not master of your destiny,” she explained, “does not imply that you have nothing to do with it or that you can afford to ignore the problem. You are abusing logic if you think otherwise. Good philosophy requires good logic.”

“Who needs philosophy?” he said.

“Now *that's* a good question.”

Again she was gone, leaving Lew to ponder the question. “The hell with it!” he said. He jumped out of the chair. “All I want to do is live my life.” *Of course,* he thought, *that in itself is a philosophy.*

Maybe, he thought, *all I really need is the truth.*

The chamber appeared to be a reading room, and Lew saw several recessed rows of books in the wall behind the chair. The sight stirred curiosity and dread. It made him think of another library, a maze of infinite possibility[8] that he was not ready to revisit.

He was relieved to find that the first book he pulled had nothing to do with him, and he was not surprised that he could read it. Reading, however, is not understanding. Lew quickly got lost in the technical discussion of local resonance fields—it was just the sort of thing for Alan, but Lew wanted something more poetic.

He found a thin, pale yellow book more to his liking. It was nearly hidden, wedged in between two tomes, one a weighty philosophical treatise and the other an advanced mathematical discussion of singularity groups. He liked the feel of it in his hands, which caused him to reflect on the sphinx's words. *Maybe I'm supposed to read this,* he thought.

The title convinced him that was so. *Humanity: The Unified Field and the Resonance of Truth, One Alethian's Historical Perspective.* For such an ambitious title, the book was preposterously thin. Lew sat down in the chair to read.

23

Integration of Powers

Jistane and Monica were talking in his den. She was taking in the view. Glass doors opened onto a porch. Jistane's terraced gardens sloped down to the shores of Lake Telamon. Monica turned her eyes from the sparkling waters to look into Jistane's dark face.

"I can hardly believe that they take such nonsense seriously!" he said. "I could almost believe that someone or some group is agitating on the campus. I haven't heard such stuff since—"

[8]*Mind-Surfer.*

"Since we were children," Monica said. "We all heard the stories as children. How the Alethians came to the earth before history, how they taught our primitive ancestors to inquire after the nature of the world and to invent explanations. These became art, science—"

"Stop! Is it infectious? Have they got to you as well?"

"Who do you mean by 'they', Jistane?"

"The students at the Academy of Gnosis, the ones everyone calls holistics."

"Of course not," she said. "I'm just repeating the old stories."

"Which is fine," he said, "as long as you know them as myth. But I'm telling you some of these students are starting to believe."

"Myth is sometimes more true than science or history," she said.

"And do *you*, Monica, honestly believe these old stories?"

"No." She sighed. "I don't. But I sometimes wish I could. We become more like a dying race every year, so alone, and now even our legends are leaving." Her voice trailed off, and she again turned to the lake.

"At least you can still separate reality from fiction," he said. "Some of the students cannot. That's why we must act. It's this silly, romantic infatuation with earth—we must finally deal with it, end it."

"End humanity on our home planet," she said.

"It is not our home! It hasn't been our home for millennia. Earthly humanity is a cancer that must be destroyed before it spreads. You have seen the prisoner. He is an ignorant savage compared to us!"

"He is merely unsophisticated in certain scientific principles," Monica said. "Will you allow them to watch the trial?"

"I don't see why not. Miranda can learn something of real justice, and the earthman might as well see the fate of his race decided."

Miranda and Ira were under house arrest. It was a comfortable house on the grounds of the Palace of the Sun.

They were allowed to wander the estate, and escape would have been easy. But Miranda's ship was under tight security, and, since the two were not charged with any crime, escape from the compound would have been meaningless.

Ira was looking down on the great city of Telamon. The palace was built on the highest point in the Atlantean capital, so the view was good. He marveled at the blend of engineering and art. Telamon was a thriving metropolis, with all the excitement and confluence of culture that this brings, but it was a beautiful place as well. There was no smog, vehicles were either horse-drawn or levity-powered. The Atlanteans seemed to like the ancient, animal mode of transportation, but since it was used primarily for romantic reasons, the animals were not overworked. An automatic drainage system kept the roads quite clean. All the animal waste was recycled as fertilizer.

"They say San Francisco is a beautiful city," Miranda said, walking up behind him.

"But it's really a mess," he said. "Like most cities on earth, it's bound by clogged freeways and surrounded by suburban sprawl, a place for cars not people."

"I suppose it is," she said. "This city is amazing. The parks are part of it, not isolated chunks of trees and greenery. And you can walk from one end to the other without fear of getting murdered or run over by a big hunk of sheet metal, spewing out poisonous fumes."

"We got the lead out of our gasoline," Ira said, turning to face her.

"So you did"—she smiled—"so you did."

"What's going to happen to us?" Ira said.

"I don't know. We are not charged with anything. Apparently it's no crime to come here, but our coming has made them nervous. Some of them at least."

"I still can't believe it," he said. "Atlantis, a real place, and floating on the other side of the sun."

"I've heard stranger things," she said.

He looked at her quizzically, but she offered no explanation.

"There is a trial. I think it involves Lew's girlfriend."

"Tana?" Ira said.

"Yes. I overheard two guards talking."

"Are they really guarding us?"

"Not really."

"Then why don't we leave, just walk out of here?"

"And go where, to do what? They have my ship—escape would be impossible. Besides, I came here to sue for peace. I am where I want to be, in the capital city at the seat of government, the Palace of the Sun." Ira looked away.

"I'm sorry," she said quickly. "I shouldn't have brought you. This isn't your fight."

"I wanted to come," he said. "Don't apologize. I'm a reporter, and this looks like a scoop."

"Indeed," she said.

They were interrupted by Monica. "I hope you have everything you need here," she said, "and I'm sorry for the inconvenience of—"

"Being under arrest," Miranda said.

"Yes." Monica's slight embarrassment made her look more lovely in her maroon gown.

"I still don't believe you aren't speaking English," Ira said.

"What did you just say?" Monica said. "Analyze the words and syntax."

"I'll be damned," Ira said, as he recalled the words and saw them in his mind as the alien speech of an ancient culture.

"It takes some getting used to," Monica said. "But all human language is essentially the same. All humanity always has the ability to communicate, but people on your planet have somehow managed to deactivate the neural pathways which make this possible."

"How?" he said. "I mean why?"

"I don't know," she said. "Maybe there is something to the legend of the Tower of Babel."

"Maybe," he said.

"I've come to invite you to witness the proceedings which start tomorrow," Monica said.

"Tana's trial?" Miranda said.

"Well," Monica said, "yes."

"What do you mean?"

"It is more than that. There are bigger things at stake. I don't know how to say this, so I'll just give it to you straight. There are certain political tensions which have been brewing for a long time, a *very* long time. Recently some students at one of our more liberal universities have helped to bring things to a head. They are talking about some old myths that have been long forgotten."

"What old myths?" Miranda said, suddenly very interested.

"Stories, legends, rumors from ancient times about a superior race that came to earth and supplied the spark that lit up the creative powers of the human imagnation."

"The *Alethians!*" Miranda said.

"Where did you hear of them?" Monica said, suddenly startled and a little afraid.

"I've heard the stories, too," was all Miranda would offer. "Are these students talking about returning to earth?"

"Worse," Monica said. "They're talking about a unified field, some sort of impossible dream—an energy field that unites all life and power in the solar system. The point is that it has galvanized the more conservative Guardians. They think it is time to deal with the problem of humanity once and for all."

"The *problem* of humanity?" Ira said.

"Yes," Monica said. "They want to cleanse the earth of humans. Destroy you. They regard your race as a planetary cancer."

"That's outrageous!" Ira said.

"Is it?" Monica said. "Humans have overrun the planet in what can only be described as an extremely irresponsible and destructive manner. Now you threaten the entire web of planetary life. No species is safe from your onslaught. Your behavior is very much like the behavior of cancer in the body. Only this time the body is an entire planet."

"But you can't be serious! All humanity—"

"I didn't say I agreed with the argument," Monica said. "I just want you to understand."

"What does all this have to do with Tana's trial?" Miranda said.

"On Atlantis we decide related issues together. We pride ourselves in streamlining justice. Tana was a terrestrial agent who tried to defect. Her case will be decided with the other larger issue."

"But that's insane!" Ira said. "One girl's impetuous rebellion can't possibly decide the fate of a planet."

"You don't understand," Monica said. "It isn't really Tana's trial. To some extent it will center around her actions. If Tana is acquitted, the question of earth will be left for at least another century. If not, Atlantis will act. We will activate the lunar resonator to initate a temproary terrestrial field disruption. That will throw the entire cultural infrastructure into chaos. Then certain viruses will be introduced that are very specific to the human nervous system. It will be all over in a matter of months."

"And you are inviting us to watch the trial?" Ira said. Monica nodded. "*Thank* you," Ira said sardonically.

"Even if the verdict is guilty," Ira said after a few moments, "it will take time, won't it? It will have to go to your executive branch of government in order to be carried out, I mean."

"In Atlantis," Monica said, "there is no executive. There is no legislative nor is there any judicial. All power resides with the Guardians, the council of ten. We don't believe in separation of powers here. Whatever we decide happens, and it happens quickly."

"A unified field theory of government," Ira said.

"You could say that," Monica said. They all looked back at the Palace of the Sun, the embodiment of the integration of powers.

Miranda and Ira dined on an enormous stuffed gourd. They were back in the spacious suite of rooms that was their prison.

"I guess they can grow stuff like this because of all

the sunlight. Atlantis is, after all, just a giant greenhouse," Ira said.

"A little more than that," Miranda said, savoring the delicate orange flesh laced with pungent spices.

"It ain't Texas," Ira said. "Did you believe what she said? That they will kill us all?"

"Yes."

"Shouldn't we do something?"

Miranda just looked at him.

"OK," he said. "Might as well enjoy dinner, I suppose. It's strange. My head tells me I should be passionately involved, outraged, and poised for action, but my feelings are curiously detached." He took a sip of wine.

The rich red tones caught the rays of Atlantis's mock evening light as their side of the continent spun out of the perpetual solar glare.

"Strange," she said, "but human."

Ira was overwhelmed by the interior of the Palace of the Sun. He had seen the Parthenon, the Sistine Chapel, and St. Paul's Cathedral. They all seemed pale imitations. The palace was much larger, but that was the least impressive thing about it. *This,* Ira thought, *is the model, the form all the other classical structures of antiquity were trying to emulate.*

It seemed curiously empty and casual. As they walked toward the far end, Ira noted a few officials milling about and meeting, the affairs of state no doubt. But there was no crowd. The fate of one young terrestrial agent obviously had not roused much public interest.

The central area was a small jungle, teeming with tropical and subtropical vegetation. Ira was drawn to giant philodendrons and fernlike plants that he imagined must have existed on earth eons ago.

They emerged from all the lushness to the final approach. Finally they were beneath the wide dais where the council of ten deliberated and decided.

"Make yourselves comfortable," Monica said, indicating ergonomically designed seats. She ascended to her place next to Jistane.

There were only a dozen or so curious spectators. Most seemed bored except for a tense couple on Ira's right. When they led Tana out, Ira noted the way the man sat forward, and the woman gripped his arm. *Her parents, no doubt*, Ira thought.

Tana took her seat at the far left of the long bench. It was at a right angle to her judges, so that the spectators below saw her in profile. When she turned to face him, Ira realized another odd thing about the few occupants of the great hall. Tana was by far the youngest person he had seen since entering. In fact, he realized, she was the youngest person he had seen on Atlantis.

Her gaze lingered on his for a moment, a look of resentful recognition. Then she looked at the couple, and Ira saw her features dissolve into those of a frightened little girl, but only for a moment. She recovered her defiance and quickly turned to look at her judges.

Most of the morning was consumed by arcane and technical parliamentary procedures. "This is worse than the Texas Senate," Ira whispered to Miranda at one point.

But then something happened that brought him back to the reality that he wasn't in Texas anymore.

Jistane spoke for the first time. "The problem is not with ourselves, nor is it in our stars. We all know where it is. We just don't want to face it. Some of you are pleading for mercy for this poor girl. I love mercy when it is called for, but I loathe false sentimentality. She deserted her post. She did so in a way that could have seriously compromised our terrestrial operations—may have already done so.

"Don't argue mercy, don't argue leniency. Facts are facts. Truth is plain. The larger truth is the one no one has dared mention. We can't go on pretending it will resolve itself. You all know that I am talking about earth. I'm talking about that planet on the other side of the sun, that houses an insane, humanoid race, a species that has become a cancer." He paused to look at Ira, and the man's intensity sent a shiver up the reporter's spine. "Some of us want to speak of earth as our home and its human inhabitants as our brothers and sisters. That's analogous to saying that our home is the sewer of Babylon and the deadly plague viruses that live in it are our friends.

"The time has come, and we all know it. The time has come for the final solution. I do love the earth. That's why we must act. I want to see something of the diversity of terrestrial life preserved.

"And now that earthly science is about to tap into the power of levity drive—"

"You know that isn't true," Monica interrupted. "There is only one, and there is no danger that the secret of levity will ever go beyond him."

"You will have your turn to speak," Aias said with the authority of his many years. "Let Jistane make his case."

"That won't take long," Jistane said, looking at Monica. "Tana is guilty. There may be circumstances that weigh in her favor. I, for one, am not interested in them. Justice demands a succint appraisal of the facts and they are clear. She must spend a minimum of two years in lunar isolation. Anything less would send a message of permissive tolerance to the young people who are responsible for her treason. The result could be disastrous.

"And linked with her fate is the fate of a world. We must use the lunar resonator to cleanse the earth once and for all of the renegade species that is destroying her. When postdiluvian humanity is gone from the planet I myself might wish to revisit mother earth. It was always meant to be a garden, a paradise for the truly human, but we can never enjoy it so long as it remains infested with the filthy scum that our ancestors have become."

Ira was shocked at the dispassionate manner in which Jistane's speech was accepted. It was impossible for him to tell whether or not the others agreed with the prescription for cleansing the earth. They were simply and calmly taking it all in, as if the matter before them were nothing more serious than the financing of a public sewage project.

A big bird with bright, outrageously colored plumage flew slowly across the hall in front of the Guardians. Aias gave it a passing glance and the others ignored it. The creature circled over the ten once and gave a soft cry, "Aieee." Monica looked up, and it settled down on her shoulder. She stroked its beak and breast for a moment and casually kissed the side of its head. It suddenly straightened itself, stretched its beautiful wings, and thrust itself back into the air, where it headed for the lush jungle in the center of the building.

It served as another reminder to Ira that he wasn't in Texas anymore.

Then something happened that was more familiar to him. A voice from the back of the hall screamed, "We will live forever! Peace, love, and harmony!"

Jistane stood and stared at the intruders, an expression of pure hatred in his eyes. "Arrest them!" he shouted.

Ira turned to see a young man running toward the ten. He was followed by two others, a boy and a girl. They were dressed in bright colors that reminded Ira of the bird's plumage.

"All fields will be unified! The old order is over. Ring in the new! Let the great cosmic dance begin!" The young man was about to ascend to the stage when two guards appeared, one on each side. They grabbed the boy roughly and flung him with great force, facedown on the hard marble surface. The other two rushed the guards, but they were no match for professional force. It was over quickly. The first youth appeared to be unconcsious, and the other two were bound. One of the guards grabbed the motionless young man and flung him over a shoulder, and the other led out the subdued pair as the hall was cleared of the disturbance.

Ira was accustomed to demonstrations in the halls of state, but the speed and efficiency with which the matter was resolved surprised and disturbed him. "I guess the trains run on time here," he whispered to Miranda.

Monica maintained a stony silence—it was impossible to read her reaction. Jistane's was one of righteous wrath. "This is what we are up against," he said to everyone, and at the same time it sounded as if he were thinking aloud. "These *holistics* as they call themselves claim to have found a beautiful vision of a sacred truth. In fact they will destroy everything we have so carefully built, they will drag us into a stupor of childish dreams that will quickly become a nightmare if we do not expose them, punish them, and destroy their message."

Monica roused herself. "You foolish man!" she said. "They are dreamers, that much is true. Maybe their dreams are nothing *more* than youthful fantasy. But they are nothing *less* either. The danger you imagine is your own private nightmare that you wish to force on the rest of us to ease your burden, which is nothing more than the lonely fear of an old man facing his own mortality."

The fury on Jistane's face was frightening for its inexpressible intensity. He fought for words but could not speak.

"We will break now," Aias said in even tones that did not quite conceal his own anxiety.

Ira saw that the big bird had returned and was circling overhead like a vulture waiting for something to die.

24

Scoop News

Leslie was sure she had enough to nail the Speaker, and possibly Ira. Drake could believe anything about Cliff, but when it came to Ira he balked.

"I can't see it, Leslie. Ira and I go back a ways. He's not your usual reporter, that's for sure. Ira's trouble is he has too damn much imagination. He thinks too much."

"I see," Leslie said. She was looking at him in a way that implied she didn't see at all.

"Not to imply that—I mean I didn't mean that you don't . . ."

"That's OK," she said, enjoying watching him squirm.

"Yeah." He looked out his window. The sun was blazing. He could see the heavy humid air hovering above the river. "I just meant that Ira always was good with the facts, a straight shooter, and I really do think he was kind of an idealist about his job. He believed a reporter's role was to go after the truth."

"Whatever that is," Leslie said.

"Yeah." Drake felt lousy about the whole thing, having fired Ira, the implications that he couldn't believe. He liked Leslie, but wasn't sure how much of that was really reducible to an attractive young woman's not-so-subtle charms.

"He's in it up to his ears, Drake," Leslie said. "You can take that to the bank." She turned and walked away. Drake's eyes followed her shapely bottom until she turned a corner.

"Damn!" He sighed, folded his hands behind his head, leaned back in his chair, and put his feet up on his desk. *If only I could talk to Ira*, he thought. *Where the hell is he?*

Back at her desk, Leslie checked her voice mail to find one message. As she listened she tensed excitedly with recognition. She quickly replayed the message to make sure it was he, the man who had given her the anonymous tip about Cliff.

She returned the call. Tantalyes answered from his room at the Driskoll Hotel. "I should meet you somewhere," he said. "This story is bigger than the last one. We should talk over coffee or something."

Even though she had never seen him, she recognized him immediately. He was wearing an expensive, cream-colored, cotton-linen suit and a green shirt open at the collar. He looked cool and collected, a sharp contrast to most of the other patrons, who were already wilting in the burning, midmorning humidity.

He stood as she approached his table on the patio under the pecan trees. "Would you like to sit inside?" he said.

"Well . . ."

"It is so much cooler in there," Tantalyes said. "But it's always cool where I come from, so I'm rather enjoying this steambath, but for you it must get trying."

"It does," she said, "but I don't mind. Let's sit outside." *What kind of accent is that?* she wondered. It sounded foreign but, at the same time, maddeningly familiar, like the name of an old favorite song that just won't come to mind.

"What will it be?" Tantalyes asked her as she sat down and crossed her legs. Her cotton skirt rested in folds across her thighs, revealing a nicely tanned knee. She idly kicked a sandaled foot as she smiled at the waiter.

"Iced latte with skim milk, please," she said.

"I'll have a machiato," Tantalyes said.

"Iced?" the waiter said, tentatively, hopefully.

"No," Tantalyes said.

"It must be cold where you come from," Leslie said.

"Not cold really, just a bit on the dark and cool side."

"London?" Leslie said.

"Yes," he lied, "London."

"I love England," she said. "It's such a," she started to say "trip" and caught herself.

"A green and pleasant land?" he said.

"Exactly," Leslie said, appraising him more closely. She would have guessed fifty, but he looked both older and younger at the same time. His hair was dark, thick and straight. He let it grow past his collar in back and just over his ears on the side. His complexion was dark in the bright sort of way one hears described as "Mediterranean." He was just under six feet and lean. He moved with an easy, athletic grace.

"You are no longer an anonymous telephone source," she said.

"No," he said, "I suppose not. You see me now, physically instantiated, in the flesh on planet earth."

It wasn't the kind of response she had expected. "Where do you usually keep yourself?" she said.

"That's not relevant to the story I have for you." He smiled, and their drinks arrived. "Ah, that's the stuff," he said, licking the foam from the surface of his brew. "Very nice indeed."

"It's coffee," she said.

"So it is," he said, "so it is. There are other drugs besides caffeine. Of course you know about the common ones of use and abuse, the stimulants, depressants, euphorics, psychedelics, etc. They are all mildly interesting at first, and ultimately quite boring." He took a sip, sighed with contentment, and looked up at the well-balanced branches of the big pecan tree. "That's one of the worst things. No trees."

"No trees where?" she said, beginning to doubt the news value of this source.

"Never mind," he said. "That's not what I came here to tell you. Your planet is in great danger. There is a drug which, like most drugs, when used with discretion is pleasant and safe, but has the potential to make the mind see and believe the most extraordinary things."

"What things?"

"That's the interesting part. The visions of mundycin are not without their basis in reality. They open the mind to the great possibility of cosmic evolution, the great dance of creation, and they also make you feel a part of it all. In some personalities, with a predilection for that sort of thing, mundycin induces a powerful messianic compulsion."

"What do you mean about a basis in reality?" she said, feeling as though the charming reality of a summer's mid-morning coffee break was suddenly at risk.

"I mean," he said, "that humans are predisposed to believe in a *telos,* a direction to things. And they are also inclined to look for prophets, extraordinary individuals who can give immediate and personal testimony to the cosmic drama that is always, everywhere unfolding before their eyes."

"*Their* eyes?" Leslie said.

"*Our* eyes, of course," he said. "It was merely a figurative, editorial detachment."

"Of course," she said.

"In any case, what is interesting is that these sorts of visions have a basis in real human experiential terms, which is why what Alan Fain plans to do now is so dangerous."

"Fain—*again*?" she said. "What is it now, a time machine?"

"No." He laughed. "Fain hasn't quite got around to that—yet. This is a plan which, although he is quite mad at the moment, he actually has the means to carry through." Tantalyes explained Alan's scheme to become the messiah of a new age.

"I don't believe it," she said.

"I'm not surprised," he said, "but my last tip proved itself, did it not?"

"Yeah." But that was different. "Cliff Sanders playing funny games with the state treasury is one thing—but this—this is just too fantastic."

"Isn't it?" he said.

"Who are you?" she said.

"It is important I remain nameless. I would have preferred faceless as well, but I decided to meet you in person to emphasize the seriousness of this new situation."

"Do you know what my editor would say if I pitched a story like this?"

"That you are crazy."

"Yeah, and it could ruin my credibility, which in turn could ruin my entire career."

"Most unfortunate," he said with a sigh.

"What?" she said, fighting to keep the anger out of her voice.

"That your personal lives are necessarily so narrowly constrained—here."

"Where is here? Austin? Texas?"

"I'm talking about your world," he said. "Very few of you feel you can take risks. You live out your lives conforming to what is expected. And you hardly ever even think to ask who makes the rules—the rules that keep you in such bondage. It's a shame really—"

"I don't know what you're talking about. What do you mean *my* world? Are you from some other planet or something?"

"Not really," he said, looking up at the quarter moon, hanging in a pale blue sky. "I can understand your reluctance to take any of this seriously. So don't pitch it to your editor—at least not yet. Wait until there is evidence."

"What sort of evidence?"

"I told you, unless he is stopped, Alan will launch his missile. I may be able to warn you ahead of time. You can be there when it strikes. Will that suffice as evidence? Pictures, real samples of the drug?"

"Won't it be too late then?" she objected.

"Not necessarily. If you know what to do, you may be able to disarm it."

"Sounds like a story for the *National Moon.*"

"It would make great copy for the grocery store tabloids," he agreed, "but this time it's true."

"How do you recognize truth?" she said, staring at him with the penetrating eye of the interrogator."

"Well spoken," he said, holding her eyes with his.

That night Leslie had dinner alone in her Westlake Hills apartment, which she could barely afford. She grilled a burger on her deck that overlooked Barton Creek. The insects were humming loudly, making the scrubby mesquite and cedar landscape seem vibrantly alive and a little alien.

As she ate and sipped a local bock beer she also idly flipped through a book she had recently purchased. It was a popular novel about some ordinary people who had stumbled across a series of coincidences that got them involved in an adventure that promised to reveal the secret of human life, the elusive goal of existence.

She didn't much care for it. It was shallow, simplistic and not very well written. But it did strike a chord deep within her. *Bizarre coincidences do happen, and they are often inexplicably significant,* she told herself. *As a reporter, I need to trust my instincts, and they tell me there is something going on here.*

Leslie ate the last tasty morsel of charred beef and washed it down with the foamy brew. The sun was disappearing in a blaze of color that seemed like a miracle even though it was a familiar sight.

Tantalyes's last words, before he got up and walked

away down Congress Avenue, still resonated in her mind.

"It may sound like pulp science fiction," he said, "but that doesn't mean it isn't true, and in your profession truth is supposed to count for something. So think about it. I'm talking about a real story here, Leslie. I know how it is with you reporters. The front page is everything—it's where you live."

"And sometimes die," she said.

"I know," he said. What he said next was what stayed with her, would not let her leave it alone. "But live or die, this is a scoop. This is *news*."

25

Peace and Love

"What happened to Don?" Alan said. He was with Raya in her villa, an elaborate living structure for the princess of Arlandia.

"Don," she said.

"Yeah, Don Fields. The former secretary of the interior. You two were rather tight as I recall."[9]

She looked out the transparent polymer wall to her left. "He's gone," she said, turning suddenly back to Alan.

"Gone?" Alan said. He was sitting in a chair that grew from the wood floor. His back was to a wall of thick, olive green cellulose growth. "Where did he go? Back to earth."

"No," she said.

"Where then?"

"What does it matter? He's gone! Gone for good."

"He went the other way," Cliff said, surprising Alan

[9]*The Gaia War.*

and Raya. The Speaker had appeared suddenly in the arched doorframe to Raya's den.

"I haven't seen you for days, Cliff," Alan said drily.

"I've been reading," Cliff said, "studying up."

"What do you mean, 'he went the other way'?" Raya said, anxious little wrinkles around her eyes.

"Just that," Cliff said. "The other way. Not the way I'm going."

"And which way is that?" Alan said.

"You wouldn't understand," Cliff said. "I'm only just beginning to. I suspect Don took one of your ships and set off for the outer reaches of the solar system. It's like this: When a man gets a taste of what it feels like to break out of terrestrial space he is euphoric. Then he gets to thinking, 'If going past the moon feels so good, so liberating, why not try heading out altogether, get out of the solar system. Now that would be really something!' And on like that. But that's wrong. Sure it frees up the mind to break free of earthly things. But it doesn't follow that you need to keep going *out* to find the ultimate ecstasy."

"What then?" Alan said. "Where do you have to go? Tell us, sir, Mr. Speaker!"

"Make fun if you want," Cliff said. "I ain't talking until I'm ready and until I'm sure no one can stop me. You think it's a joke—fine. You're the *crazy* one."

"Do you know for sure?" Raya said. "That he's headed for interstellar space?"

"Most likely," Cliff said. "It's a common mistake. It's all in the book." Cliff left them as suddenly as he had come.

"Have you tried to contact him? Surely, if he is in a levity drive craft you can raise him on an Asklepian channel through the aether," Alan said.

"I've tried," she said, looking back outside on the lush tangle of vines, ancient-looking trees, and giant, multicolored ferns, "and tried." She put her hands up to her face and then lowered them in a gesture of resignation. "It's no good. He is either dead or does not choose to hear."

Alan saw an opportunity. "Listen, Raya," he said,

"this is just what I've been telling you all along. You can't trust humans. Why not? Because, like Don, like Cliff, they are all madly seeking after foolish dreams, the nonexistent and the unattainable.

"They throw their lives away in the process. That would be OK if it were not for the fact that their vain ambitions can cause suffering to others. Who cares what Cliff does with his life, or Don for that matter? But I see that Don's crazy flight into the void has left a good deal of pain in its wake, and that is not cool. No, that is definitely most uncool."

"You're almost making sense," she said. "Are you feeling better?"

"I'm feeling fine!" he said.

"And your plan to—"

"Save the world?" he said, laughing. "Don't you see, Raya? Think about what I've been telling you. My plan doesn't sound so crazy anymore, does it? Humans are pathetic creatures. Cliff's loony obsession with the Golden Grail, Don's space odyssey into never-never land.

"I know what you're thinking. You think my plans are just more of the same. But nothing could be farther from the truth. Think about it. While most people chase phantoms, I create reality! Can you deny it? After all, didn't I create *this* place? Without me there would be no Arlandia!" He opened his arms wide and threw his head back.

"Yes," she said, "but you really only tinkered with the empathetic aether, and you had Miranda's help. It was no less than brilliant science, but it was no more either. You aren't a god."

Alan laughed. "What's a god? And who cares anyway? All I'm saying is that I get results. I don't waste my energies on mere figments and next-to-nothings. I like reality. Don't you?"

"Yes, I do," she said quietly.

"Then help me bring reality to earth," he said. "The people are hungry for it, Raya. You can see that. Why would Don leave you, a virtual Eve in Eden? Only one reason. He is possessed like most of his planetbound brothers and sisters—possessed by the unreal, the impossible, the always unattainable. Together we can bring a true vision to earth. Together we can heal a planet. The mundycin is nothing more than a drug. I know that. But if we use it right—we quench the thirst of a people, a world. I ask you again, will you help me?"

"I have to think," she said.

"There isn't much time. We don't know what will happen with Atlantis. If we wait, we may be too late."

"I have to *think*," she said. "Now leave me alone." It was a command, meant to be obeyed and Alan responded like a queen's subject, but there was nothing humble about the smile on his face as he left her.

Cliff found Alan later in the cycle that passes for days on Arlandia. Alan was sitting in a grove of huge hardwood trees. "I wish I could explain it all to you," Cliff said. "Until recently we seemed to be on the same wavelength, but now—well, you've *changed*."

"I'm the same man I always was," Alan said, not bothering to turn and face Cliff. "It's just that now, I'm *more* the same."

"Because I think you, of all people, could truly begin to grasp the significance of Golden Grail," Cliff said, as if he weren't listening to Alan. "If I am successful—"

"If you are successful"—Alan suddenly turned and stood up to face Cliff—"*what*?"

"You have changed, Alan Fain. No doubt about it. You've lost your center. The grail when found and handled rightly can bring about a radical transformation of the entire solar system. I'm talking about a harmony beyond your wildest dreams."

"I doubt that," Alan said.

"A harmony that will do more than bring mankind to together. It will bring all the energy fields into a superfunctionality—light, electricity, the nuclear forces and gravity, all of them will become what they were intended to be."

"What's that?"

"Simply components of the great cosmic dance. We are all called to that dance. It's—"

"I know," Alan said, "It's *in the book.*"

"We should work together," Cliff said.

"Sorry, my plans don't include crazy religious quests. I'm a scientist."

"A scientist," Cliff mused. "Well as a scientist you should be interested in cosmic harmony, the greatest harmonic equation ever conceived."

"Yes," Alan said, "I'm interested in something like that. But I'm afraid I don't believe in your grail and that crazy book. My way is real. It is something I can actually *do.*"

"But you do want harmony—*don't you*?" Cliff sounded worried.

"Oh yeah," Alan said, "most definitely. Like they used to say, only now we're gonna do it."

"What did they say?"

"Oh, you remember, I'm sure. You're old enough. Peace and Love man, Peace and Love!" Cliff could not hear much of either in the voice.

26

Reverberations

Tantalyes left his comfortable hotel room in Austin, Texas, planet earth, somewhat reluctantly. It was tempting to blend in, take a vacation among the natives, but he had business on the moon.

He brought his sleek ship in gently and reflected on how long it had been since he had explored the lunar interior.

Have we lost all curiosity? he wondered, as he unbolted the ancient hatch on the surface. Despite evidence that went beyond legend, no one from Atlantis had bothered to investigate the subsurface structures of the moon for hundreds of years.

Tantalyes knew how to activate the powerful field resonator in the temple of Alethis, deep within the lunar bowels, but he had not been there himself for decades, and his fellow citizens of the lost continent seemed to have forgotten all about the place.

This is strange—the force of the sudden realization surprised him, *that he and his people had all but forgotten the mysteries of the moon. Who were the Alethians? Where did they come from, where had they gone, and what was their connection to humanity?*

The task of descending the long ladder forced him to abandon these speculations. It was a safer way down than the fall Lew had taken. The hatch was inside a small chamber, at the bottom of a shallow crater about a mile away from the main station. Tantalyes had discovered it many years earlier. It opened to a narrow tube that went straight down. The diameter was just wide enough for a man, and the rungs were spaced too far for an easy descent. His legs, back, and arms had to stretch for each one.

When his feet touched the rocky bottom he was drenched in sweat despite the coolness. He let himself drop and sat down, leaning his back against a large boulder. It was covered with the phosphorescent moss, which gave him a cushion as well as light. *I'm getting old*, he thought. *I don't remember its being as exhausting as all that.*

After he had rested, he got to his feet and surveyed his surroundings. The cavern looked smaller than he remembered. The air was still, damp and cool. He thought the quality of the light remarkable. *Splendid riches everywhere,* so colorful, soft, and shimmering it was, wherever he looked.

There was slight movement of air in the direction of the passageway that Tantalyes knew led to the falls. He stretched his legs and set out.

Before long he could hear a sound like the ocean one hears in a seashell pressed against the ear. It got louder and resolved into a roar as he stepped out into the huge cavern on the edge of the falls. *He can't have survived this*, Tantalyes thought, staring at the falling wall of water. Miranda's conviction that Lew was somehow still alive seemed a vain hope. He dreaded the prospect of finding a body, even as he quickened to the search.

He wondered why he hadn't visited the sublunar landscape more often. As he made the steep descent to the riverbed he was impressed by the sheer enchantment of it. The path was narrow and cleverly hidden against the cavern walls. He emerged from behind a boulder by a pool with lazy eddies, where he rested and ate from his pack. It struck him as extremely odd that he had never really explored the temple of Alethis. He knew it as the place of the massive lunar resonator, was intrigued by its beauty, but it seemed to Tantalyes, as he ate his dried meat and sipped a dilute red wine, that something had actively occluded his mind, preventing him from investigating it.

And so, while he still had little hope of finding Lew, he was excited by the image of the temple so long mysteriously absent from his mind.

"With the technology currently available there is no possibility of extending the unified field to the entire cosmos," Lew read, "but it is certainly possible to do it locally. The solar field extends far beyond the orbit of Pluto. Within that sphere of influence, all energy fields can become as one—the theory is sound. What are now distinct nuclear, electromagnetic, and gravitational dimensions of force would merge into a seamless whole—a unity.

"It can be brought about through a chain reaction initiated in the heart of the solar furnace. But it requires a special substance to set it off. I have just begun to experiment with a material which I believe to be something really new—not matter in the ordinary sense at all, but the pure particulate precipitate of thought. I call these elementary particles nouons—"

Lew let the book fall into his lap. "Not again," he said

softly. Lew had some experience of nouons[10] and he wasn't sure he wanted any more.

"But we always have things again, don't we?" Lew recognized the feline, feminine voice of the sphinx. She was behind him.

He started to get up, but stopped when she said, "Don't."

He gasped when she came into view, standing in front of him.

"I told you, did I not?" she said. "The real is seeming?" She laughed softly.

"But you're . . ."

"I'm what?" she said.

"Beautiful," he whispered.

Her head and face were the same, lovely black eyes and long, wavy, thick black hair. But her body was no longer that of a lioness. She was a woman.

"It's not polite to stare," she said. Lew was gaping, mouth open. "Did you like me better the way I was before?"

"No! I mean I—"

She laughed again.

She was lovely in the classical sense, reminding Lew of Artemis, goddess of the hunt and the moon. She was extremely well proportioned and clearly human from head to toe, except for one stunning feature—from the waist down she was covered in golden brown fur—a little of the cat remained.

"Is there anything I can do for you?" she purred. "Anything you need?"

Tantalyes was following the path by the river, his mind full of a strange contentment. Then he saw the footprints. There were the indentions in the dust made by ancient feet in ancient times, but there were also new ones. He quickened his pace. *Miranda was right,* he thought. *He lives.*

* * *

---

[10]*Mind-Surfer.*

"There must be something else I can do for you," she said. They were lying on a sofa in the upper chamber, and Lew was running his hand through the soft fur on her thighs.

"Do you play tennis?" he said.

She laughed, and the sound frightened him, bringing to mind her earlier form. "No," she said, "I don't, but I think something could be arranged. Tell me about tennis." She pulled him closer.

"OK," he said, "but not right now."

"No." Her voice was full of the animal. "First things first."

When he woke a few hours later, she was gone. He got up and went back out to get a drink from the fountain. As he was sipping the water from his cupped hand he saw the net.

The court was in a grove of trees. The surface was something new. Lew had never played on clay, but he imagined it would be like this, hard, but somewhat springy. It was blue, reminding him of the Pacific Ocean seen on a clear day from the hills of Marin.

He walked slowly around the court. At the other end, just off the court, underneath a tree, he found a tennis outfit, folded neatly. The shorts, shirt, and shoes were cream-colored. Next to these were a racket and a basket of balls. The racket was wooden. He picked it up, tested the strings on the heel of his hand, and found it good.

After he had put on the clothes and served up the basket of balls he hit for a while against the backboard. He said aloud, "Tennis anyone?" but remained alone.

The racket intrigued him. He hadn't played with wood in years. The wood was dark, and the grip was a soft material, not leather, but it didn't seem synthetic either.

As he was examining the grip he noticed something strange at the bottom. Against the classic wood it was a strangely high-tech–looking piece. It was a disk that appeared to be a dial set into the butt of the racket.

Lew put his thumb and forefinger to it and twisted. It moved a notch making a soft clicking sound. There was a slight, momentary disturbance in the air around the court, and he thought he heard a low humming sound. It was over almost before he noticed it.

He bent to pick up a ball and heard, "Shall we take serves?"

"What?" He wheeled around to look across the net.

"Shall we take serves?" the man said, stretching his arm. "I'm already warm, but I'd like a few serves before we start."

"Start what?"

"The match," Lew's opponent said. "You do want to play, don't you?"

The days went by in an idyllic rhythm of tennis and eros. Lew wondered if the latter might not really be love, but decided it didn't matter.

His tennis opponent conveniently disappeared when he twisted the dial on his racket in the other direction. They were a perfect match. Lew found that he could win only when he made most of his shots. If his serve lost any depth or his forehand faltered, as it did occasionally because of the old injury, the other was quick to take advantage.

At the end of one match he made a discovery. He accidentally turned the dial one more notch in the "on" direction. When he looked he saw his opponent ready for another set. Realizing his mistake he was about to shut him off, but decided to play a little longer instead.

The opponent won the spin and opted for serve. The ball came in deep and fast, Lew could just block it back. What followed was a game in which Lew could just hang on. He lost.

Testing suspicion, Lew cranked the dial one more notch. He hit a good serve, but the other blasted it back with tremendous topspin. Clearly the dial controlled the level of play.

Just to see how far it could go Lew cranked it all the way. This time he was able to handle the return and he started in for the net. The ball came back right at him. He tried to block it with his racket but it hit him in the solar plexus. He went down, gasping for air and wracked with pain.

The next thing he knew his opponent was helping him up. He had been out for over a minute. "That's pushing it a bit," the tennis player said. "You should probably back off. This could get dangerous."

Lew shut him down and walked stiffly off the court. The pain in his middle throbbed as he walked beneath the trees. Later, on the couch, after she had massaged his chest, he said, "The gravity is normal on the court. How is that?"

"The resonator," she said.

"Where is it?"

"In here, in the temple."

"But where?"

"It's here, that's all. What's wrong, don't you like the court? Tennis in lunar gravity wouldn't be nearly so much fun."

"No," he said, "I suppose it wouldn't. What should I call you?"

"Call me?"

"Your name?"

"Ah, who am I? Who are you?" She flashed her eyes at him, and he was momentarily seized with the old fear. But then she laughed. "You may call me Diotima."

"But is that really your name?" He idly stroked her soft fur.

She silenced him with a kiss.

Tantalyes did not remember the way being so long. His supplies were running low. *How had Lew survived*? he wondered. There was no sign of weakness or stumbling in the footprints. His quarry's stride, if anything, showed signs of increased vigor.

He rose after a few hours' sleep and ate the last of his meat and dried fruit. Sipping water from the river he thought he heard music, but it was faint, and before he could identify it the notes drifted into silence.

But as he walked he heard it again—far away came the sounds of an electric guitar, rock riffs and chord progressions that he recognized from his time on earth in the late 1960s.

The light ahead took on a different quality as well. He quickened his pace. When the path diverged from the river and began to ascend, Tantalyes was almost jogging. When he got to the double stairway he stopped.

"I had forgotten," he whispered. The lush greens and blues of the big trees and the art of the stone steps held him for several heartbeats before he started up.

He walked through the keyhole and looked at the temple. Standing by the fountain, wielding a blond Stratocaster, stood Lew. He was playing the introduction to "Purple Haze." The notes came cascading out of the Fender twin reverb amp, but when he got to the chorus he hit a sour one.

"I never could get that part," he said, putting the guitar down. Tantalyes noted that he appeared to be dressed for tennis.

"Mr. Slack?"

"Yeah," Lew said. "Are you real?"

"Seems to be the case," Tantalyes said.

"Seems," Lew said. "I know seems."

"What more *can* you know?" Tantalyes said.

"I don't know," Lew said, "but something tells me it's not that easy. I've had a few scrapes with reality."

"Yes," Tantalyes said. "Nice guitar. Do you know any surf songs?"

"I can do a passable 'Miserlou,' " Lew said.

"*That's* the one. Do you mind?"

"Not at all." Lew picked up the guitar. Soon the place was drenched in reverb and a thumping, wailing sound that seemed the perfect music for the Temple of Truth.

27

Visions from the Heart of the Sun

Raya found him with his plants. Alan had identified the mundycin as an alkaloid in a number of different varieties of fungi and grasses that grew in Arlandia. He had gathered a large number.

"Soon I'll have enough," he said.

"Do you really believe you can change the world?" she said. "Bring love to humanity?"

"Sure, don't you?"

"I don't know," she said. "It seems hopeless. You are all so crazy down there."

"Yeah, but you will help me now, won't you?"

"Yes."

"I need access to her lab."

"But—"

"I *know* she has one," Alan said. "I've got to do two things—extract the mundycin and build the missile. I'll need resonance technology to do the latter. The extraction should be fairly simple once I have the necessary equipment. Show me where she works, Raya. It's the only way."

Miranda's lab was located in a heavily forested area, well hidden. Like everything else in Arlandia it was difficult to tell what had grown from the ground and what was made by human hands. There were solar-powered burners that were definitely crafted, but the walls seemed to grow and the windows were made of the same organic polymer that shielded the colony from the killing radiation and freezing emptiness outside.

"Perfect!" Alan said after he had inspected the place.

"You don't need me for anything else do you?" Raya said. She wanted to leave, but was afraid of what she had done.

"Where are the resonators?" he said. "She must be testing them."

"I don't know. I have to go."

"No, wait!" It was too late. She had vanished outside into the wood. "Damn!" Alan said. He began rummaging about. Before long he had a mass of organic material heating in a large flask, the first phase of his extraction.

He had his own crude resonator with him. He had called it a truth resonator, but knew it was not even close. Alan understood the metaphysical principles of resonance theory well enough to know that what he had been able to create would not even levitate with any consistency. And truth was something else. The three were inextricably bound together: gravity, levity, and truth. Humans had got as far as gravity. Alan, with help, had managed to tease a little levity out of his resonator, but nothing like what he needed for his missile, and truth—that was still very far away indeed.

He didn't find any resonators in the lab, but he found something that he was sure Miranda had used to calibrate the resonator in her own ship. *It just might work*, he thought. If he could tune his own resonator, he reasoned, it would be accurate enough to deliver his payload.

Alan Fain got very busy. He worked on his two projects like a man possessed. The extraction itself demanded careful attention to the smallest details, the sort of technique acquired only through years of patient work in an organic chemistry laboratory.

His work with the resonator was not nearly so precise. He alternately sent everything at one end of the lab flying, then nearly crushed himself with sudden, suffocating weight. But by the time he collapsed from exhaustion to claim a few hours' sleep, he was convinced that he would be able to do it.

Miranda learned that the young holistic leader of the demonstration was named Phoenix, and it was surprisingly easy for her to get to see him. "Why not?" was all the guard said when she asked.

He was being held in a room at the other end of the Palace of the Sun. The trial had begun to bore her. Ira was still interested, but he had a greater capacity for legal and political maneuvering. Miranda could tell from the questions that the vote would be close—there was nothing more to do but wait for the final outcome. In the meantime she wanted to find out more about the holistics.

"What is it you are trying to accomplish?" she asked the young man. They were seated in his room, she in a stuffed chair and he on a chaise-style lounge.

"We think it is time to reconcile our differences with the earth," he said.

"And what are those differences?"

"That's just the point," he said. "No one knows anymore. They say you are barbaric, savag—"

"I'm not of the earth," she said.

"Where then?" he asked suspiciously.

"Arlandia," she said.

"So it's true," he said. "There is another continent like ours."

"Not a continent," she said. "We are a little colony, and not like you at all."

"But you have the levity drive?"

"Yes."

"And you came from earth?"

"Yes."

"Then we are alike. That's all we are trying to say—that we are all human and should face our destiny together. We only stand to gain."

"But what was that you said about unifying the fields?" Miranda said. "Surely that was something more than a harmonious confluence of cultures?"

He got very quiet. There were no windows in the room, but he stared at the wall as if he were looking out. Miranda noted his dark good looks and imagined Lew might have looked like that as a youth.

"It's no secret," he said finally.

"What?"

"The unified field," he said. "Everyone knows about it, but very few believe anymore. What do you understand of science?"

"A little," she said, smiling.

"Then you know about the four basic force fields, and you understand that levity is a first step."

"Toward what?"

"Levity is the beginning of resolution," he said, growing more excited as he spoke. "Levity allows us to modulate the gravitational force in much the same way we use the electromagnetic. But gravity is still more mysterious than the other three forces. This is because gravity is closer to home. We live with gravity in a more immediate, more human way than we do the other force fields.

"So when gravity is resolved into levity its opposite, we are at the beginning of the great adventure."

"And what is that?"

"The cosmic dance! The unified field. There are legends. Most here dismiss them as myth but—"

"The Alethians," Miranda said.

"So you *know*." he said.

"I don't know," she said, "but I have heard. Do you really believe in this ancient race that came from God knows where and gave humans the spark of—"

"I don't know!" he said. "Prometheus is the myth that survives, the god who gave us fire, but the Alethians could be more than myth. Without them we would never have started to dream. Language is really nothing more than a dream, you know. What are words? Ephemeral things. The word stands for the real—it stands between ourselves and the Universe, and somewhere in that strange relation we find truth. Words are miracles; we have just forgotten the magic of it, but it is old magic, an ancient gift, and the Alethians are our benefactors."

"You are quite a philosopher for one so young," Miranda said.

"We are outnumbered," he said.

"The philosophers?"

"No, the young."

"Why is that?"

"Our race here on the lost continent has gradually, over many generations been learning to live longer. They would have us believe that we learned immortality along with levity all those millennia ago, when our continent ascended to the heavens.

"But that's a lie. Initially our life spans were quite ordinary, but through genetic tinkering we have extended it past the thousand-year mark. But there is a worrisome side effect. The birthrate has steadily declined. Jistane is typical of the elders; he refuses to acknowledge what is staring him in the face. If we don't change, we will slowly die, and Atlantis will be no more than a legend."

"What has the reuniting of Atlantis with earth got to do with this unified field?" Miranda said.

He smiled. "That's a good question. No one really knows. We are young and desperate, so we make a big noise. It has Jistane and his crowd worried. I don't know if I really believe in the unified field. The ancients knew about atoms, the smallest units of material substance.

"We now know that atoms are not the smallest things—they are themselves composed of constituent parts. But the atom is possessed of a degree of integrity that gives it unity. An atom of gold is purely gold and resonates with all the properties of that substance.

"The solar system, while it resembles an atom in structure, is highly differentiated. One theory has it that at one time, so long ago as to be inconceivable, atoms were as differentiated as our solar system. But atomic resonance resolved the three forces of electromagnetism and the strong and weak nuclear forces. Atoms, the building blocks of our world, were crystallized out of a dissonance of force fields and resolved into existence.

"Gravity remains the one unresolved force. Gravity is our force. It is the solar reality, and the history of humanity is one of gravity. The resonator, which gave us levity, was the first step in this final resolution.

"But my ancestors saw levity merely as a means to isolate us from the rest of humanity. For three millennia we have circled the sun removed from the sight and mind of earth. Three millennia wasted. Our mission as human beings is to resolve the force of gravity with the three atomic forces, unify the solar field. Maybe our solar system can become the first superatom in the Universe.

"There are some who believe that this will cause a chain reaction, and all other star systems will spontaneously resolve their gravitational fields as well."

"And what then?" Miranda said.

"Who knows?" he said. "What's outside the Universe? Maybe then we will see.

"But back to your question. We don't know precisely what we are doing. But we do believe that our isolation from earth has been a mistake. We need new blood. We need the earth to bring us back to ourselves. Only then can we begin again to understand our mission, and how to get on with the work of resolving gravity within the solar sphere and bring about the unified field.

"Some of us believe that the Alethians came to terrestrial space before humans could speak or even think much. They saw our strange destiny and chose to fire our minds with language and the notion of truth anyway. Why? And where are they now?"

"I don't know, but I'm convinced we must act. Do you know why?"

"Why?"

"As humans it is our destiny. We are the gravitons. It is through us that the unified field will come about. We will be the fundamental particles of a new solar atom!"

A silence settled over the room. Miranda broke it after a long minute. "You think the Alethians knew all this before humans were truly human?"

"Yes," Phoenix said. "And they left records. No one knows where they are, although it is rumored that there is something on the moon."

Miranda had a sudden vision of Lew, deep underground in a temple, and then it was gone. "Of course!" she said.

"You know? Have you seen them?" Phoenix said.

"No, just a flash of intuition," she said.

"But if this was all known before history began," Miranda said, "why didn't the Alethians simply unify the fields themselves?"

"We have to do it," Phoenix said.

"Why?" Miranda said.

"It is our solar system," he said.

"And the Alethians. Where did they come from?"

"Somewhere else. Maybe they were truly gods and have returned to Olympus."

"Now you are talking like a child!" she snapped. Miranda was irritated. There was something to what the young man said. It confirmed many of her own suspicions about humanity, gravity, and levity. But something was missing, something important, and she sensed danger in Phoenix's vision of a unified solar field.

"You're right," he said. "This is no time to confuse myth with truth. But there is one myth that deserves mention."

"What?"

"The Golden Grail," he said.

"Oh no," Miranda said.

"You've heard of it?"

"Yes." She sighed, thinking of the big Texan and his preposterous book.

"Well we think the grail exists. It is a superdense material, not really matter. Crystallized thought is the closest thing to describe it. The Alethians created it. It contains the essence of the potential of human consciousness. And with the grail lies the secret of unifying the solar field."

"What do you mean?"

"A human being must deliver the grail personally into the heart of the sun," Phoenix said, "and that will do it. It must be a personal, conscious act of human will. It won't do just to hurl the thing into the sun with an unmanned missile. That's where one human being becomes the graviton that creates the solar resonance."

"And you believe this?"

"Not really," he said as if he regretted his inability to believe.

"Where's the grail?"

"I wish I knew." He sighed.

Miranda suddenly thought she understood him. He passionately desired to burn himself up in the heart of the sun, to be the catalyst for the birth of a superatom the size of the solar sphere, but he lacked conviction and courage.

"You are appropriately named, Phoenix," she said.

"I don't think so," he said.

28

Golden Age of Tennis

When Lew finished playing he unslung the Strat and leaned it against the amp. The quiet sounds of the fountain replaced the rolling chords.

" 'The real is seeming, bright as any sun,' " Tantalyes read.

"Do you understand it?" Lew asked.

"Not really," Tantalyes said, "but it has a certain ring to it, don't you think?"

"The ring of truth?"

"Well spoken," Tantalyes laughed. "Are you by any chance a philosopher?"

"Not by profession," Lew said.

"Philosophy makes a poor profession anyway," Tantalyes said. "It's a game better left to amateurs."

"Like tennis?"

"There's something to be said for professional tennis, I think. Do you play?"

"A little."

"I used to, many years ago. I don't like to think how many nor how it is I ever forgot how much I enjoyed it."

"Care for a game?" Lew said.

Tantalyes's left eyebrow went up. "Certainly," he said.

Lew led the way to the court. When he turned the dial

on his racket, Tantalyes uttered an exclamation of surprise followed by, "Of course, the resonator."

"What do you mean?" Lew said.

"Later," Tantalyes said. "Let's play. I need a game."

Lew had Tantalyes borrow his mysterious opponent's racket. The opponent acted as referee.

When it was over, Lew had won but not easily. "That's a vicious, crosscourt backhand you have," Lew said.

"Thank you. I'm a bit rusty." Tantalyes was euphoric. The game and his return to the temple after so many years had quickened his spirits.

"What did you mean about the resonator?" Lew said, toweling his face and neck.

Tantalyes led the way back to the temple entrance. They went inside. He pointed to the globe on the marble table. "That," he said, "is the most sophisticated resonator I have ever seen. It could move the moon from its orbit. Reversing its polarity makes it a dissonator, and, as such, it could disrupt the entire gravitational field of terrestrial space."

"But what has that got to do with the imaginary tennis player?" Lew said.

"Imaginary?" Tantalyes said. "He seemed quite real."

"Real?" Lew said.

"Seeming and bright!" Lew recognized the voice. Tantalyes spun around to face the sphinx.

She had reverted to her earlier form. "*Seemingly* real?" she said, taunting the newcomer. "How do you decide, what is real and what is"—she paused to lick a large paw—"illusion?" she shrieked, and pounced on Tantalyes, knocking him to the floor.

Lew ran up to her, "Stop!" he said. "What are you doing?" She brushed him away casually, and he went spinning across the hard, smooth marble floor.

"Please," Tantalyes said when he recovered his breath.

"Please what?" she said, still pinning him down with her great paws.

"I'm not your enemy."

"Enemy?" she said sarcastically. "What have I to fear from enemies?"

"You have nothing to fear from me," he said.

"Who *are* you?"

"Tantalyes of Atlantis."

"Atlantiss," she hissed the final "s." "Yes, the lost continent of legend. And so, Tantalyes of Atlantis, *who are you*?"

"None of us can know the answer to that," he said. "A man cannot be one with himself."

"That's not what the great philosophers of the antediluvian age said," she said.

"They were mistaken."

"One is easily misled about such things," she said. "Why are you here?"

"I came for Lew, and to discover the nature of this place."

She lifted her paws from his chest and backed away. A transformation began, so gradual that neither man noticed at first. "This," she said, "is Alethis, the temple of truth. Surely you know that."

"Yes," Tantalyes said. "But what does that mean?" He began to discern the change in her limbs and torso.

"That could mean any number of things. Would you like me to launch into an explication of the three main branches of truth theory: correspondence, coherence, and skepticism? Compare and contrast?"

"No," Tantalyes said, fascinated by the beautiful form emerging before his eyes.

"Good," she said, turning to Lew, who had regained his feet. She walked to him, and by the time she reached his side the transformation was complete. "So, Tantalyes of Atlantis, you have come for Lew." She slid her arm around his waist. They made the most preposterous couple, Lew in his tennis clothes and the cat woman by his side. She pulled him close and kissed him, pressing against his chest. The she rolled her head lazily back to Tantalyes and said, "I'm not sure I'm ready to give him back."

"And what does Lew say?" Tantalyes said.

"I think," Lew said, "there is plenty of time to discuss these matters, and that now is not the best time."

"Do you remember your friend, Alan Fain?" Tantalyes said.

"Of course."

"Alan's situation lends some urgency to the problem."

"Damn!" Lew pulled away from Diotima. "Why is it always Alan? I'm not sure I care anymore. I've come a long way, Tantalyes. And now, here—I don't even know if I'm happy here. And that's the beauty of it, don't you see?"

"We all desire happiness," Diotima said in a smooth, silky voice. Her soft fur shimmered in the even yellow light streaming from the resonator.

"Maybe we do," Lew said. "And I have pursued it with varying degrees of success. But what I am saying is that here, wherever this is, none of that seems to matter. I have music, I have tennis, wonderful books, and—"

Diotima walked back to his side and said, "What else?"

"I don't know," Lew said, looking at her. "I don't know whether I should love you or fear you, but I'm not sure I care about that either. I'm tired of caring—not because I don't want to, but because it really doesn't seem to do much good."

Diotima kissed him passionately. Lew broke free. His face was hot and flushed when he said to Tantalyes, "So you see?"

"Alright," Tantalyes said, "I think I do." He looked to Diotima, but she was gone.

"She does it all the time," Lew said. "Now maybe you can tell me what you meant about the resonator."

Tantalyes was already moving toward it. He put his hand on the globe and quickly pulled it away to pick up the grail standing next to it. He looked inside and read the inscription that matched the words etched in stone outside. "What is *this?*"

"I found it," Lew said.

"Where?"

"Beneath the falls. In the water. It caught my eye."

"Yes," Tantalyes set it back down, "it would," and

added, thinking out loud, "and I am really not so surprised—by any of this."

"What do you mean?" Lew said.

"The pattern, it all fits, or at least it is beginning to."

"Maybe you could fill me in on the details, because it doesn't mean much to me," Lew said.

Lew's sarcasm was not lost on Tantalyes. "No," he said, "I don't suppose it would. You mentioned books?"

Lew gestured below.

"Show me, please."

Tantalyes dived into the literature. He was like a hungry beast going after raw meat. "I never knew this was here!" he said.

"You've been here before?" Lew said.

"A long time ago," Tantalyes said, "but I only saw what I was meant to see."

"*Meant* to see? And who controls that? Are they still here?"

"The Alethians?"

"Yeah."

"In a way," Tantalyes said. He was piling books on a table, flipping through pages and scanning the shelf.

Lew wandered back upstairs. He looked for Diotima and was relieved not to find her. He went outside and wandered down to the river. He drank deeply and looked around. Tantalyes's arrival had changed his perception of the place, and he found himself thinking of home.

Later, when Lew was playing his guitar by the fountain, Tantalyes came out to listen.

"Nice blues," he said.

"You and Tana?" Lew said, and played a haunting riff.

"Yes?"

"You're from the same place."

"Yes."

"Atlantis?"

"You must find it hard to believe."

"Really?"

"Maybe not," Tantalyes conceded. "Yes, I'm from Atlantis. The lost continent—but not really lost, we just went our own way.''

Lew threw some Phrygian modulations into the chord progression, giving the music a Moorish flavor.

''We built a resonator that could levitate our continent and keep it together. We left and hid ourselves on the other side of the sun.''

''Why?''

Tantalyes laughed. ''Why not? I thought, you would understand.''

''Yeah,'' Lew said, ''I guess I do.'' He launched into one of his own tunes, a song he had intended to record with the Resonators.

''Your own composition?'' Tantalyes said when Lew finished.

''Yeah.''

''Not bad. You would be a hit on Atlantis.''

''The legends are true,'' Tantalyes said later, when they were sitting in the library.

Time had resumed its peculiar course—Tantalyes's presence was more felt than seen since he had immersed himself in the literature.

''What legends?'' Lew said.

''There are stories that tell of a race before humans. They came from somewhere else—''

''Somewhere else? Aliens?''

''Are the two necessarily the same?'' Tantalyes said.

''Depends on your definition,'' Lew said.

''Exactly. Anyway the stories of Alethis still persist on Atlantis. They have given rise to a new youth movement—they call themselves the *holistics.*''

''Was Tana one?'' Lew said.

''She was being recruited,'' Tantalyes said. ''They *corrupted* her.''

''I see,'' Lew said. ''Tell me about the Alethians.''

''They're the ones who taught us levity. But that came much later.''

''Later than what?''

''You know the myth of Prometheus?''

"Sure," Lew said.

"He was a god, a Titan in some accounts. He gave mankind the gift of fire. One interpretation of that myth is that the gift of fire symbolizes the spark of creativity. Prometheus gave us the ability to imagine and with that—"

"The rest is history," Lew said.

"Yes. Imagination gave birth to language, mathematics, science, philosophy, even truth."

"Truth? But—"

"Think about it," Tantalyes said. "Without imagination there is no separation between you and reality. Without that there is no possibility of untruth, hence truth is meaningless. Truth is the congruence of the word and the real. The Alethians gave us imagination and hence truth."

"Sounds to me like they gave us the ability to endlessly deceive ourselves," Lew said.

"That too. Anyway, they knew, long before we had the capacity to know, that truth is intimately bound up with gravity."

"Gravity?"

"The most mysterious of the four forces. Yes, gravity. I'll try to explain, but I don't fully understand either. If I did, I don't suppose I would be here."

"Where would you be?"

"Levitating my way through the cosmos, I guess." Tantalyes laughed. "Gravity is essentially different from electricity and the two nuclear forces. This much is obvious when you consider the way it works. It is the only cosmic force that acts at such great distances, and it is weak compared to the other three. Antigravity is levity, and the Alethians taught my people how to make crude resonators many thousands of years ago."

"What is a resonator?" Lew said.

"A resonator is any device that can vibrate to a particular frequency. In that sense everything is a resonator. But I'm talking about devices that resonate to the gravitational pulse—such resonators can modulate the force of gravity so that it becomes levity. But artificial levity is rather crude. We haven't made much progress in all these millennia. We can alter our local gravitational field so that our orbit is stable and our world does not break apart, but that is all. Do you know what the most advanced resonator is?''

''No,'' Lew said.

''You,'' Tantalyes said. ''Me. Each human being has the potential to levitate and more, but very few have ever realized this potential.''

Lew started to speak of Miranda, but held his tongue.

''We are all gravitons,'' Tantalyes said. ''At least potentially.''

''But what has this got to do with truth and imagination?'' Lew said.

''Everything. When gravity becomes levity, the gulf between imagination and reality becomes smaller. In a very real sense truth is resonance. Surely you must have sensed this yourself.''

''Yeah,'' Lew said. He had, in fact, thought along similar lines. ''When the music is really flowing—we've had a few gigs like that, me and my band—I almost feel like I can fly, like the Universe is capable of becoming one song that we all can sing—forever and ever . . . '' His voice trailed off wistfully.

''Indeed,'' Tantalyes said. ''And then, of course, there is the unified field.''

''What? Isn't that what Einstein was after?'' Lew said.

''Yes. Now the scientists call it grand unification theory, and they don't really know the significance of it.''

''And what is that?'' Lew said.

''I didn't believe it, but now I wonder,'' Tantalyes said. ''Maybe the kids are right—that crowd of *holistics* that compromised your Tana. Maybe all the fields can be unified into one incredible resonating superatom.''

''You've lost me again,'' Lew said.

''Yes—and if it happens we may all be lost.''

''How?''

''Think about it,'' Tantalyes said. ''It is the separation of the fields that makes life as we know it possible. Things are discrete. The nucleus has its own sphere of influence. It interacts with the biological through the atomic interface, and then we move up to the molecular level of DNA and protein chemistry. The electrical also affects us but remains a separate force. Gravity we have already discussed. It is the separation of these forces into their respective spheres and modes that gives us our world. You are separate from me, as I am separate from the air I breathe and the sun that lights my world.

"If all the fields are unified, these differentiations are all annihilated. There is only the one superresonance."

"But wouldn't that also be a supertruth?" Lew asked.

"Either that or the end of truth," Tantalyes said. "The Alethians had the power to create a solar unified field, a conversion of the solar system into a giant resonating entity—and they did not do it."

"Why?" Lew said.

"Yes, 'why?' I think they pulled back at the brink because they saw a higher truth. Maybe the unified field is not the future, but the past. It was meant to be fragmented. Maybe they realized this and abandoned the quest."

"Where did they go?" Lew asked.

"I'm tired," Tantalyes said. He rose from his chair and stretched. "Care for a game?"

"But you're tired," Lew said.

"I can't sleep yet. I need something to take my mind away from all this."

It was one of the best matches Lew ever played, but Tantalyes was much improved and won it. Lew asked him where he learned to play.

"We invented tennis," Tantalyes said, "a long time ago. Before the glory that was Greece and the grandeur that was Rome, there was a golden age of tennis in the middle of the sea."

29

The Telamonian

Ira was finding the trial a tedious affair. *Worse than the Water Commission hearings,* he thought, as witness after witness testified to the primitive and dangerous nature of earthlings. According to Monica it was not going well. A majority vote for acquittal would settle the matter in Tana's favor and spare the earth, but Monica could only count on four votes, with one undecided.

Ira asked her what would happen in the case of a tie.

"Then things begin to get interesting," she said.

"What do you mean?" Ira said.

"A tie may be the best we can hope for," Monica said, "but I'd rather not go into the details. Our law can be arcane and convoluted."

"I'm from Texas," Ira pressed her. "That stuff doesn't worry me."

But she refused to explain. "If it comes to that" was all she would say.

"I don't understand what all the fuss is about," Ira said to Miranda one evening. They were standing on the bluff overlooking the lake. The angled solar light through the dome brought out subtle colors along the shoreline.

"These people have been so long away from earth they see your race as alien and dangerous," Miranda said. "That's part of the problem. But the real issue is Alan—his experimentation with resonance technology. If I could only convince them that Alan is an exception, and his understanding of the science poses no threat—"

"You may have to do just that," Monica said, surprising them both. "The lake is lovely, isn't it."

"Yeah," Ira said.

"Are you going to call me as a witness?" Miranda said.

"No, that wouldn't do much good. I'm surprised at the hold Jistane has over them. If I could only convince Selena, that would at least give us a tie. And she wants to find a moderate solution, but Jistane has her wavering. As things stand I think she might actually vote with him."

"So what do you propose?" Miranda said.

"If Selena could just meet with this Alan Fain, and the others—"

"Cliff?" Ira said. "But surely, they can't take him seriously!"

"Exactly," Monica said. "I'm sure Selena, at least, would grasp the situation if she could see them, talk to them. But, as it is, Jistane is able to paint his own picture of brilliant and dangerous minds plotting a dark conspiracy. We need to bring these people here, including that Lew Slack person, demonstrate that we are dealing with marginal forces that offer no serious threat."

"How?" Miranda said.

"Leave that to me. It will be dangerous, but I think I can get you a ship. Are you willing?"

"Of course," Miranda said.

Later, when Ira and Miranda were alone again, she said, "I have to confess that I did not like her patronizing tone."

"What do you mean?" Ira asked. They were in his room, and he had poured them each a glass of wine.

"I mean Monica's dismissal of Alan, Cliff, and Lew as inconsequential flakes." She raised the glass to her lips. Ira admired the way a few drops clung there until the tip of her tongue darted out and in.

"Aren't they?" Ira said.

"What do you think?" she said.

Ira thought for a moment. "I see what you mean," he said.

"We are all inconsequential flakes," Miranda said, "some more inconsequential than others, and that is largely a matter of timing. This Atlantean chauvinism is stifling."

"But you are going to do it? Bring them here?"

"I have no choice," she said.

"I still can't believe these people are real," he said.

"You had better believe it."

"But Atlantis! I saw a movie when I was a kid. The continent sank because some guy was playing with solar power, or atomic power—or something. But this is stranger than anything I could have imagined."

"Isn't that usually the way of truth?" she said.

Ira stared at her for a moment. "What is really going on here?" he said. "I mean, who are you—really, and what has it got to do with me?"

"Feeling paranoid?" she said.

"Yeah, I guess so."

"Don't. There is no grand conspiracy. And it has no more to do with you than it does with me. We just happen to be involved. Me, because I'm who I am, and you because you're a reporter. And there is something to report, don't you think?"

"What *exactly* are we reporting, anyway?" he said.

"What?"

"Never mind," Ira said. "That's something my editor used to say to me. I don't think he would easily accept any of this as true."

"No editor would," she said.

"Editors have a hard time with the truth," Ira said.

"Like the rest of us," she said.

The next morning, after a long boring session where Jistane presented a ten-thousand-year history of earth showing the planet's inhabitants as immoral barbarians, Monica motioned for Miranda to follow her. Ira started to get up, but Monica shook her head sharply.

Great, he thought, and got up to wander the palace. The light was particularly interesting. He went to the garden in the center of the vast place. *I'm going to be left here alone*, he thought. *I may never get home*. Visions of Miranda's spacecraft being shot down by the Atlantean filled his head, and he also vividly imagined the earth's destruction after the inevitable verdict.

A chill passed through him. He could not ever remember feeling so alone. Opening himself to the brilliant colors helped. He had noted the sensation before when they had passed through the little jungle. Something about it convinced him that he wasn't dreaming, that Atlantis was real and ancient. The garden seemed familiar. The lush smells triggered memories. They weren't memories in the ordinary sense, because they weren't from his own experience. They were vivid feelings that carried the imprint of a rich past. He could almost believe in something like a collective consciousness of the species, so compelling were the feelings.

The garden was big enough to hide in, and Ira wandered farther into the dense primordial growth. A big colorful bird with long striped feathers cooed down at him. He rounded a big tree and stopped.

"Hello," she said.

Ira was stunned by her beauty and her youth. She was younger than Tana, and her hair was even darker.

"We have a window of opportunity," Monica said, "but I need to get you to Eidon."

"How?" Miranda said.

"Train. The last leg, over the pass, will have to be by horseback."

"Horseback?"

"Charming, isn't it?"

"I could fly," Miranda said.

"We allow very few aircraft, and those that do fly are closely monitored," Monica said.

"No, I mean I could *fly*." Miranda gave a demonstration, soaring to the top of a nearby tree and quickly back down.

"How—do you have a miniature resonator?" Monica said, incredulous.

"I am my own resonator. Resonance and levity are latent in the human nervous system. By a strange set of circumstances I was able to actualize them."

Monica continued to stare.

"It's a long story,[11] Monica, and there isn't time," Miranda said.

"No, of course not," Monica said. "Can you fly for long distances, hundreds of miles?"

"Yes, as long as I have sunlight."

"Your green skin?"

"Harbors advanced photosynthetic cells, yes."

"Alright," Monica said, "but you will still have to ride over the pass. We have very sensitive monitors around Mount Poseidon, and I'm afraid you would be detected."

Monica produced a map and explained the route. "My friend has an outpost here. He is expecting you, but not for a few days. How long will it take you to fly?"

"Hours."

"Alright, I'll have to call him."

"When should I leave?"

"Now," Monica said. "Go now."

"You'll look after Ira?"

"Of course."

"Do we have time?" Miranda said.

"I hope so. You've seen the pace of Atlantean justice. I think I can drag it out for long enough, but Jistane is getting impatient."

"Won't he get suspicious? With me gone?"

"I'll tell him you're sightseeing. Fly low." Monica watched with a measure of jealousy as the woman took off. After Miranda had gone, Monica sighed and turned to go back to the law. *Why do we waste our time on such foolishness*? she thought, the image of Miranda vanishing in the distance vivid in her mind.

"You're one of the earthlings, aren't you?" She asked it with a mixture of challenge and curiosity. She was standing beneath an enormous tree.

"Yes, I suppose I am," Ira said. He examined her as closely as he dared. She was wearing loose silk pants and a long tunic tied at the waist. Her build was petite, making

[11]*The Gaia War.*

her appear even younger, almost childlike, and her eyes were stunning, dark burning black.

"I know her."

"Who?"

"Tana. We were friends at school. It's not fair. She didn't do anything really."

"Didn't she desert her post?" Ira said.

The young woman laughed bitterly and leaned back against the tree trunk. "Her post! Yes, she did, I guess. So what?"

"So nothing. I don't know your law. I'm just stating the facts."

"The facts. Do you like the facts?" she said.

"I'm supposed to find them out," he said.

"That's a funny job."

"I'm a reporter," Ira said. He watched her closely to see if the word would carry any meaning for her. He had seen one trial observer reading a newspaper, but the man had left before Ira could get to him.

"A *newspaper* reporter?" she said.

"Yeah." Ira was starting to get excited. He very much wanted to see a newspaper in this strange place. "How many do you have here?"

"One," she said.

"Oh," Ira said showing disappointment.

"One big one. There are a few small papers in the towns. Eidon may have one of its own. I don't know. Not that many people read them."

"Why not?" he said.

"What's news?" she said, and smiled. It took Ira completely off his guard, so cryptic and intriguing was her expression.

"I—uh—news is what's happening, news is the truth—or something."

She laughed. "Yes, but I can get you a copy of *The Telamonian*, if you want."

"The what?"

"*The Telamonian*, our big newspaper."

"I'd like that."

"Well come on then, *earthling*!" She began walking, an easy flowing motion.

Ira hesitated for a moment, wondering what would happen if he deserted the proceedings—but only for a moment.

She took him to a café not far from the Palace of the Sun. "Stay here," she said. "I'll be right back."

Ira sat at an outside table. The street was busy, but seemed quiet to Ira since there were no internal combustion vehicles. He watched the easy confluence of people, horse-drawn vehicles, the occasional levity drive car. *Maybe these people are right about us barbaric earthlings,* he thought.

"Here." A newspaper plopped on the table. Ira picked it up and admired the masthead. *The Telamonian*, it said in bold print, slightly extruded to give a 3-D effect.

There was a front-page story about a recent murder, bringing Ira back to the reality that Atlantis was not Utopia.

"There is nothing here about the trial," he said.

"Somewhere in there you'll find it. It's not front-page stuff anymore. Maybe when they sentence her to lunar isolation," she said.

"You think they will?"

"Of course. They have to. To make an example of her."

"But, it's crazy!" Ira said. "I can understand that, unfair though it may be, but to destroy the earth as well!"

Ira noticed she was looking behind him. He turned to see a waiter. "Are you the earthling?" the waiter said.

"Yeah," Ira said.

"What are you up to, Phaedra?" the waiter said to the girl.

"Not a thing. Bring us two café stanzas, please," she said.

"He knows you," Ira said.

"He *thinks* he does," she said.

The drinks were a blend of coffee and something Ira could not identify. They were iced and Ira found the effect euphoric.

"So, tell me, earthling," she said.

"What?"

"What do you know about the *unified field*?"

Miranda flew into the foothills of Mount Poseidon. There she hiked for several miles until she came to a station. It looked like the one Monica had described.

"Not many people around here," she said to the proprietor behind the counter. He was reading, and it took a few seconds to look up.

"No," he said. "I like it that way. This pass is seldom used. It's steeper and rougher than the main road. Will you be wanting a horse?" He made the question sound like a challenge.

"Yes, please."

"Headed to the port?"

"Yes."

"Business?"

"Sort of."

"Well I guess it's none of my business anyway, is it?"

"Not really," she said.

"Big doings in Telamon," he said.

"What do you mean?"

"The trial," he said. "That traitor, and the earthlings."

"It's old news now," she said.

"Not out here," he said, pointing to his paper. There was a picture of Miranda and Ira on the front page.

She started to back out. "It's alright," he said, "I've been expecting you. Monica sent word. Have you ever ridden a horse before?"

"No," she said, still suspicious.

"Then you better let me come with you partway."

Soon Miranda was perched on a small mare winding up the narrow pass. Altinous was following on a larger horse. "You're doing fine," he said after a few hours. "I'll turn back now. She knows the way."

"But—" Miranda began. She was worried. The trail was getting extremely narrow and steep. Her powers would not necessarily help much in a sudden fall. She would not have the time necessary to focus her energies and levitate.

"You are doing fine," he repeated. "Just go slow—don't make any sudden moves." He wheeled his horse around and started back down.

Miranda's mare snorted and raised her head, nostrils flaring. "Come on, girl," Miranda said. "I'm going a lot farther than you."

30

In the Ordinary Sense

Raya was thinking deeply as she worked. She had no doubt that there was something fundamentally wrong with humanity. She wanted to do something about it.

But things were so complicated. Complexity she could handle—the missile she was making for Alan was complex, involving delicate genetic and synthetic architectures. Complications of desire, love, and compassion she could do without.

The earthman she still loved was off on a fool's errand, unlikely ever to return. That had helped convince her that humans needed a new mode of being. Alan was clearly mad, but there was a logic to his plan Raya found hard to resist. A radical change in human consciousness was overdue, and if not now, when?

The lab in which she worked was, like everything else on Arlandia, a living structure. It was underground, where temperature could be more easily regulated. The walls were an organic polymer that had grown to conform to giant underground root systems. Pulsating light spread out in a soft yellow glow from recessed, living photocells in the ceiling. The place had the look and feel of a living heart's interior.

"How's it going?" Alan's voice startled her. "Sorry," he said. "People say I'm like a cat, but I don't do it deliberately—I'm just naturally quiet."

"That's alright," she said, startling him with her beauty as she turned around.

"This light flatters you," he said. "You look like a goddess. And this place reminds me of my lab. Of course my little basement is only wood, brick, and Sheetrock. Still, it has the same kind of charm, an inner sanctum. Don't you feel a special peace in here?"

"I don't know," she said. "Lately I'm confused."

"Don't let that worry you. We're all confused."

"I wasn't always," she said.

"Welcome to the human race."

"But surely—I mean there must be some among you who aren't, some who are—"

"Wise?" he said.

"Yes."

"Maybe there were once. There are stories about that."

"What stories?" she said.

"Never mind," he said, suddenly quite irritated. "Ask Miranda about that, or Cliff—even Lew."

"I'm sorry, I just—"

"Yeah, I know, forget it. Anyway, I've brought the resonator. Are you ready to install it?" he said.

"I suppose. But shouldn't we wait?"

"Wait for what?"

"Miranda will come back. I know she will, and she can tell me if this is a good thing or not."

"I thought we had already agreed on that point," he said. "It is most definitely a good thing. How could it not be a good thing to usher in a new age of harmony on the earth?"

"It might not work," she said.

"Let me worry about that." Alan placed the polished wooden box on her workbench, where it contrasted sharply with the bright green missile, a gleaming, meter-long projectile. The head was a rounded point, and the tail sported a triad of evenly spaced fins.

"This resonator is a crude one, but it's the best I could do with what I had. I think it will work." He opened the box and pulled out the living sphere of densely packed nerve cells. "It's not conscious," he said, "not in the way we are. This is a specialized organic computer, an advanced neural net that has one function only, it resolves the gravitational force field. After I program it, nothing will be able to divert the missile from its target, not even the powerful lunar resonator."

"Why do you call it a truth resonator?" she said.

"Hyperbole on my part," he said, "but not without significance. I'm convinced that the mystery of gravity and the answer to Pilate's question, 'What is truth?' are linked. But that's another research project. The work goes on, and I'm afraid my advances are incremental at best."

She installed the resonator in the center of the missile. Alan programmed it with a portable nouancer. "We mustn't forget the payload," he said when he had finished. He pulled a small vial from his inside coat pocket. It held a clear fluid that could have been easily mistaken for water except for the way it refracted the light, sending little rainbows streaming to the bench and floor.

"No," she said, "I suppose not."

"You've designed the dissemination mechanism properly?" he said.

"It will explode and spread the mundycin spores over an area with a radius of a least two hundred miles," she said.

"That should do it," Alan said. "We'll hit North Dakota, wheat and barley country. Every slice of bread, every glass of beer—man it will be beautiful, a nation gone crazy!"

"Crazy?" she said. "But I thought—"

"Good kind of crazy!" he said. "Beautiful crazy. And it should easily spread in a matter of months to all the grains of the world. Then we will make our move."

"We?" she said.

"You can do as you like!" he said. "But you know what I'm going to do."

"Yes," she said. "I suppose I do."

They armed the missile. "We'll launch it in a few hours," he said, "when our rotation angle is more favorable."

"I suppose we should," she said.

"Of course we should. There are those that dream, like Cliff, and there are people who actually make things happen. We are about to launch a new chapter in history."

Alan was waiting, wandering in a grove of trees that produced huge nuts. He found Cliff eating one. "These things are like pecans," Cliff said, "only better."

Cliff offered one to Alan, who shook his head, "Not hungry," Alan said.

"I know what you're up to," Cliff said.

"I suppose you're going to try and stop me," Alan said, sounding more weary than angry. "You better act fast. We're going to do it before dinner."

"Of course not," Cliff said. "What do you think this is? Some old movie, an adventure story where things are settled by brute strength. This is a spiritual battle, and you are unknowingly serving a higher cause."

"Am I?" Alan was interested.

"Definitely. You're going to try and change human consciousness. It doesn't matter that your pathetic attempt will fail—it will have an effect. Some folks will notice. In fact you may plunge a good deal of the planet into a mad confusion with your drug. But that's insignificant to what's coming, and it will probably do a little good, wake up a few souls who are ready to comprehend the real change."

"I see," Alan said.

"You don't believe me, but since I've been here I've been able to figure out what the book is saying. The grail was created for one purpose. Its superdense structure is mental, not physical—"

"It's made of nouons then," Alan said with disgust, "thought particles!"

"Yeah," Cliff said, "and it was designed to start a chain reaction. Once it is thrust into the heart of the sun, the solar field will be as one, the *unified* field. It is all clear now. The book speaks in metaphors of course. But out here my eyes have been opened. I *see,* I understand."

"Except you don't have the grail," Alan said. "It's a myth, a dream. I deal in realities, and I'm about to launch one."

Cliff laughed, which greatly annoyed Alan. "Science!" Cliff said. "I respect your science. It was science that freed us from our earthly bonds. It was an ancient science that designed the grail.

"But tell me, scientist—what's underneath your fabric of reality, your photons and mesons and nouons? What lies outside it, before and after it?

"*That* is the origin of our myths. And what is more, behind the veil where the story begins and lives forever, there, my friend, you find not abstract structure, energy, and particles—no, there you find something far more interesting."

"What?" Alan said, somewhat shaken by Cliff's sudden eloquence.

"A human face," Cliff said.

"You're crazy!" Alan said. "And you can't stop me."

"I won't even try," Cliff said. "There is no need. Once I unite the grail with the celestial fire, our solar field, you, me, the earth, all the planets, asteroids, and comets will become one, a unified, resonating atom on a tremendous scale—perhaps the first the Universe has ever seen."

"Your grail exists nowhere outside your books and your imagination," Alan said.

"I think not," Cliff said, "and I think I will find it soon." He wandered off, leaving Alan alone and frustrated.

"Where did you get this stuff?" Drake said. He dropped the folder and ran his thumb across his fingertips as if he feared contamination.

"The Speaker's office," Leslie said. "You should see the painting he has of himself in there—"

"I have," Drake said. "Everyone knows about Cliff's rather inflated view of himself."

"Well, it seems that the picture is more than an embarrassing piece of art," Leslie said. "At least it is to him. Apparently he was working with someone on a spaceship. Or he thought he was. That's where the money went. You've got to admire him sort of—I mean at least he didn't embezzle the funds to support an expensive habit in call girls and cars."

"But you don't seriously believe—"

"I don't know what to make of it, Drake. You know as much as me now." *But not quite as much,* she thought.

"We can't print this, you know," Drake said.

"Why *not*?" Leslie was eager to get the story out as a way to prepare the public and her editor for the more bizarre story to come.

"Think about it, Leslie. What *exactly* would we be reporting?"

"Can you read, Drake?" Leslie said, unable to control her temper. "It's right there in the lead for God's sa—"

"I know you're disappointed," he said. "You've worked hard, but this will just confuse our readers."

"You misjudge our readers, Drake. They may not be brilliant, but they do read. You're being unfair to them. It's that rare story that happens to be both true and entertaining."

"Keep reporting on it if you want to. I can't promise you anything, but if you turn up something else—we'll see."

"Thanks, Drake. I'll see you—" She left his office with a new feeling of disgust for her profession. It wasn't the wasted effort, it had been easy to get the information—she had just walked into Cliff's office and rifled his desk—it was the stifling lack of imagination. *No wonder newspapers are dying*, she thought.

"So you know something of the theory of nouons?" Tantalyes said.

"Yeah," Lew said. "More than I care to."

They had finished a tennis match and were sitting under

a nearby tree. The match had been particularly strenuous, Lew having won it in an impossible tiebreaker thirty-two to thirty. His game was better than ever, but Tantalyes was improving rapidly.

"Think of your mind as another sense organ," Tantalyes said, "like your nose or your eyes."

"What does it sense?"

"It senses the nouonic pulse transmitted through the aether. When an artist paints a picture, you see it. You say, on one level that the picture isn't real, but on a deeper level, if it is a good painting, it is very real. You see with more than your eyes—your mind is acting as a sense organ.

"A sophisticated resonator can do more than modulate the gravitational field—it can modulate the pulse of nouons, the fundamental particles of consciousness.

"That explains all this—the tennis court, your partner, and even—"

"Diotima?" Lew said.

"Yes. I hope I haven't shattered any romantic illusions you may have had about her."

"When we first met, and she still assumed her ferocious form, her claws actually drew blood. I saw it, felt it. But within a few hours, all traces of the wounds were gone."

"It was a nouogram," Tantalyes said.

"A what?"

"You have heard of holograms—3-D laser images?"

"Yeah."

"Well these are mental images. They are analogous to laser-produced images, in that the nouonic frequencies, like laser-produced light rays, are highly resolved; most of the random dissonance has been artificially removed."

"So none of it is real," Lew said.

"Ah, now there you are!" Tantalyes said. "That's a question for the philosophers. What is reality? That's what you are really asking. These nouograms, where do they exist? Do they exist at all? I suppose when you are with Diotima it feels real?"

"Yeah." Lew's mind was momentarily filled with images and scents, her soft fur and warm body.

"The kinds of images we are dealing with present new analytical dilemmas. It is one thing to say a movie or a hallucination is not real. A movie exists only in light and film, and a hallucination is not something shared. But that tennis match felt quite real, and Diotima—I would not want to treat her as a mere figment."

"But these nouograms," Lew said, "are all produced by the globe, the resonator?"

"Yes."

"Why?"

"You would have to ask the Alethians that," Tantalyes said. "They must have liked tennis, and I suppose Diotima serves as a guardian of sorts."

"But you have been here before, and you never saw her?" Lew said.

"No, but I'm beginning to think your arrival acted as some special trigger."

"How?" It made Lew uneasy to think that he played any special role in the adventure.

"I don't know, but our race has been strangely uninterested in this place. I never explored it very carefully, and that seems very strange to me now. The only explanation is that, to some extent, the resonator controls what we see and feel here."

"But is the entire place an illusion, or a nouogram?" Lew said.

"I doubt it. I think the temple and the library, most of the infrastructure, is 'real' in the ordinary sense."

"Whatever that means," Lew said.

"You're beginning to get the idea," Tantalyes said.

31

Cold Fact

''Why are you helping me?'' Miranda said. Her tired horse was stabled and she was eating across the the table from her host, a man named Xanthius.

''You don't trust me,'' he said.

''I don't know. I—''

''There are few things you really need to understand in life,'' he said.

''I'm sorry, I—''

''Stop your mindless chatter and listen to me,'' he said. ''You must learn the proper way to receive that which is given, and the appropriate way to give. The wisdom of our race is all about those two things. Study the great myths and legends—you will see. If you can accept your gifts on your life's journey and give properly in the right measure, you will reach your goal. But if not, if you look too closely at the gift, or cannot be a proper host and giver, you will suffer much and may perish, a sun-bleached sack of bones by the side of the road, a warning to those who come after.''

''Oh,'' she said. She finished her fish and wine in silence.

''More?'' he said.

''No thank you.''

Xanthius laughed. ''The reason I am helping you, by the way, is simple. I trust Monica. She is from here—a good, capable woman. She seems to think you need to retrieve your ship. That's enough for me.''

''Thank you again,'' Miranda said.

''You are welcome,'' he said.

* * *

After a restful sleep, Xanthius took Miranda to the port. She was struck by the classical beauty of Eidon. The architecture of Telamon seemed merely to pay lip service to an ancient tradition, while that of Eidon had the refined, understated air of true art.

Getting into the port was no problem. Xanthius knew how to grease the right palms. But getting access to Miranda's ship was not so easy.

The man outside the air lock was a special agent of the Guardians.

"We are here to inspect the ship," Xanthius said.

"Where are your papers?"

Xanthius did not hesitate. He gave the guard a powerful kick in the solar plexus. He grabbed the collapsed man's keys and opened the outer door.

"But what about you?" Miranda said, hesitating while Xanthius furiously motioned for her to go in.

He shoved her inside. The last thing Miranda saw, before the door slid shut, was the guard rising, weapon drawn, behind Xanthius, who was sealing the inner door and opening the outer.

I can't just leave him, she thought, as the outer door opened to reveal the stars.

But she did.

"I need some time off, Drake," Leslie said.

"Sure," the editor said uneasily. "How much?"

"I don't know."

"Vacation?"

"Yeah, but it may be a while, longer than what I've got."

"Don't worry about it," Drake said. "I mean, I want you back. Losing Ira was tough. I need you on the beat—so take as much time as—"

"I'll level with you, Drake," Leslie said. "You gave me the job, my big break, so I owe it to you. I'm going to follow some leads I have on this thing."

"The spaceship?" Drake said, suddenly very weary.

"That and more," she said.

"So where are you going?"

"North Dakota."

"North Dakota? But—"

"My source told me—well never mind what he told me—you don't want to hear, not yet. But he said it would probably happen near some major wheat-farming country."

"But that could be Kansas, Nebraska—"

"Except that Alan Fain is from North Dakota."

"Who?"

"Never mind, Drake. I'll explain it all when I have the story. Anyway, I checked on it. This Alan Fain is from Grafton, North Dakota. He grew up on a wheat, barley, and potato farm. That's where he'll strike, I'm sure of it!"

"Strike?" Drake ran his hand across his sweating brow. The August sun of Texas was streaming in through the big window behind him.

"Never mind, Drake, just give me some time, a few weeks, a month maybe, and when I get back we'll have the biggest scoop ever." She waited a few moments, and when he failed to reply she said softly, "OK?"

"Yeah, OK."

Leslie got up and turned to leave. "Leslie?" Drake called after her, as if he had just woken up from a nap.

"Yeah?"

"Take care of yourself. I mean, be careful."

"Sure, chief," she said. "And you too."

What? he thought as he watched her walk out. *No one has ever called me chief.*

Lew woke up in the arms of Diotima. He ran his hand down the curve of her back and stopped just where the smooth silky fur began.

She opened her eyes and kissed him. His hand went lower.

"Who are you—really?" he said when the tension had left him, and she was stretching like a cat.

"Ssss!" she hissed playfully.

"But if you aren't real, then—"

"Why are you so obsessed with what is real?" she said.

"I'm not. It's just that sometimes you need to know. It's about action. Truth may be hard to define, but the truth is what you need for the purpose of acting, otherwise what chance do you have?"

"Chance to do what?" she said.

Lew was suddenly angry with her, and he jumped to his feet. "You're mocking me!" he said. "How easy it is for you. Down here reality seems irrelevant, but I have to try and believe that what I do is based on something, that it makes sense. I—"

"Yes," she said, "I know. Come here." She rolled into a seductive pose.

"No," Lew said, and walked out of the room.

He found Tantalyes by the fountain eating a white fruit from the trees that lined the entrance.

"Breakfast?" Tantalyes offered some to Lew.

They ate in silence for several minutes.

"We should leave," Tantalyes said.

"Why?"

"I have learned enough for now," Tantalyes said. "It may be futile, but I hope I can get back in time to influence the proceedings. You do want to help Tana, don't you? After all, it was partly because of you that she's in such trouble."

"But she never cared about me," Lew said. "It was all part of the game she was playing, her mission or whatever it was."

"Don't be so sure," Tantalyes said. "I think she cares quite a lot for you—and she is quite real, unlike your pussycat here."

"Real. Yeah, she seemed real enough. I thought we might get married back in San Francisco. I would have my band, play tennis a few times a week. None of it seems real now."

"You can't stay here," Tantalyes said.

"But we can't just leave this place," Lew said. "There is something here—isn't there?"

"Yes, and we have discovered as much as we can for now. I plan to come back. Maybe you will, too."

"No," Lew said. "If I go, I will never return. And, of

course, I know that I must go. I can't say that I've been happy here. Happiness, or the lack of it, has been irrelevant. That has made it like a vacation, a vacation you want to last forever."

"So," Tantalyes said. He splashed some water from the clear, glassy pool in his face and stood up. "Are you ready?"

"Now?"

"Why not now?"

"Sure," Lew said. "But I'd like to say good-bye."

"You'll probably get your chance," Tantalyes said, a cynical edge to his voice. "There is something I want to take back with us."

"What's that?"

"The grail. I want to study it in a proper laboratory."

Lew's feet were light with a strange sense of dread as they walked back up the steps and under the columns.

She was waiting for them, standing beside the resonator.

"Hello, boys," she purred.

"Diotima," Lew said, approaching her, "I—"

"I know," she said. "You have to get back to reality. I understand. Do you think I will try to stop you, deter you from your destiny? I might as well try to alter the course of the stars. It is your fate as a man to strive for truth and reality." She gave him a long lingering kiss.

How can I leave this? he thought. *I'll never find anyone like her.*

"No, you won't," she said, running her hands down the fur on her thighs. "The women of your world don't run with the cats."

Tantalyes was beside them, and he reached for the grail.

"What do you think you're doing?" She turned and grabbed his arm.

"You won't mind if we take this," Tantalyes said, picking up the golden cup.

"What I think or feel about it doesn't matter," she said. "But you will not take it."

Tantalyes pulled his arm away and started to run. He was almost to the door when she leapt. She had reverted to her terrifying form, and she covered the ground in an instant. He screamed as a sharp claw dug into his back.

Lew was pounding on the sphinx's back while she turned Tantalyes over. Lew's efforts had almost no effect on her tough hide.

"Give it back," she said to Tantalyes, who still held the grail.

"Why? Lew found it. It belongs to us."

"It belongs here!" she said. "It was lost for so long, and now it is found."

"What is the secret of the grail?" Tantalyes said.

She lowered her face close to his, her breath again the hot, fetid wind of the jungle cat. "I thought you knew the secret," she said. Tantalyes turned his face away, so pungent were the fumes from her mouth.

"I have guessed," he said, "but I wanted to hear it from you."

"Give it back."

"No." She bore down on him more closely, her face only millimeters from his.

Lew saw the small pool of blood forming underneath Tantalyes, and he screamed, "You're hurting him, Diotima! The game has gone far enough!"

"Game?" She rolled her head to look at him. "This is not a game, lover, this is for real." She pressed her paws into Tantalyes's chest and extended her claws a little.

Tantalyes was able to move his arm enough to thrust the grail from his side. It went spinning across the marble floor. "Take it, Lew!" he said. "Get out of here!"

Lew picked it up and bolted. He ran down the steps, past the fountain, and down the long staircase. He set the grail on a rock ledge and ran back the way he came. All the way he looked for a weapon, something sharp. A piece of the stone railing that had broken off caught his eye. It was a heavy chunk of rock with a sharp point, and he picked it up.

He went straight for her face, swinging the jagged edge with all the momentum of his motion. It struck her between the eyes with a dull chunk.

She shrieked in fury and pain as she jumped up. Lew

tried to strike her again, but a powerful paw slapped the stone from his hands. It hit the floor and shattered.

She came at him, but Lew was able to sidestep her charge. He could see that he had done some serious damage. Blood was filling her eyes, and she was unsteady on her legs.

Tantalyes was crawling toward the door. "You hurt him," Lew said.

"In life is much pain," she said.

"Why be the cause of it?" Lew said.

"I?" she said. "I am the cause of nothing. You are the cause of things." She was sitting and trying to wipe the blood from her face with a large paw.

From the corner of his eye Lew could see that Tantalyes, on his hands and knees, was almost through the doorway. Lew began slowly backing away.

He helped Tantalyes out to the fountain and tried to wash the blood from his chest, but it kept coming.

"You got the grail?" Tantalyes asked in a weak voice.

"Yes."

"Take me to it. I want to see it again before—"

"Before what?" Lew said. Tantalyes just shook his head.

Lew had to support most of the Atlantean's weight as they slowly descended the steps. When they finally arrived at the bottom Lew was practically carrying the man.

"Yes," Tantalyes whispered, picking up the cup. "Now I remember hearing about this when I was a child."

"When was that?" Lew said.

"Too long, too long," Tantalyes said.

"You must take this back!" Tantalyes said with a sudden energy that left him drained.

"Me? Aren't you coming with me?" Lew said.

"I'm not going much farther," Tantalyes said, looking at the blood still running down his chest.

"She scratched me," Lew said. "I told you about it. The wounds were gone in a few hours."

"I don't have a few hours," he said.

"But it isn't real!" Lew said, looking at the blood.

Tantalyes smiled weakly and lay down on the shelf of rock where Lew had left the grail. It looked disturbingly like a funeral bier.

"You take it back," Tantalyes whispered. "Some will recognize it. Maybe we should do it."

"Do what?" Lew said.

"The unified field," Tantalyes said. He was staring straight up at the glittering cavern ceiling, but his eyes seemed to be looking straight through the rock.

Lew sat there long after the man's breathing had stopped. He touched the body a few times, feeling it grow colder.

This isn't how people die, he thought. *He can't be dead.*

Lew walked back up the staircase. Each step registered as an act done only after much deliberation.

He stood at the fountain for a few minutes and stared at the inscription on the temple. Then he approached.

She was waiting for him, outside the door underneath the columns.

"Why?" he asked. She was a woman again. Her hands idly stroked the fur of her thighs.

"Bring it back," she said.

"Why did you do it, Diotima?"

"The grail belongs in the temple," she said.

"Then go get it," he said. "I won't help you." She didn't move.

"You can't get it. You can't leave the temple, can you?"

She said nothing.

"You're a fucking illusion!"

She smiled, and the expression brought the image of Tantalyes, cold and pale, to life.

"Illusions don't kill," he said. "He's not dead!"

"And if he is dead? Would that make me real?"

"Do you care?" Lew said.

"No, it means nothing to me—real or unreal, true or false."

"And death?" Lew said.

"Death means even less," she said.

"It means something to me," Lew said.

"Yes," she said, "I suppose it must. Poor man."

"You are the poor one," he said.

She laughed.

"What's so funny?"

"You silly man, projecting your myriad structure of beliefs on me! It's a house of cards, built on shifting sand."

"There is more to it than that," Lew said.

"I suppose you must believe that," she said.

"You aren't real," Lew said with false conviction. "You can't even walk out that door. You are a projection of that globe in there—a nouogram, an image in my mind."

She walked out from under the columns and down the wide steps. Lew watched her with a mixture of fear and desire. She was so beautiful, so perfectly the blend of animal feeling and human intellect.

She pulled him close and kissed him passionately. He had to fight hard to keep down his desire.

"Oh well," she said, letting him go, "I guess you can't make love to your friend's murderess. Quaint and charming, but I am disappointed."

"He isn't dead," Lew said, realizing it sounded more like a question than a statement.

"I wouldn't know," she said.

"Or care?"

"I told you, death means nothing to me," she said.

"Because you don't exist," Lew said. "You're a hallucination."

"Can something be a hallucination if everyone perceives it in exactly the same way?"

"Of course," he said.

"Then how can you ever tell the real from the unreal?"

"Reality is more than shared perception," he said.

"Maybe it is and maybe it isn't. I am only showing you that you can never know."

"Tell me whether or not you are real, Diotima. Please?"

"I would be the last to know," she said. She walked back up the steps and into the temple, her tail swishing and flicking. Lew looked fondly at her beautiful form and glistening fur. He wanted to follow her. The thought seized him like a desperate criminal pleading with the judge for his life. *I could stay here, make fantastic love with her, play guitar, play tennis, and read for the rest of my life, maybe forever. Maybe this is heaven and that's how it works. It's a test—I can refuse it or take it, but I only get one chance!*

The image of Tantalyes forced its way back on him. It felt like an icy weight on his back. It stayed with him until he was halfway down the staircase, and then the thought came that Tantalyes might be alright and his steps lightened. He ran the rest of the way.

He was convinced of it as he bounded down the last few steps and rounded the rock to where he had left the man.

Lew hugged himself to fight off the chill that consumed him as he stared at the corpse, as real and dead as it gets.

32

Rave On

Miranda stared at the sun. It drew her like an ancient memory, sweet and sharp. *I should just leave this ship*, she thought, *and fly free in the light*. But she knew that her body was still changing and wasn't yet ready for naked space.

It is good to be alive out here, she thought. *Why do the affairs of humans keep us all so bound*?

There was no answer from the blazing font of energy. She reluctantly turned away.

She had a warm sense of home when Arlandia came into view. It was like a little jewel hanging in the vast solar field. So much smaller than Atlantis, it was that much more precious to her.

Raya was waiting for her inside the air lock. "It's good to see you," she said when Miranda stepped out.

"It's good to be back. How are the guests?"

"Fine—I suppose."

Miranda found Raya's voice disturbing. "And Alan? Has he finally come out of his delusion?"

"No." Raya turned away.

They walked silently out into the filtered light and rich tapestry of color that was their world.

"Any word of Lew?" Miranda said.

"No."

"What's wrong, Raya?" Miranda said, stopping. "Tell me."

"I can't stop thinking about him," Raya said.

"Don?"

"Yes. I know I should forget him, but—"

"It's difficult I suppose. I don't understand humans very well, either. Although you and I, Raya, we are—after all—human. That much is clear to me now. We are just farther along in the evolutionary scheme of things."

"Yes, we are, but that doesn't make dealing with them any easier."

"It's hard for all humanity," Miranda said. "I'm not sure why, but I think the moon holds some of those secrets. Maybe Lew can tell us something if we find him."

"Where is Alan? I need to talk with him and Cliff."

Raya looked away.

"They are still here?"

"Of course. Where would they go?"

"Don left—for the outer reaches of the solar system, the next great leap."

"No," Raya said, "nothing like that."

They found Alan sitting under a giant tree in a clearing. He looked up at them and smiled. "Evening, ladies," he said. "Or is it morning? I lose track here."

"Evening," Miranda said, "and it doesn't matter—you're supposed to lose track."

"Yeah," Alan said. "Paradise maintained. Cool."

"I need to talk to you and to Cliff," Miranda said.

"It sounds serious."

"I suppose it is, if you take the fate of your world seriously," Miranda said.

"The earth?" Alan said.

"The earth."

"I have taken care of the earth already," Alan said.

"What?" Miranda looked at Raya. "You haven't—?"

Raya looked away.

"Oh no," Miranda said.

"We only need to wait now," Alan said.

"How *could* you?" Miranda said to Raya. They were alone in the lab. Alan had gone to look for Cliff.

"But he's right," Raya said. "About humanity, I mean."

"Maybe, but not about the solution—A world full of crazy, drug-induced visions won't solve anything!"

"But it didn't seem that way at the time. I thought we—"

"Never mind," Miranda said. "How is it guided?"

"Alan's resonator."

"Then we can't stop it."

"What will we do?"

"I don't know. The problem is that Alan may be misguided, but he's brilliant. This missile is not going to be easy to stop. Maybe I can intercept it before it detonates."

"Will it be dangerous?"

"Maybe."

"Let me do it," Raya said, "It was my—"

"No," Miranda said. "It wasn't your fault. I should never have left you alone with that man. You haven't the experience. Humans are too clever for their own good, and it's all too easy to get caught up in their madness."

"Aren't we human too—sort of?"

"Yes, and I guess that's the problem."

"Stick with me, ladies, and your problems are over." It was Alan. he was descending the stairs with Cliff.

"Things are now more complicated," Miranda said, after they were all seated, ''but the fact remains that I must take you back with me to Atlantis.''

''I have a date with destiny on earth,'' Alan said.

''He is going to be the new messiah, the prophet of the axial awakening,'' Cliff said.

''And you?'' Miranda said.

''I, too, have a date with destiny,'' Cliff said, ''which is why I may go with you to Atlantis. The Golden Grail is not here. If Atlantis is what I suspect, I hope to find it there.''

''Alright,'' Miranda said, looking back at Alan. ''The effects of the drug must have worn off by now, Alan,'' she said. ''You can't still believe that stuff.''

''I see it differently now,'' Alan said, ''and I've had to take a few more doses, just to keep it all in focus.''

''You call yourself a scientist! Don't you see that your objectivity is gone!''

''Yes and no,'' he said. ''I'm starting to believe that what we call objectivity is just a temporary phase. It's a necessary phase. We need it to get around the accretion of nonsense that is our legacy as humans. The ancients knew about atoms, but it took scientific objectivity to overcome thousands of years of superstition, to finally *do* something with that knowledge.

''But I'm functioning at a higher level now. What is objective? What is real? We have only our methods and our perceptions. Once these are disciplined, fine-tuned, the whole Universe begins to open up. Things are actually more, not less, fantastic than the priests, philosophers, and scientists can imagine.''

''Your problem,'' Miranda said, her anger showing, ''is that you are too damn smart. It is difficult to argue effectively against you because there is much truth in what you say. I have come to some of the same conclusions myself. But there is one truth you have missed which I am compelled to put to you.''

''Yes?''

''You're full of shit, Alan! Don't you see that you have fallen into the same trap as the priests and the philosophers! You have let keen perception and much knowledge get distorted by your own filter, until what you see as truth is nothing more than megalomania.''

''This talk is getting us nowhere,'' Alan said. Her words had stung him; the analysis was too good, too much like his own thoughts.

''You're right,'' she said, ''and there is something more important. While your missile with its psychoactive payload speeds its way to earth, deliberations on Atlantis could make your plans irrelevant.''

''What's happening?'' Cliff said.

''They are trying Tana, Lew's girlfriend.''

''She was just using him,'' Alan said. ''I knew it all along.''

''It doesn't matter! She's on trial.''

''So?'' Alan said. ''What do I care for the fate of one alien traitor?''

''If she goes down, so does the earth. They do things efficiently on Atlantis. And they have the power. There is a powerful resonator in the moon that can disrupt the entire terrestrial gravitational field, and there are powerful forces in Atlantis that want to use it, to cleanse the earth once and for all of the pernicious species known as man.''

''Well, well,'' Alan said.

''So you see,'' Miranda said, ''if they do that, your dreams are nothing. You will have no world to save.''

''It's all beginning to make sense now,'' Cliff said, ''but in my case it is irrelevant.''

Miranda ignored him. ''Will you come with me then?'' she said to Alan. ''It's our only hope. We need to let the Guardians see what they are so afraid of.''

''Alright,'' Alan said, ''I'll go. Why not. I'll save the earth twice.''

Ira couldn't take his eyes off Phaedra. She was dancing. Her rhythm suggested passion. The dance floor was full of other kids, and they were all swaying to the monotonous beat. *It's like religion*, Ira thought. The kids reminded him of dervishes, who danced themselves into visions and trances.

She moved to his table and motioned for him to join

her. He shook his head. She moved her lithe body more deliberately and ran her hands along her hips and thighs. She threw her head back and shook out her long black hair. When she looked back at him her eyes were full of fire.

Ira reluctantly got up, as he could see she wouldn't take no for an answer. He tried to remember how to do it, how to make his body move to a beat. He felt as if all eyes were on him, evaluating, laughing. It was horrible, and he would have sat back down, but for her eyes pulling him deeper into it.

Slowly he realized that, except for a few curious glances, no one was paying him much attention. He let the throbbing pulse of synthetic sound in, and his body began to respond.

They danced for hours. Phaedra wouldn't let him sit down, and he was surprised at how he felt—not tired but energized. When she finally did lead him to a booth behind a sonic screen he was reluctant to go.

"Probably shouldn't overdo it," she said.

"That was great. How does the music do that? Make you dance so well, I mean."

She laughed. "It's not magic, it's just the beat, the rhythm of life. You let yourself feel it, that's all."

"It's been so long," Ira sighed, "since I did anything like that—felt like this."

"How do you feel?" she said.

Ira was too overcome by feeling to answer. He was so attracted to her—it had the urgency of a high school crush, and he was also exhilarated. He wanted to kiss her tenderly and, at the same time, to scream out his newfound sense of freedom."

"Never mind, don't answer," she said. "Better drink." A waiter had brought two large glasses of water. She drained hers easily. Ira admired the action of her slender neck muscles as the liquid slid down her throat. "Drink," she said. "You need it."

Ira picked up his glass and took a little sip. His dehydrated body responded and he drank half the glass before setting it back down.

"Who are all these kids?" He said.

"Kids?" she laughed.

"Young people, I mean."

"Some of them are friends. I know them all. This is our place. The rest of Telamon is so old."

"But who are they—are they the *holistics*?"

"The *subversives*, the *radicals*, you mean."

"Yeah."

"You *are* a reporter aren't you?"

"I suppose so," he said, disappointed in himself.

"It's OK," she said, as if reading his mind. "You can only be who you are."

"The kids where I come from would like this place," Ira said.

"Kids?"

"Young people, I mean. They call them raves."

"The 'kids' are called raves?"

"No, the dance scenes," Ira said. "They dance to music like this all night—go into trancelike states."

"You go to these raves?"

"Only once. I did a story about one. Human interest angle. Are they bad for our youth, ruining the children, or is it just good clean fun—that sort of thing."

She laughed and pulled him back onto the dance floor. Ira was surprised at how easy it was to keep dancing. *It does feel kind of like a trance,* he thought.

When they arrived at her house in a neighborhood close to the shores of Lake Telamon he was in a state of euphoria. "I should be exhausted," he said, "but I feel great."

"Maybe the 'kids' have something to offer," she said, opening the door.

"I'm sure you do," he said. "I know I thought so when I was young."

"When was that?"

"Long ago and far away—in a place called Texas."

"Texas? That's a funny name."

"It's a funny place."

She passed her hand over a panel in the wall, starting some music. It was more mellow than the dance music, the beat less insistent. She went into another room and returned with drinks. ''Essential nutrients for your mind and body,'' she said, handing him the glass. ''Stuff you need after dancing for so long.''

He sipped and sat down on the long sofa. The drink tasted slightly bitter, with a complex mix of sparkle and spice. ''Hits the spot,'' he said.

She laughed and sat down beside him. He looked around, admiring the classical simplicity of the room. A skylight dispersed the sun's rays evenly. The floor was marble, with thick carpets tastefully arranged.

''I feel wonderful,'' he said honestly when he had finished his drink.

She took the glass from him and set it on the low table. ''Would you like to feel even more wonderful?'' she said, moving closer.

''Yes,'' he said, letting her arms wrap around his neck.

She pulled him close and kissed him. He felt his body come even more alive, delicious sensation in every part.

Hours later they were eating at her desk, which overlooked the lake. She had prepared a delicious meal of red beans and eggs. The eggs had purple yolks and tasted slightly sweet. She had also made some of the best coffee Ira had ever tasted.

''We don't have coffee like this back in Texas,'' he said, sipping in ecstasy.

''The Telamonian bean is famous,'' she said.

''You could make a fortune exporting this to Austin,'' he said.

''It is a shame,'' she said, ''that our worlds must remain so far apart.''

''Why must they?'' he said.

''Maybe they don't. That's what we are all about. We want to bring things together, into a unity a whole.''

''You *are* a holistic,'' he said.

''Isn't a holistic view better than the divisive philosophy of people like Jistane?'' She sounded slightly defensive.

''Yeah, I suppose it is. I was like that once. We've had

some times in my world when the young were speaking out about the same sort of thing."

"And you were one of them?" she said hopefully.

"Sort of," Ira said. "I mean, I agreed with the general principles—harmony, peace, love—but I guess I've always been a reporter, which means I stay somewhat detached."

"You observe," she said.

"Yeah, I guess I do," he said, sounding disappointed in himself.

"That's alright! We need observers. That's what we are all about. A perfect unified whole. Everyone has a place, the ultimate harmony, each fulfilling his or her own mission yet merging with the ultimate unity."

"Do your own thing," Ira said.

"Yes, I guess you could say that."

"But it sounds a little too metaphysical," Ira said. "Where do you propose to find this unity?"

"There are legends and stories," she said. "We believe they are true. We aren't just talking empty theories. This is much more than political philosophy. It can be real, *physical.* The fields can be unified! That's what the legends tell us."

"And you believe them?"

"Yes!"

"But how? How will this happen?"

"It has something to do with the sun," she said. "There is a real physical process that can be triggered. It's irreversible and will bring all energy within the solar field into the same structure—no more strife, no more isolation and separation."

"No more diversity?" Ira said.

The question threw her off-balance. "What do you mean?" she said.

"I'm just playing the devil's advocate," he said. "Maybe there is something to be said for separation in that it provides diversity. Do we all really want to be the same thing? Maybe some strife and conflict are necessary."

"Necessary?" she said.

"So we can have the experience of self and separation, the beauty of love, and making love." He took her hand.

"And then maybe not." The voice came from behind in the doorway to the deck.

"Phoenix!" Phaedra said. She jumped up and hugged him.

Ira watched with a sinking feeling as the embrace turned from something that could be called sisterly or friendly into something more serious. *I haven't felt like this since high school,* he realized, as the pangs of jealously cut like a knife.

33

The Watchers

Lew sat by Tantalyes's body for a long time, moving only to eat and relieve himself. He slept fitfully for a few hours. Finally he started to believe that the man was really dead.

I can't bury him, he thought. *It could still be an illusion.* He did look peaceful, as if in a deep sleep, stretched out on the rock ledge beside the sculpted staircase leading up to the temple.

Lew hated to admit it, but he was still drawn back up those stairs. He knew she would not hurt him, and in some ways it was an ideal existence. *It could go on forever*, he thought. *In the temple of truth I need not die.* But the body of his friend was like a teacher with an insistent lesson, *you can never go back; you must go forward to meet your life.*

But why should I return to a life that never seems to make any sense? he asked himself.

Again Tantalyes's corpse supplied the answer: *Because it is yours.* Lew could almost believe that the man was still alive, that he had won some kind of victory just by living his life and giving it up.

Lew picked up the grail and stared up the stairs for a long time. He wanted to fix the scene in his memory, so that if he ever got back, he would think of it when he gazed up at the moon.

He took one last look at Tantalyes, hoping against hope, but there was nothing more to see, so he started walking, the fine dust soft against his bare feet.

Alan was troubled. The three of them were seated in Miranda's ship. Cliff was thrilled to be out again with the stars, sun, and planets, but Alan was beginning to have a change of heart.

"How do you feel?" Miranda said, sensing his mood.

"Alright," Alan said, not sounding it.

"You ingested a substantial dose of the mundycin. I thought it would wear off eventually, but I wasn't sure. The action of that class of substances is subtle, and in such a large amount—"

"Yeah, but all good things come to an end," Alan said bitterly.

"You made some mistakes," Miranda said.

"Maybe."

"It isn't too late," she said.

"But it is too late," Alan said. "The missile can't be deflected, not with the resonator built in, and it will have a devastating impact. It could easily dose the entire planet if the carrier fungus is as robust as I think it is. What have I done?" He looked at her.

"You have succumbed to one of the oldest temptations in the book," she said. "The messiah complex. Maybe we can intercept the missile."

"How?"

"Tell me the trajectory," she said.

Alan rattled off some figures, acceleration vectors and reference coordinates. "But I told you we can't deflect it, not even if we catch up to it in this ship."

"Maybe I can disarm it," she said. She proceeded to query Alan about the precise mechanism, how the warhead was set to trigger at a certain height and air pressure. She activated the ship's nouancer and altered course.

"What are you doing?" Alan said.

"There is a chance I can intercept it," she said.

"It won't matter." Cliff finally turned his head from the cosmic view and spoke.

"Cliff's been working on a messiah complex longer than I," Alan explained. "He's in politics."

"I'm no messiah," Cliff said. "I'm just the Speaker of the House."

"I'd say that gives you a leg up," Alan said.

"What is about to happen will leave no room for messiahs," Cliff said. "There will only be one, a center that subsumes us all."

"I'm picking something up," Miranda informed them. "I think it's your missile." She activated a speaker, and Alan listened to the pings.

"Sounds like it," he agreed, "but how do you propose to stop it? It won't show up on any radar, so even if we alert the authorities, they won't be able to shoot it down, and we have no weapons."

"Leave it to me," she said. Alan was startled at the seriousness of her tone, and something more, which he seldom heard from Miranda. She sounded worried.

"So," Alan said, "this business about Atlantis—it's hard to believe."

"Believe it," Cliff said. "It's all prophesied in the book—'That land which rose from the sea, the same shall, in later generations, return to pass judgment on the earth.' "

"Is that really what's happening?" Alan asked Miranda, trying to ignore Cliff.

"Something like that," Miranda said. She was distracted, concentrating on the ever-louder pings from Alan's missile.

"They are the Phaeicians." Cliff said.

"What—" Alan said,

"From the *Odyssey*," Cliff said.

"I *know* the reference," Alan said. "I just find your ever more elaborate fantasies hard to take."

"They were a people of stories," Cliff said. "They

lived inside of stories. When Odysseus was stranded there even he was temporarily distracted from his purpose by hearing his own story sung by the Phaeician minstrels. He did recover himself and return home to Ithaca. But the joke was on him as it is on us each and all, because you can never escape your own story, even when you find your home.''

''Charming analysis, Cliff,'' Alan said, ''but I don't think the classical scholars would think much of your equating a mythical culture from the *Odyssey* with an obscure reference in Plato.''

''So what?'' Cliff said. ''The truth still stands.''

Alan was humiliated. It was becoming clearer to him with each passing moment just how carried away he had been with his own cosmic conception of truth. It didn't help his conscience that he could blame it on a massive drug overdose—that had merely been a catalyst. Those crazy ideas must have existed, must still exist in his mind.

''So,'' Alan said to Miranda, ''you are taking us back to Atlantis to do what?''

''To convince them that the earth is not a threat. Some of the Guardians, the rulers, think that because you have been able to utilize the levity drive, the rest of humanity will follow, an invasion of a barbaric culture. We need to show them it was an isolated incident, that they have nothing to fear.''

''And that we are just a few total flakes,'' Alan said, and was not surprised that Miranda failed to contradict him.

''What about Lew?'' Alan asked suddenly.

''I thought you would never ask,'' Miranda said.

''Did you find him?''

''Not yet.''

''Then we have to—''

''Tantalyes is searching for him. You need to get to Atlantis as quickly as possible. I'll tell you how to get in touch with Monica. She's the closest thing to an ally we have there''

''What do you mean?''

''You can fly the ship,'' she said, ''and the coordinates

for Atlantis are programmed into the nouancer.''

''And you?''

''This is where I leave you.'' Miranda got up and removed her clothes.

''What are you doing? This is insane,'' Alan said, panic rising in his voice.

''It's the only way,'' she said. ''The missile is nearing terrestrial space. There is no way to deflect or intercept it in the ship. My body is still evolving, but you know that I can metabolize sunlight. My skin is tough, and my vascular structure can withstand a near vacuum without damage.''

''Out there''—Alan pointed at the earth hanging like a big blue marble against the starry black void—''is a total vacuum. And the cold. You will die.''

''I don't think so,'' she said, sounding unsure.

''We can pick it up in the ship,'' Alan said.

''It's too late,'' she said. ''The only hope is to disarm it in the atmosphere, and the only way to do that is to ride it down.'' She was on her belly, wriggling into the air lock.

Alan grabbed her foot, but was no match for her great strength. She easily kicked his hand away. The hatch slammed shut. There was a whoosh of air, and both men saw her beautiful green body shooting away from the ship. ''Like Aphrodite,'' he whispered, watching her.

''No,'' Cliff said, correcting him. ''More like Athena, the bold and brilliant warrior, than Venus the love goddesses.''

''Yeah,'' Alan said, although he hated to agree, ''you're right.'' He hung his head and turned back to the panel. ''Atlantis,'' he said.

''And the Golden Grail,'' Cliff said with such conviction that Alan almost believed it.

The cold stung with violent force. Miranda instinctively gasped for air and cried out silently at the pain that emptied into her lungs. Her head ached and the blood throbbed painfully in her veins, but her system held against the cruel vacuum. With grim determination she accelerated toward the earth and the missile.

She was not suffocating. Her skin was processing energy directly from the sun. It was where she wanted to be, flying free in the spaces between the stars, but she wasn't ready for the challenge—her body was too young, not yet efficient enough to protect her from the cold and the void.

She pressed on, using her mastery of the gravitational field to gain velocity. They were just inside the lunar orbit when she jettisoned. She estimated contact with the earth's atmosphere in a few hours.

The pings from the missile were getting louder as she picked them up on the aether. *It's like hunting*, she thought. *I'm a falcon intercepting my prey.*

Except, she realized, a falcon is more at home in its element. She closed her eyes and hugged herself, but it just focused her attention inward on the deathly chill that was touching her too deeply. She directed her gaze out to the shimmering sliver of air that was the earth's blanket. The warmth of the tropical oceans beckoned her.

Hours later something stung her face. It was the outer layer of air, only a few molecules, but they were slamming into her skin. She had lost consciousness, an instinctive survival tactic, to shut down all nonessential life functions.

She tried to move and found she was paralyzed. Her limbs were cold and lifeless. She was helplessly buffeted by the increasing density of the atmosphere. *I will burn up in violent friction with the air*, she thought.

She struggled, but all she could do was blink her eyes. The pings were more distinct—the missile was very near, which meant that she had maintained her trajectory of interception. She was able to move her head a little, but could not see it.

A fireball, this is how it ends. She felt no warmth, only turbulence. The pings became insistent. Off to her left she could just make out a gray needle. It was growing larger. She tried flexing her leg muscles, and was rewarded by sharp, shooting pain up her thighs and back.

She concentrated on closing the gap between herself and the missile. It was like trying to run in one of those dreams where your legs just won't move. But she was moving, slowly, to the missile.

When she was only a few feet away from it, she tried to move her arms. The pain was intense, but she was able to extend her hands. Her fingers brushed the missile's surface. She felt nothing.

Inching closer she wrapped her arms around it. Her only chance would be to ride the missile. Alan had programmed the resonator to slow down its entry into the atmosphere. Miranda was too weak to slow herself down, but if she could lock herself tightly to the missile, she might not go out in a blaze of combustion.

She was pummeled by the thicker air. The missile was still moving fast. She hugged it with feeble strength and struggled to get her legs around it. The air was trying to tear her away from it.

And finally there was heat, but it was not the deep, comforting warmth for which she longed. It was a searing surface burn that only accentuated the numb cold inside.

Leslie was drinking coffee in Grafton, North Dakota. She didn't like it. "Are there any espresso bars around here?" she asked the waitress behind the counter.

"Any what?"

"You know, places where you can get good coffee."

The waitress looked at Leslie's cup and then back at Leslie, a weary expression on her face.

"I'm sorry," Leslie said. "I didn't mean—"

"Don't worry about it. Where are you from?"

"Texas," Leslie said, sipping her coffee, trying to look like she liked it.

"Long way. What brings you up here?"

"That's a long story," Leslie said.

The waitress looked around the empty diner, and then back at Leslie.

"OK," Leslie said. "I think something is going to happen here."

"Here?"

"Not the diner, but out in the fields where they're harvesting the wheat."

"And barley."

"Yeah, barley. Do you know any astronomers?"

"Astronomers?"

"Or better still," Leslie said, leaning close, "are there any UFO groups out here?"

"You mean like flying saucers?" the waitress said.

"Yeah."

"Flying saucers, I can do," the waitress said.

"Really?"

"Yeah, and something else. I don't much care about it myself, but there is a new place that serves those coffee drinks you were talking about. I'll take you if you want."

"But what about this?" Leslie looked around. The empty, red vinyl–covered stools and seats stared back.

"We're closed," the waitress said. "Come on."

She led Leslie out the door, locked it, and turned the sign around.

The brilliant blue sky seemed alive to Leslie. "It's an electric time of year," the waitress said.

"Harvest time?" Leslie said.

"Yeah, grain is everything here. Potatoes in the fall, but it's not the same. Have you ever ridden in a combine?"

"No."

"It's really something to see all those golden kernels come pouring up and into the bed—a fountain of life."

"Sounds wonderful." Leslie noted the small-town hardware store and shoe repair shop.

"Not like Texas, huh?"

"Oh, I don't know," Leslie said. They were standing in front of Home Ground, Grafton's new espresso bar.

Leslie got a latte with skim milk, and the waitress got a Coke.

"I'm Helen," she said when they were seated with their drinks.

"Leslie."

"Now, Leslie," Helen said, "what brings you to North Dakota in search of flying saucers?"

"You first," Leslie said.

Helen appraised her for a few seconds. The she reached into her battered, stained leather purse and retrieved a business card which she handed to Leslie.

Leslie was impressed by the professional look of the card. The paper was cream-colored. There was a stylized yin yang symbol that also looked like a space vehicle. In an impressive black font that leapt out in an extruded 3-D design, the card read "The Watchers."

"I don't understand," Leslie said.

"We believe there is life out there." Helen looked up. "We believe they have been here and they are coming back."

"And?" Leslie said.

"Now it's your turn," Helen said.

Leslie told her some of the story, emphasizing the part about the missile.

"So you think it will land here?"

"Yes," Leslie said, finishing her coffee.

"Telescopes and radar won't do any good," Helen said.

"Why not?"

"They have ways to get around all that. But I can take you to our station. We have some equipment that can detect it."

"How?" Leslie said. She was confused. A short time earlier she would have thought the waitress crazy, but she found herself accepting Helen and her statements at face value. "Synchronicity," she said softly.

"Indeed," Helen said, finishing her Coke. "I don't think this coffee place is going to make it though," she added. "People up here just aren't ready for it."

34

Compromise

Ira could tell that the trial was winding down, and he didn't care. The fate of the earth seemed an abstraction compared to his new passion. Ira was in love.

It was not an easy love. When Phaedra did not sleep with him, he knew she was with Phoenix; nor did she try to hide the fact from him. "You can't be possessive." He recalled the scene vividly. "Especially now that we are truly on the verge of a higher unity. Don't you see that when it comes all will be totally free and completely possessed by each!" She hugged herself.

"That doesn't make any sense," he said.

"Of course it does, but if my making love with Phoenix bothers you, then you should do something to distract yourself. You haven't been to the trial in several days."

"It's boring," he said.

"I hear they will be voting soon," she said. "That should interest you."

"Yeah," he said glumly. They were seated in her dining room. The sun was low on the horizon, and Ira was staring through the glass, directly into it.

"The fate of your world?" she said.

"I love you," Ira said.

"And I love you," she said.

"Then why—"

"Don't!" she said, and got up.

"Where are you going?" Ira said as she moved away.

"To a meeting," she said.

"The holistics again!" Ira said, but she hadn't heard—she was already gone.

So he was watching the trial, trying to soothe his lovesick heart with the proceedings. It was clear to him that unless something could sway Selena, the swing vote, Tana and the earth would be convicted.

Crazy kind of justice, he thought, even as it occurred to him that he had seen crazier things as a political journalist. In a way the system made sense—one body for legislative, judicial, and executive authority. Ira had seen enough of the inefficient mess the American system had become. *Of course*, he thought, as he had thought many times before, *maybe that, too, is for the best. Efficient is not always good.*

But the stakes in this trial were too high. One of the brightly colored birds from the atrium gardens flew past his line of sight. Ira had the absurd conviction it was a sign telling him that the fate of the world always hung in a precarious balance, that this trial was not a freak event but simply an enactment of something that was always the case.

Nonsense, he told himself, even as the bird alighted on Selena's shoulder, just as her eyes met his.

The farther Lew got from the temple, the more driven he became. *I have to get back*, he kept telling himself.

He felt as if a mist was lifting, that he was waking up. And what he was waking to was a sense of urgent duty, a mission. When he reflected on these thoughts he found them ridiculous since he no idea what that mission might be.

But the feeling grew stronger, and he picked up the pace. He was in better shape than at any time he could remember. Even as young man he had not had the muscle tone and new strength that he felt. Occasionally he would stop to look at his reflection in the water and was pleased at the sculpted definition of his shoulders, chest, and abdomen.

So it was that he reached the falls in less than half the time it had taken him to descend to the temple.

He searched in vain for a way up. Tired and frustrated, he sat on a rock and looked at the falls. *How did I survive it?* he wondered, and the thought reinforced the impression that there was a purpose to his adventure, and possibly more, which made him uneasy, so he pushed the matter from his mind.

Lew began to feel drowsy. He hadn't had much sleep, but fought the fatigue. With the effort came a wave of exhaustion that forced him to lie down. He was asleep as soon as he closed his eyes.

Alan and Cliff were taken into custody by the Guardian's agents as soon as they emerged from the air lock. "Nice badge," Alan said, referring to the metal sphinx emblems.

To his surprise the agent laughed. "Yeah," the man said.

Alan felt relieved, believing for a moment that their reception party was a benign, welcoming committee. Then he realized the man had cuffed him during their exchange. He looked at Cliff, who was similarly bound, and shrugged.

When they arrived in Telamon Monica took charge, reprimanding the agents. "There was no need to restrain them," she said.

"One of the prisoners escaped."

"So what? Where is there to go?" Monica said.

"I don't know," the agent said. "I'm only following orders."

Monica dismissed them with a weary gesture and took the two men to their quarters in the palace.

"The Palace of the Sun!" Cliff said as they walked through the massive space.

"How do you know that?" Monica said, appraising him with sudden suspicion.

"These things are known in certain circles," Cliff said in hushed tones as he admired the surroundings.

"Cliff is a bit of an afficionado," Alan said.

"Of what?" Monica said.

"Various things," Cliff said. "You don't get to be where I'm at without running into people who know—certain things. Now there's plenty of good ol' boys don't ever pay attention, but I do."

"I see," Monica said, wondering whether it was such a good idea to expose these two to the council after all.

They had rooms next to Ira's. "Where is Ira?" Alan said.

Monica obviously wanted to leave them. "Out," she said.

"Where?" Alan said.

"He's found a new girlfriend," Monica said sharply.

"What's wrong?" Alan said. "Don't you approve us barbarians fraternizing with the natives?"

"I couldn't care less who or what you sleep with," Monica said. "But the object of Ira's lust is likely to get him into trouble." She turned and left.

"Now what?" Alan said to his empty room.

"We look for Ira," Cliff said. "Something tells me he's onto something."

"You like these space women?" Alan said.

"You know I'm not talking about that," Cliff said, "although that Monica's got a nice little—"

"Yeah," Alan said, "she does. But what do you mean about Ira?"

"The man has a nose for news," Cliff said. "Always has. He would have found the source of the action here, and it may be just the action I'm looking for. Are you game?"

"Obviously," Alan said.

"Then let's go." Cliff led them back the way they had come.

Alan was amazed to find that they were free men on the lost continent.

But what surprised Alan even more was Cliff. The Speaker was at home. He could have been wandering the halls of the state capitol. He even began greeting people who crossed their path.

"How y'all doin'. Hey there, good to see ya!"

What kind of a place is this? Alan wondered, because, except for a few curious stares, most people responded as if Cliff Sanders belonged there.

"Horses!" Cliff said. A lightweight, two-wheeled buggy had passed them on the street.

"They're good horses, too. I've checked it out. Probably an ancient Arabian breed." It was Ira. He was standing behind them.

"Damn it's good to see you, Ira!" Cliff said. "That Monica woman said you were off with a ladyfriend."

"I was," Ira said, "but she's—busy right now. I've been watching the trial. How are you doing, Alan? You were a little around the bend the last time I saw you."

"Yeah," Alan said. "I'm alright now, but Miranda's having to deal with the fallout, I'm afraid."

"What's the trial business like?" Cliff said.

"Come on. Let's get something to drink, and I'll tell you about it." Ira led them to a bar. The architecture and finishings of the place were curiously art deco with some Greek classical on the side.

Alan commented on it. "Yeah," Ira said. "Everything here is like that. It reminds you of something—sometimes you're not exactly sure what it is, but it's usually there." He ordered drinks.

"Tastes like an English bitter, but—"

"Not quite," Ira said. "Yeah. It's a different kind of grain—not wheat, not barley. I think it's a more ancient variety, something we don't have anymore on earth. And they don't use hops. They throw in some kind of weed ball that smells like marijuana."

"You smoke any?" Alan said. Ira just smiled. "This stuff is good," Alan said, taking another sip of his brew, "really good."

Ira told them about the trial and the fact that it was winding down.

"So we don't have much time," Alan said.

"No."

"What about these kids, these holistics. Can you introduce me to any members?" Cliff said.

"Unfortunately, I can." Ira said.

"So," Cliff said, "this girl you've found. She's—"

"She is," Ira said, "and so is her other boyfriend. They believe in free love."

"Hippies!" Cliff said, draining his glass. "Let's have another!"

Ira obliged them. "Where do you get your money?" Cliff said.

"Monica gave me some cash. I'm sure she'll give you guys some spending money. She's pretty well off as a Guardian."

"I don't like taking money when I don't know why it's being given," Cliff said.

"Good political ethics," Alan said. Cliff just laughed it off.

"Well they don't expect us to be around for very long," Ira said. "We will be returned to earth when the trial is over."

"Returned to our death sentence," Alan said.

"Something like that," Ira said.

"To hell with all this doom talk!" Cliff said. "I *know* it now! I'm close to the answer. Can you get me to a meeting of some of these holistics?"

"Yeah," Ira said. "They're meeting this evening. Phoenix is going to talk."

"Phoenix. Is he—"

"The other one," Ira said. "Yeah. Her name is Phaedra, and she will probably be there. Actually the meetings are kind of interesting. I'm half-convinced these crazy kids are right."

"When?" Cliff said.

"We can go now." He got up, and Cliff followed.

"You're not coming, Alan?" Cliff said.

"I'll let you guys chase the holy grail," Alan said. "I think I'll have another drink and try to get my head together."

"There is unity. Unity which goes beyond a mere common purpose. There is unity of light, unity of sound, a universal resonance!" Phoenix was addressing the gathering.

Cliff was immediately captivated. He looked at Ira and nodded. The hall was large and shaped like a giant ellipsoid. It was ornate, gilded, and plush. The seats were covered in red velevt.

Phoenix spoke from a podium on the stage. Ira and

Cliff sat in the balcony. Cliff could just make out the young man's features. But the acoustics of the place were excellent—they could hear every word clearly with no amplification.

"You know we have visitors from earth. I've told you what it means. Soon it will be time. Are you ready?"

"Yes!" The crowd roared.

Cliff stood, and when the noise died he yelled, "Which one of you has it? Who has the Golden Grail?"

The place was suddenly very quiet. The only sounds were of young heads turning to look at the big speaker. Cliff waited a few moments for dramatic effect. "Which one of you has it!" he repeated. "The time has come, and I'll do it if no one here will take the risk, but we need the grail!"

Phoenix finally spoke. "You speak boldly, sir. Who are you?"

"Just a seeker," Cliff said.

"Where do you come from?"

"The Lone Star State!"

Ira squirmed in his seat. He was embarrassed and a little frightened. He could feel the eyes boring down on them from all directions.

"What makes you think we possess the grail?" Phoenix said.

"Call it hope," Cliff said. "I don't know. Only thing I'm sure of is I'm ready to rock. You are right, young man. The time has come!"

Another man, in the lower level, stood to speak. "He's right, Phoenix! We have been talking too long. When will we act? Some of us are beginning to wonder if this is just more of the same we hear from the elders—"

"The elders are blind!" Phoenix yelled back. "We all know that! Don't let this earthling tell you differently."

"I'm not telling you anything!" Cliff said. "I know about the blind elders. We got 'em in the Senate, we got 'em in the House. Hell, we got one in the governor's mansion!

"No sir, I'm not gonna tell you anything you don't already know. See, I'll let you young folks in on a little secret. You don't get where I am, by trying to tell people what's what or what to do. You got to talk to 'em like you're talking *with* them.

"People *want* to be told, but they don't want to *think* they're being told. So you make it sound like you're just saying what they would say if they had the time and energy to get up on stage and do it. But I don't have to tell you that, young man. *Do* I?" Cliff finished his little speech, staring right at Phoenix.

Phoenix stared back, frustration and anger showing all too clearly on his face. Cliff had the rare political gift of knowing when to shut up and sat quietly back down.

How does he do it? Ira wondered. *He's got them eating out of his hand now.*

"They're just kids," Cliff whispered to Ira, as if reading the reporter's mind.

As Lew was coming out of his deep sleep he dreamed of the temple. He was standing by the fountain, looking up at the columns and the inscription.

"This is real," he said in his dream. "I'm not dreaming this." He tried to hold the image as he felt himself waking up, but it was fading. He opened his eyes and gasped. Diotima was standing before him.

Her long, shapely legs with their soft fur made him ache with desire. Suddenly her tail flicked out to the side, the tuft on the end pointing, and then she vanished.

Lew opened his eyes again to find himself alone. "That was no dream," he told himself. "She was here!"

But she wasn't there even though the image of her was still vivid. He looked in the direction her tail had pointed and noticed a space behind a large boulder.

It was just large enough for him to squeeze between the rock and the cavern wall. He went a few paces and saw the steps leading up. They were so well camouflaged in the wall that one might never notice them unless directed that way.

Lew went back to his sleeping spot and grabbed the grail. He looked around, but there was nothing—no one.

But as he began the ascent, the words formed unbidden on his lips, "So she remains," he said softly.

Alan was lying down back in his room when Monica entered. "Where's the other one?" she said.

"You mean Cliff. He's gone. Ira took him away—some sort of youth gathering."

"Yes," Monica said, "I see. Oh well. I want you to come with me."

"What for?"

"You need to meet someone. Someone very special. She holds the fate of your world in her hands."

"OK."

Monica led Alan out of the palace. They walked along a quiet avenue until they reached a large, low-slung house. It reminded Alan of the "modern" style of architecture, popular in the twenties.

They entered a tastefully sparse foyer. The colors were soft grays and ivory creams. They found Selena sitting in the central courtyard, amid her flowers and greenery.

"This is Alan Fain," Monica said unceremoniously.

"Please sit down," Selena said.

"You can find your way back?" Monica said.

"Sure," Alan said, sitting down in a chair opposite Selena. The legs scraped against the sandstone patio tiles.

"Then I'll leave you two to talk," Monica said.

"Monica?" Selena said.

"Yes?"

"What about the others?"

"One is with Ira at a holistic society meeting. The other one, Lew Slack, is most likely dead on the moon."

"No, he is not!" Alan said. Monica shrugged.

"Thank you, Monica," Selena said. Monica quietly made her way out.

"Can I get you anything to eat or drink?" Selena said.

"I am hungry," Alan said.

Selena rang a little bell. A servant appeared. "Bring us some food," Selena said.

A few minutes later Alan was eating some of the most succulent fruit he had ever tasted. It was complemented by a rich brown bread, mellow cheese, and light red wine.

"So," Selena said, "you're the cause of all this."

"I wouldn't say that," Alan said, sipping his wine.

"I would. You have tampered with some powerful forces—a little unwisely, I might add."

"It's not my fault!" Alan said.

"No?"

"No! I didn't know that my experiments would lead to the secret of levitation. Nor did I know that you people existed out here. Atlantis! It's a story for children."

Selena smiled. "But we aren't children anymore—are we?"

"No."

"What were you trying to do when you grew the vehicle that Tana used?"

"She stole it," Alan said.

"Fine. She is a thief. Don't worry. She will likely pay for her crime. What were you seeking?"

"I'm a scientist," Alan said.

"So?"

"So I seek the truth."

"The truth can take many forms."

"Maybe."

"Why did you want to leave the earth!" Selena said with sudden force. "Answer me!"

"That you would have to ask that question!" Alan said. "What irony! You disdain all earthly things. Now you threaten to destroy it."

"We won't destroy the earth, only the human population," she said.

"*That* puts my mind at ease," Alan said.

"I want to help you, Mr. Fain."

"Good. What can you do for me?"

"I don't know. I will vote my conscience. Right now, I'm inclined to agree with Jistane. Your planet could use a cleansing. There is nothing wrong with it that a lack of humanity won't cure."

"Indeed," Alan said, and took another bite of delicious cheese.

"But I have an open mind."

"I'm glad."

"Would you care to share my bed tonight, Mr. Fain?"

"I suppose that would be nice," Alan said after he got over the initial shock. "But won't it compromise your—"

"My what?" She smiled and bit a juicy fig.

"Your judgment," he said, watching her lips.

"Not in the least," she said.

35

What Exactly Are we Reporting?

Millard Hatlestead was a square-shouldered, Norwegian farmer with a barn full of strange toys. Leslie sat surrounded by equipment that looked as if it came from the set of a 1950s science fiction movie.

"We watch the skies," Millard said.

"Why?"

"Because we have seen them."

Leslie looked at Helen, who nodded.

"Them? Who are they?" Leslie said.

"We don't know. But we think they are the bearers of truth. We think they are the angels of religion and legend. We think they have been here longer than we have."

"What do they look like?" Leslie said.

Millard laughed. "A bit like the pictures. They are tall, about seven feet, and they have large heads, big eyes, but are more human-looking than what you see in those books that everyone reads nowadays."

"So what is all this equipment?" Leslie said. "Radar?"

"Oh no. They are much too sophisticated for that. We can detect subtle vibrations in the gravitational field.

That's how they travel, you know, antigravity.''

"No,'' Leslie said, "I didn't know.''

"Now tell me why you are here,'' Millard said.

Leslie started her story for the second time that day. Millard listened patiently—he appeared to enjoy the tale.

"So,'' Leslie said, nearing the end, "that's why I think he will have targeted this area. He's got megalomania, he has roots here, and he wants to contaminate a large, grain-producing area. I'm willing to bet I'm right. I just don't know how long we'll have to wait.''

Millard suddenly motioned for her to be quiet. A red light was flashing on the console in front of him. "Not long, I think,'' he said.

They piled into Millard's pickup and went cruising down the straight, flat roads. He tuned the car radio to a frequency which, he said, "wasn't on regular channels,'' and followed the strength of the signal.

"Looks like the old Fain place,'' he said.

"He was accurate,'' Leslie said. "He hit the farm on which he grew up. Is it deserted?''

"Oh no,'' Millard said. "The place is run by a big agribusiness outfit. We still call it the Fain place even though the Fains sold out a long time ago.''

"What were they like?'' Leslie said. "The Fains I mean.''

"Peculiar family,'' Millard said. "Old Dr. Fain—he was some kind of Ph.D. or something—bought the place back in the forties. There were all kinds of rumors that he had been involved in the atom bomb project or a secret government UFO operation.

"But he settled in and started farming. Married the prettiest girl in Grafton, too, one of the Thorstadts. He ran a good farm, wheat and potatoes, but they never seemed to quite fit in. And Dr. Fain was of two minds about their boy.''

"Alan?''

"Yes,'' Millard said, "Alan Fain.'' He took a sharp left, and the truck plowed into an ocean of amber wheat. "They'll be combining tomorrow,'' Millard said.

"What do you mean about Dr. Fain being of two

minds?'' Leslie said over the high-pitched sound coming from the radio and the roar of the engine.

''He wanted his boy to take over the farm. I think that's what he wanted more than anything. But he also wanted him to study science, to know the things that he knew. And that's what made him afraid?''

''Afraid of what?''

''I don't know,'' Millard said. He stopped the truck. ''But something in Dr. Fain's past, something he came across in his work as a scientist, had spooked him pretty bad. He wanted both to protect his son from it and, at the same time to see his son conquer it, do what he had failed to do.''

''Which was?''

Millard stopped the truck. ''I told you,'' he said. ''I don't know.'' He looked out the window. There was a plume of blue-gray smoke rising from the wheat, through the still air, into the harvest sky. ''Maybe,'' he said opening the door, ''this is it.''

They got out and waded through the wheat. Leslie plucked a head of kernels and rolled them in her hands. Then she blew on her palm, and the chaff flew away, leaving the kernels. *So this is how it all began,* she thought. Images of ancient Egypt and Mesopotamia filled her mind—and other, unfamiliar images: tall, humanoid creatures instructing nomads and hunters on the right way to plant and till, and later how to brew a tasty beer from the grain. ''Beer before bread,'' she whispered.

''What?'' Helen said.

Leslie didn't have a chance to answer. Millard said softly, in a tone of voice Leslie had heard before, when she was on the police beat, at accident and murder scenes, ''Oh my God!''

The missile was half-buried, its nose sunk into the rich earth. But clinging to the part of the cylinder that protruded was the barely recognizable form of a naked woman. Her arms were locked around it in a deathly grasp. Most of her skin was burned away. The smoke was coming from her as well as the missile. What remained of her lips were drawn back, exposing blackened teeth in a horrible grimace. She had no hair, the top of her skull showed in places. Her right hand clutched a small canister about an inch in diameter.

The three of them stood speechless for a few moments. Finally Leslie whispered, "What should we do?"

"We sure as hell don't call the police," Millard said, "and it's obviously too late for a hospital."

"Maybe she isn't dead," Helen said.

Millard just looked at his niece and shook his head. "We need to get the missile and the body away from here, back to the lab," he said.

They had to wait several hours before the missile was cool enough to haul onto the truck bed. Miranda's body was another matter. They pried her loose and laid her down in the compartment behind the cab. Millard covered her with a canvas tarp. The smell of burned flesh filled the silence as they returned to his barn.

Millard put what was left of Miranda on a workbench. The three of them hefted the missile up beside her.

"Looks like that thing in her hand came from inside the missile," Millard said, pointing to a place just below the nose cone. A small panel had been peeled away, revealing an interior that looked more like the inside of an alligator than a smart bomb.

Leslie tried to pull the small cylinder from Miranda's clawlike grasp. She had to pull hard before it came loose, along with some blackened skin. She dropped it and the canister bounced off the concrete floor.

Bending down to pick it up, Leslie noticed a tiny amount of fine white powder that had seeped out on impact. "Careful," Millard warned.

She ran her finger through the powder and held it up to her nose to smell it. "It's nothing," she said, "probably a fuel sup—"

Before she could finish her eyes rolled back up into her skull and she collapsed on the floor.

Lew was exhausted. *I can't have fallen this far,* he thought. He was stopped, resting his legs in the shaft that just kept going up. The rungs had obviously been designed for creatures with longer legs.

He looked up, but the light was too dim—all he could see were a few more rungs and a little more shaft. *It can't go on forever*, he thought, and immediately his tired mind answered, *Why not*?

"Because," Lew yelled, "nothing lasts forever!" The sound echoed and reverberated up and down the tube. He used the catharsis to consolidate his energy and began slowly climbing again. *Einstein was right*, he thought. *Gravity is relative, but the most significant relativity of all is in the relation to human strength. I don't care if it is the moon—I can't go on much longer.*

It felt like many hours later when his head banged against steel. He cried out from the sharp pain. Lew realized that he had been virtually unconscious, operating from a robot sense of survival.

He reached up to find a wheel. He still held the grail in his left hand, but the effort of trying to open the lock with his right hand caused him lose his grip with the other. The grail fell.

Lew twisted sideways and kicked. His foot just caught the grail, and he jammed his toe against it, which caused him to shriek again with pain. The grail flew up and banged against the shaft, where he was able to catch it. He wedged it between the rungs and the shaft wall and grabbed the wheel with both hands.

After struggling for several minutes he felt the lock begin to open. *I hope there's air out there,* he thought. He pushed up gingerly and was relieved when the hissing sound resolved into a slight change of pressure. He grabbed the grail and emerged into a small hangar, which housed Tantalyes's ship.

It was a sleek structure of smooth, dull gray metal. He made his way inside and sat in the comfortable captain's chair. He found a lever marked with the sign of the sphinx. He pulled it.

The dome above slowly opened, revealing the stars. There was no sun; it was nighttime on that part of Luna. The ship rose in a smooth motion, the dome below closed, and Lew felt a rush of acceleration. "Home, James," he said, and immediately fell asleep.

Millard had Helen help carry Leslie into the house, where they put her in the guest bedroom. Then he went back to the barn. He opened a locker that was full of weapons, automatic and semiautomatic rifles and cases of explosives. On a shelf in the back of the locker was a gas mask. Millard retrieved it, and after examining the rubber and testing the straps he put it on.

He took the little canister from the floor to a bench in the corner of the building, where he fired up a blowtorch. When he was satisfied with the seal he locked the canister away in a wall safe.

Then he pulled a coffin from a small storage room in another corner of the barn. He put Miranda's body in the coffin and bolted it down tight. He dragged the coffin back into the room and locked the door.

Finally he sprayed the floor and much of the air with a powerful fungicide.

"What's wrong with her?" Helen said. Millard was back in the house.

"She got a dose of whatever that missile was supposed to deliver, I suspect," Millard said.

"The story she told was so wild," Helen said.

"Alan Fain," Millard said. "That boy is following in his daddy's footsteps after all."

"Is she going to be alright?" Helen said.

"I don't know. I suspect that stuff is pretty concentrated."

"That poor woman—the other one, I mean. All burned up like that. What did you do with her?"

"I put her away," Millard said. "She'll keep for a while, and I'm going to want to study her. She is obviously not one of *them,* but there is something strange about her."

"There is something strange about everyone," Leslie said, causing Millard and Helen to jump.

"Are you alright?" Helen said.

"I am *beautiful,*" Leslie said.

There was no denying it. Leslie was an attractive woman in her own right, but she was all aglow with a new, surreal beauty. It radiated from her eyes and shone from her hair. For a moment Millard thought he detected a halo around her head, until he saw it was just the intense luster of her hair.

"I am beauty itself," she said.

"Sit down, Leslie," Helen said.

"Why?"

"Don't you want to rest?"

"Rest? There is no more rest for me," Leslie said. "All is now work. The glorious work of the new beginning."

"What beginning is that?" Millard said.

"The axial awakening!" Leslie said, and her whole body quivered with passion. She turned to go.

"Wait," Millard put his hand on her shoulder. Leslie grabbed it and twisted, pulling him to her. She quickly had him pinned, so that if he struggled his wrist would break.

"I don't want to hurt you," Leslie said. "Will you let me go now? I have work to do."

"OK," Millard said. She released him.

Back in Grafton, Leslie called Drake. It was Sunday night, and the editor was home, watching TV.

"How are you, doing?" he said. "Enjoying your vacation?"

"I have the truth, Drake," she said.

"That's good," Drake said. An uneasy feeling began to creep over him.

"The beginning is here," she said, "and I have been chosen to lead the world into the new era of peace, love, and harmony. Do you know what I'm talking about?"

"What?" Drake said.

"The unified field! Here, now!"

"Does this have anything to do with that business about Cliff—and the spaceship?" Drake said.

"Of course it does. But that's all irrelevant now." Leslie proceeded to describe how she would teach the world a new way to live. It was a messianic ramble, long on image and short on substance.

Finally she finished, and when Drake said nothing she said, "Well?"

"What?"

"I'm giving you a story, Drake! The biggest story ever. Front-page news, the scoop of the millennium!"

"You want me to—*print* this?" Drake said.

"Hell yes, I want you to print it!"

"But Leslie," Drake said, "what *exactly* are we reporting?"

36

Possibly Anything

What is the distance around the sun and how long will it take to get there? Lew was dreaming of a ship, an old clipper ship from the 1890s, tacking across the solar winds, beating its way around the sun.

He opened his eyes to a white-hot glare that he could feel in his brain. He quickly shut them and turned his head. He had been staring straight into the sun. When he opened his eyes again he was looking at stars. *How long*, he thought again. That he was not going home was obvious. He only hoped that he was going somewhere.

To drift forever in the void was a notion full of such terror that his mind recoiled before he could even contemplate it. With no points of reference, it was impossible to estimate speed. He recalled Alan explaining that one of the side benefits of levity drive was the elegant way it completely sidestepped Einstein's speed limit. As speed increased to an order of magnitude of c, the velocity of light, mass approached infinity, so that the energy requirement at such speeds was beyond anything remotely imaginable.

But Einstein's equations all assumed the normal relation of mass to gravitational force. Levity subsumed that relation, thus nullifying c as the cosmic speed limit.

All it meant to Lew, as he gazed at the stars, was a reasonable hope that he would arrive somewhere before he perished. "That's all one can ever expect," he said aloud, "a reasonable hope."

He found some dried fruit mixed with a nutty grain in a bag tucked under his seat. And, more importantly, water. He sucked at the bottle. It seemed his thirst was fueled by the white light of the sun and the burning of the stars.

"Aaah!" he sighed, and sank back into the cushions. It occurred to him that thousands of years of human history and millions of years of evolution were as nothing in the vast solar field. And yet he felt as if it were somehow significant, that the solar system itself was evolving toward something. *Maybe there is a unified field for us here*, he thought, *somewhere in the distant future*.

"Where is the grail?" Cliff said, and slammed his fist on the table. He and Phoenix were sitting in Phaedra's living room.

"The legends say it was part of Lucifer's crown," Phoenix said, "a jewel in the crown that was dislodged when the archangel Michael smote the rebel and sent him plunging from heaven to earth."

"Nice story," Cliff said, "but I'm talking about a real piece of hardware. That it is in the shape of a grail and is beautiful is merely incidental. It is made of a substance both denser and finer than matter—*nous*, solid *spirit*. When it is united with the fusion furnace of the sun we will realize the dream, the unified field. It will set off a chain reaction the likes of which the Universe has never seen. The solar system will be melded into one superatom, where all is synchronized energy, dancing to a higher frequency.

"This is not fantasy, this is science! Now where is it? You must have a clue."

"I do not," Phoenix said. He was beginning to dislike the earthman. Cliff had inspired the young holistics in a new way, supplanting Phoenix's own leadership.

"You don't really want it," Cliff said. "I see that now. You want to exploit the desire of your followers for your own purposes. I can't hold that against you. I've made a career of it myself, but you must understand, young man, we are no longer playing games here. We are playing with fire."

"And where do you think the grail is?" Phoenix said.

"I thought I would find it here," Cliff said.

Phoenix laughed. "Here? There is nothing in Atlantis. All is as it was since a very long time ago, and nothing will ever change."

"So tell me what you are doing," Cliff said, "leading a movement that promises change?"

"Just what you said," Phoenix said. "I'm young. I have to do something."

"And all those young people, the ones who look to you for hope and inspiration?"

Phoenix merely shrugged.

"Alright," Cliff said, "enough of that. What does Phaedra mean to you?"

"Phaedra is a very desirable woman," Phoenix said.

"Do you love her?"

"What is love?" Phoenix said.

"Ira loves her," Cliff said. "I know the look. If she means so little to you, why not let him have her?"

Phoenix laughed. "She isn't mine to let anyone have or not have," he said. "What a primitive notion. I could step aside, but she would not willingly give herself to him and him alone. She is, as we all are, a free spirit."

"A free spirit!" Cliff said in disgust. "You are all slaves to your concept of freedom. I just thought a little consideration on your part could spare Ira a lot of pain. He is eating his heart out over that silly girl. But soon it won't matter."

"What won't matter?" It was Ira. He had come in alone through the front door.

"Where is Phaedra?" Cliff said.

"I don't know," Ira said despondently. "I thought she was with you." He nodded toward Phoenix.

"You see," Phoenix said. "I told you she was free." He got up to leave, and Ira glared at him as he walked by.

Ira collapsed in a chair opposite Cliff.

"I know what you're going through," Cliff said.

"Do you?"

"Yes, love is not easy. Sometimes what you need is something to distract you, a project, a great work."

"A great work," Ira said cynically.

"Like the unified field," Cliff said.

"Oh yeah," Ira said, full of indifference.

"I tell you," Cliff said, "we are close. I sense it. I'm going to find the grail, and when I do, I'll need help. Can I count on you?"

Ira stared at Cliff for a moment. The reporter had seen the same compelling look in Cliff's eyes many times before—on the House floor, in press conferences, and he had never been taken in by it.

But this time he found himself willing to be lured by the man's political skill. "Yeah," Ira said.

"It may be dangerous, we may have to risk our lives. Are you with me?"

"Sure, why not?"

Alan let himself be lost in the splendid indolence of life with Selena. He had been there a number of days when she asked him what he wanted from life. They were eating a delicious dinner of scallops on a bed of pasta with a sauce that reminded Alan of his days in India.

"What I want," he said, "is—" He stopped and sipped his wine. "I think I have been working too hard," he said, putting the glass down.

"So you want rest?"

"You are so beautiful," he said.

"I know," she said. "Stick to the point please."

"Oh yes," he said, "I almost forgot. You are evaluating me, trying to decide what to do about the pesky earthlings. Are we a threat, or merely a bunch of harmless flakes."

"I would never call you harmless," she said, leaning

back in her chair and fixing him with her large eyes while she sipped the rich red wine. They ate in her garden courtyard. The small fountain beside the table complemented their conversation with soft sounds of falling water, and her flowers added to the exotic aroma of the food.

"The question is whether you are harmless to us. So tell me, what do you want?"

"I don't think I want rest," Alan said, "although I have to say, this is all very nice—better than nice.

"But I need my work. Unfortunately my work has, for most of my life, completely consumed me. I could tell you the whole story—how I went to India and Tibet, how I made a mess of my personal life and initiated the most insane adventures. It has all come to nothing."

Selena suddenly felt empathy. It took her completely off guard. She knew it was unwise, unprofessional, but the sincerity of the earthling was too much for her defenses. "So you are lost," she said, with such quiet intensity that it shook Alan from his self-indulgent memories.

"Yes," he said, "I am. So you see, I cannot rest. I can't even change direction, because I wouldn't know which way to go. I can only go forward."

They finished their meal, and when it was over she took him by the hand and led him closer to the fountain. She pulled her long, flowing dress over her head and stood naked, watching him undress. They made love on the limestone slabs by the water.

Selena was strangely silent at breakfast the next morning. "Did you always have coffee?" Alan said, trying to draw her out.

"What?" she said, spilling some coffee as she set her cup down. "I think so."

"I heard the drink came from nomads in Arabia, who chewed the bean," Alan said.

"Oh, maybe it did! What's the difference?"

"What's wrong?" Alan said.

"You don't know?" she said, lifting her eyebrows in an expression that could have been easily mistaken for comical.

But it wasn't meant to be funny, and Alan knew it. "I'm afraid I don't know," he said.

"That's right," she said, "why *would* you? You have been lounging around here in indolence, not bothering to—"

"Indolence, is it?" Alan said.

"I'm sorry, but it does strike me as odd that you don't know. The trial ends today. The fate of your world is to be decided and you—"

"I am completely ignorant. What can I do anyway? I can ask you not to be a party to the destruction of billions of people. I suppose that's the least I can—"

They were interrupted by one of the servants. The young woman handed Selena an envelope on a silver tray and left.

Selena picked up a knife and sliced the envelope open. She pulled out a folded sheet of ivory-colored paper and set it down, opening it and smoothing out the creases. "Hmm," she said.

"What?" Alan said.

"You just keep coming," she said. "Another of your kind arrived in Eidon a few days ago. He should arrive this morning. He was in Tantalyes's ship—*without* Tantalyes."

"Yes!" Alan said, laughing triumphantly. "Lew, you old mind-surfer!"

"Your friend is in a lot of trouble," Selena said, "arriving in a stolen ship belonging to a special agent of the Guardians. If he cannot account for it, if Tantalyes cannot be found—"

"What?"

"He will almost certainly die."

"Over my dead body," Alan said.

"Possibly," she said.

"Can't you do anything to help?" Alan said.

"It all depends," she said.

"On what?"

"On what happens today."

"But Lew has got nothing to do with it—Tana's disloyalty and your crazy plans to destroy humanity."

"That's one way to look at it," she said, getting up from the table. "But this Lew person was involved with Tana and is of your race. You can't separate things so neatly. If Tana is spared, if your world is spared, I may be able to do something for your friend, but otherwise, he is probably doomed. Now, if you will excuse me, I have to get ready."

"How are you going to vote?" Alan said.

He saw a look of fear pass across her face. It was gone in an instant as she recovered her aristocratic composure. "I don't know, and if I did, I wouldn't tell you."

"But you might save us?" Alan said.

"I might do anything!" she said hotly, and abruptly left him alone in the courtyard.

Her words gave Alan a strange rush of euphoria. He sipped his coffee and stared at the lovely fountain as he let the waves of feeling flow through him.

The fate of a world is at the mercy of some small whim, a detail here or there, he thought. *And truly, each one of us, might do anything!*

37

Hit Single

The agents were rough with Lew. Arriving in a ship stolen from one of their highest-ranking officers earned him special consideration.

He was still naked when they reached the train station on the other side of Mount Poseidon. They chained him in a car with livestock. A large cow stood beside him and periodically voided his massive bowels. By the time they reached Telamon he was covered in fresh cow dung, splattered with urine, and dehydrated.

The guards laughed uproariously when they removed him. They made him walk, hands cuffed behind him, stinking filthy, and naked through the station. Monica met them in the special rooms reserved for the Guardians near the front entrance.

"What is the meaning of this?" she said when they brought Lew in.

"Apparently he was mistaken for some sort of animal," one of the agents said with a deadpan expression.

"You," Monica said, "are the animals!"

The other agent smirked.

"And," she said, "I will deal with you later. But for now, unchain this man and get out of my sight."

They both saluted and did as they were told, but Monica noted the schoolboylike delight, barely concealed.

When they had gone she said, "I'm sorry for the indignities. Go wash up. There is a bathroom over there." She pointed to a door.

Lew was greatly relieved to let the water flow over him. And when he was clean he drank, gulping it down so fast that he nearly choked. He emerged with with a towel wrapped around his waist.

"I found you some clothes," Monica said, handing him a tunic and narrow cotton pants.

He went back into the bathroom and changed. The material was so light, the clothes felt like pajamas, which made him realize how tired he was.

"Where is Tantalyes?" Monica said as they rode to the palace.

"On the moon—or *in* the moon I should say."

"Why isn't he with you?"

Lew turned his head to look out the coach at the smooth clay streets and classical architecture.

"Is he *alright*?" Monica said with insistence.

"He's dead," Lew said, looking her in the eye, noting the features so like Tana's.

"Oh no," Monica said. "How did it happen?"

"I don't know," Lew said. "I mean you wouldn't believe me."

"What were you doing inside Luna?" Monica said it as if it were rape, a violation of a wife, mother, or daughter.

"I didn't want to be there!" he said angrily.

"Alright," she said, "you have been through a great deal, but try to understand you're in serious trouble."

"I understand," he said, sounding strangely indifferent. "Where are we going?"

"Today is the last day of the trial," Monica said.

"Whose trial?"

"I believe you know her. Tana."

"What is she on trial for? What did she do?"

"She deserted her post, disobeyed orders, tried to—"

"What will happen to her?" Lew said.

"If she is convicted she will almost certainly face lunar isolation—and she will lose years of privileges. But it isn't Tana you should worry about. She won't die, and in time she can regain her position."

"I see," Lew said sarcastically. "I should worry about myself."

"Well—yes, I suppose," Monica said, "but that's not what I meant."

"What then?"

"Your world."

"My world?"

"May end soon," she said, as the carriage pulled up in front of the Palace of the Sun.

"I've seen this kind of architecture," he said as they approached the broad steps.

"Oh? Have you been to Greece?"

"No. It was—somewhere else."

She stopped and looked at him for a moment. "I see," she said, and led the way up the steps and under the columns.

Inside Lew marveled at the light, shade, stone, and glass. It was all so exquisite. They lingered for a while in the gardens. "This would be a great place for a tennis court," he said. She was momentarily startled by his words and gave him a strange look.

Alan was sitting in a row not far from the dais. He jumped up and moved quickly down the aisle when he saw Lew.

"Man, you're looking good," he said, and grabbed Lew's hand.

"What do you mean?" Lew said.

"Fit," Alan said. "Positively athletic."

"Well, I've been playing some tennis," Lew said. Alan looked puzzled.

"They're going to decide today," Alan said.

Before Lew could respond a hush came over the small audience as the Guardians took their places. When Tana came out to take her place her eyes instantly found Lew's.

Her expression made Lew want to run up the steps, grab her, and get her quickly away. Alan reached over and put his hand on Lew's arm. "There's nothing you can do now," he whispered.

After lengthy procedures that accomplished nothing and took half the morning Jistane announced the vote. He went first and the condemnation was no surprise.

All but Monica abstained on the first round. It was an elaborate game they played. Most were decided, but each was maneuvering for the maximum effect. It stayed tied at one–one for several more rounds.

Gradually the tally began to take shape. The votes alternated between conviction and acquittal for two more rounds. Then there were two votes for conviction.

It stood at five–three for a few more rounds. Only one more vote was required to condemn the earth. Zeno surprised Alan by voting against Jistane. Zeno had been particularly hard on Tana and critical of terrestrial culture. It was five–four and the final vote was Selena's.

She stood up on the next round. "You know the procedure, Selena," Jistane said. "No speeches."

"No speech," she said, and looked straight down at Alan, "I cannot side with you this time, Jistane. Let the poor girl go, and spare the miserable earthlings for another century, when we can take the matter up again." She sat down.

"It's a tie!" Alan said.

"What now?" Lew said, completely bewildered by the spectacle.

A partial answer came in a rambling, incomprehensible speech by Jistane.

"What was the meaning of that?" Lew asked Alan when it was finished.

"I don't know. It sounds like the final decision depends on some obscure process," Alan said, watching Selena, who disappeared behind a door at the far end of the palace. Then Alan leaned close to Lew and said, "These people are very strange."

"Are you a prisoner?" Lew said.

"I suppose," Alan said, "but they are very casual about it. Cliff is here—Ira, too, but they have taken up with a bunch of radicals, Tana's people I think. I haven't seen them in days."

"They don't keep you locked up?"

"What does it look like?" Alan said. "I told you they are strange. I know I'm watched. This is a very orderly society."

"But what about the radicals?"

"The holistics," Alan said.

"Yeah, them."

"I am beginning to suspect that their form of rebellion is just part of the overall structure to the society," Alan said. "This is an old world. They have lived here on the other side of the sun in a big greenhouse for millennia. That kind of life does things to you."

"I guess," Lew said.

"Let's get out of here," Alan said. "I know a good bar."

"So what happened to you?" Alan said when they were comfortably seated with their beers.

"You wouldn't believe it."

"Oh *wouldn't* I? Who do you think you're talking to? I'm not from Kansas."

"But you are from North Dakota," Lew said. "I doubt

if a single potato farmer up there would believe the story I could tell.''

''Potato farmers can surprise you,'' Alan said. ''My father was one, you know.''

Lew watched Alan closely, hoping he would open up and talk about his past, but he didn't.

''Later, Lew,'' Alan said finally. ''That's another story. We need to figure out what to do now. So tell me what happened.''

Lew gave Alan as short a version of his adventures as he could manage.

Two beers later, wiping the foam from his mouth, Alan said, ''So what about this Diotima. Did you—''

''That is none of your business,'' Lew said. ''She wasn't real anyway.''

''It sounds to me like her reality is still a matter for debate,'' Alan said.

''Maybe,'' Lew said with a note of defiance.

''But what about this grail?'' Alan said. ''If it's what I think it is, that could be the key to the whole thing, and our ticket out of here.''

''The guards that seized me at the port took it,'' Lew said. ''I don't know where it is.''

''We have to find it!'' Alan said. ''If for no other reason than to prevent Cliff from getting hold of it.''

''Why?''

''Because,'' Alan said solemnly, ''unfortunately there is a grain of truth to all the nonsense he has been spouting. I was pretty wigged-out until recently, full of my own grand designs. Those were, I must admit, based on little more than dreams and altered brain chemistry.

''But the unified field! That's a real possibility. I looked at the theory years ago, back in India. The science was good. But the technology to create the required catalyst—that was possible only in theory. But these Alethians you describe—''

''I never saw them,'' Lew said, and the memory of that fleeting image when he first came upon the entrance to the temple returned for a moment. ''Really,'' he added softly.

"That sphinx, the cat woman Diotima, these are exactly the kinds of images you would expect from a race like that," Alan said.

"A race obsessed with truth," he added.

"But why would they create such elaborate illusions if they—"

"Because" Alan said, "truth is resonance! They were pushing the limits between the real and the unreal, trying to find the place where it all resonates in a single, shining . . ." His voice trailed off.

"Single shining what?" Lew said.

"I don't know," Alan said. "That's just it. You can't know until you confront it yourself. And that's why they would invest the enormous amount of time and energy required to make a structure of superrefined crystalline nous like the grail. You remember the crystal[12], the one the professor gave to you?"

"Sure," Lew said.

"That was crude compared to this. The crystalline symmetries required to trigger a unified field reaction inside a star are so complex that I know of no mathematics to model it."

"What makes you so sure that's what the grail is?" Lew said.

"Very unscientific, I grant you," Alan said, "but I know when to trust my intuition. Call it a coherence of fact and fiction—I just *know.* And that's why we have to find the grail. If we don't, and those kids get hold of it—God help us all."

Two guards entered the bar, followed by Jistane. The guards came to the table and jerked Lew to his feet.

"What's going on?" Alan said.

"You earthlings are all prisoners here," Jistane said. "Personally it offends me to see you walking around free, but I can't do much about it. Except"—he looked at Lew—"when we are dealing with murder. Take him away."

---

[12]*Mind-Surfer.*

The guards cuffed Lew and led him out.

"Lew!" Alan called.

Lew looked back, but he kept quiet.

"Lew," Alan said again, softly, and watched his friend disappear through the door.

Leslie was heading west. She deliberately stopped in small towns to preach her message. She usually found interested listeners, some abusive and some sympathetic.

She was replaying a recent scene in her mind from a small farming town in eastern Colorado. "Why, you may ask," she had said, "would the voice of truth choose to come through me? Here? Now?

"Why anyone! Why anyplace or anytime? I am here to tell you it has always been here and now in me and you and each and every one of us?"

"What about God?" a man in the small park across from city hall had said.

"God?"

"The Bible. You are saying some mighty powerful words, young lady, but you're not saying where they come from."

"The truth comes from everywhere," she had replied.

"And what is that?"

She hadn't lingered there. The small group had turned aggressive. Her plan was to hone her message in Western towns along the way and then unveil the full force of it in San Francisco.

She turned on the radio. The song immediately caught her attention. It was arresting both for the simple, yet alien chord progression and the lyrics.

"You may seek across the stars for the only thing
that matters
Never understanding how it all began.
But it's the same story in the end.
I flew into the sun and fell into the ocean,
The legend goes on and on.
The preacher said wisdom is best.

I never found time to put it to the test,
And still I ask the question,
What is truth?''

''That's a new single from a band out of San Francisco,'' the DJ said. 'What Is Truth?'—from the Resonators. They are getting rave reviews and, I understand, are featured on the cover of this month's *Rolling Stone*. I talked with the bass player earlier in the week:

''So where did you get those lyrics?''

''They came from our former lead guitar player.''

''And the chord progression is unusual. Where did that come from?''

''That came from him as well.''

''Your *ex*–lead guitar player?''

''Yeah, he wrote most of our songs.''

''What happened? Did you have a falling out?''

''He just disappeared, right before we were supposed to go into the studio to record 'What is Truth?' That's when we got Alex, our new guitar player. Everything just took off after that.''

''You must be very happy. You guys are the hottest new band to come along in a quite a while.''

''Yeah, things are finally breaking our way.''

Leslie pressed the seek button, hoping to find another station playing the song. It didn't take long. The next Denver rock station was playing it. The Resonators were everywhere.

38

Lone Star Man

"What happens now?" Alan said.

"Apparently you didn't understand Jistane's closing remarks," Selena said with an ironic smile. They were back in her courtyard.

"Did you?"

"We must seem strange to you," she said. "But think about the differences between our worlds, and you might understand. On your poor planet you have spent the last several thousand years lurching form one paradigm to another—polytheism, empire, monarchy, Christianity, Buddhism, communism, capitalism—with no end in sight. The result is that you barely have time to establish cultural traditions before another wave of change comes along.

"Here it is different. We have lived much as we do now for a very long time. The traditions are stable and deep. If you begin to peel them back, you see it is like a great onion, delicate thin layers upon layers."

"Alright," Alan said impatiently, "but what happens *now*?"

"I'm trying to explain." She motioned for the servant to pour them a drink of iced coffee with a touch of exotic mint. Alan usually disdained flavored coffees, but found it delicious.

"There will be a contest to decide," she said.

"A contest? What kind of contest?"

"That's up to us. I will meet with Jistane to work it out."

"Why you?"

"His was the first vote to condemn, and mine was the

last to acquit. The responsibility lies with us."

"But what will actually decide it?"

"It could be something as simple as flipping a coin, or as complex as a pattern of shifting sunspots."

"What would either have to do with the trial?"

"Don't you see?" she said. "We did our best to reach a conclusion based on the evidence. We failed, so now it's up to nature."

"But random events!"

"What appears random may be the the surface layer of the workings of a higher law."

"How can you know that?"

She shrugged. "Who is to say it is not so? Our lives are mostly determined by forces beyond our control, beyond logic. That's why culture exists. All our traditions and knowledge are really attempts to put a wrapper of predictability over what is essentially unpredictable."

Alan watched her closely as she spoke. The soothing sound of the fountain and her beauty seemed in sharp contrast to the sense of what she was saying. "This is wild," he said.

"We are never far from the wilderness," she said.

"So, what will decide it?"

"Jistane wants some kind of contest. A game. I'm not in favor of that. It isn't unheard of, since the outcome is unpredictable, but it leaves too much humanity in it for my liking. We failed; now it is time to look elsewhere for a decision."

"And Lew? Will his fate be decided by some random series of events?"

"It could be," she said, "but more likely we will take it up as a separate case."

"He's innocent," Alan said.

Selena's eyes opened wider in an expression of feigned interest.

"I don't expect you to believe it," Alan said, "but I know it's true."

"I'm glad someone does," she said in an ambiguous tone that caused Alan to search her eyes more deeply for some sign that she might help.

"More coffee?" was all she said.

"Sure."

Phoenix was uneasy around Cliff. Conditioned all his life to regard earthlings as inferior, it was particularly galling to feel so dominated by one. He squirmed on Phaedra's couch, trying to invest himself with the sense of importance that was so diminished in the Speaker's presence.

"Hell, man!" Cliff said. "The time for talk is long gone. I've been making speeches and winning elections all my life, but I didn't come here for more of that."

"What makes you think you could win power here?" Phoenix said.

Cliff just laughed and said, "Politics is politics, young man. I love it. It's been a good life, but now it's time to move on—beyond politics."

"To what?"

"To the thing you kids have been talking about. The unified field! The grail must be close at hand. I know it! These things may appear random to the untrained eye, but I've learned to read the pattern behind the thin veneer of daily human desire. I've had to—it's how I remade myself into the most powerful man in the greatest state of the Union.

"So I'm seldom wrong about these things. Now, Phoenix, tell me"—the Speaker's eyes bore deeply into the youth's—"what have you heard?"

Phoenix fought to find a mask behind which he could hide. "Nothing I—"

"Don't lie to me!" Cliff used the voice he saved for special occasions. That was the key to its effectiveness; it had the resonance of reserve. He had used it twice in the House to save bills that were about to go down, votes he had to win to keep his authority. It was also effective in disciplining children, who have ears for such things.

"There are rumors, but I don't believe them," Phoenix said, head lowered.

"I'll tell you what to believe!" Cliff said. "Now what have you heard?"

"Phaedra's been contacted by someone claiming to have it. He wants money—"

Just then Phaedra walked in. She immediately took in the nature of the conversation and frowned disapprovingly at the two men. "Where is Ira?" she said.

"Drowning his sorrows no doubt," Cliff said, returning her look. "If you care about Ira, then help us."

"Why should I help you?"

"Because we both want the same thing," Cliff said. "Phoenix apparently wants nothing, but I know it's different with you—and me."

"I was just leaving," Phoenix said.

Phaedra watched him leave, then said, "What did you do to him? He had his tail between his legs. I've never seen him like that."

"People often don't like the truth," Cliff said. "He just got a dose of it. Now will you tell me what you know?"

"Not now," she said. "I'm tired."

"We may not have much time," Cliff said.

"There is always time for sleep."

When Ira walked in Cliff was still up. "We have to talk," Cliff said. "Sit down."

"Is Phaedra here?"

"She is, but sit down, man! Things are coming to a head. We must act."

"Did you hear about the vote? It was a tie. I don't understand their laws here. The fate of the earth will now be decided by some sort of contest, or chance occurrence."

"Not if we can act!" Cliff said. He told Ira about Phaedra's contact.

"What am I supposed to do about it?" Ira said dejectedly.

"I think she really loves you," Cliff said. "She doesn't care about Phoenix. You're twice the man he is. Go to her. Now. Make her see. We need her help. I think she wants the same thing. She has money. The girl comes from one of the wealthiest families in Telamon. Get her to—''

''You're asking me to make love to her and then use her for—''

''Dammit, man!'' Cliff said. He stood up, and Ira was impressed by the big Texan's height, as if he were seeing it for the first time. ''I know you love her! I'm not asking you to betray that love!

''You're too good, Ira. And too full of nonsense. You've read too many romantic stories and seen too many movies. Don't you see? Love is meant to be used. People in love use each other all the time. There is nothing wrong with it. That, in fact, is what love is all about.

''It's when they don't use each other in truth. The lie is the betrayal. I'm not suggesting you lie to her. We are working on something that is bigger than you, her, all of us put together. You might even say the unified field is the ultimate love trip.

''But it won't happen without the key, and right now she has it.''

Phaedra murmured with pleasure when Ira got in bed beside her. They made love, and afterward Ira said, ''Do you love me?''

She was silent for a few moments, snuggled against him, then said, ''Yes, I guess I do—a little bit anyway.''

''Can't we get away from here?'' he said.

''Where would we go?''

''Back to my world,'' Ira said. ''It isn't so bad there. I could make a good life for us. I—''

She put a finger on his lips. ''They still might destroy your world,'' she said. ''Let's not talk. Just hold me.''

''No,'' he said, anger suddenly rushing through him. ''We both know it's futile. It will never work.''

''It may not matter,'' she said.

''What do you mean?''

''I have the grail,'' she said.

''You have it? How?''

''One of the guards that brought your friend from Eidon,'' she said. ''He had no idea what it was, but suspected it was worth something. I got it cheap, really.''

''How do you know it's the real thing?''

''I know,'' she said.

''What will we do?''

Suddenly she was all awake and sitting up next to him. He ached at the beauty of her petite body and long dark hair. She was so animate, so fiery.

''I can get a ship,'' she said. ''All you have to do is take the grail and fly into the sun!''

''Will you come with me?''

''I can't.''

''Why not?''

''I'm afraid,'' she said. ''But it won't matter. Once the process is compete we will be together forever, united in a total fusion of love.''

Ira felt a thrill of ecstasy rush through his body.

''Will you do it? If I can get you to a ship?''

''Cliff will want to come,'' Ira said hollowly.

''It doesn't matter,'' she said, eyes boring into him, all question.

''Alright,'' Ira said.

She lay back down and pressed close to him, her passion aroused.

''Not now,'' Ira said. Suddenly he felt very tired.

Jistane was interviewing Lew in his room. ''No one will believe your story,'' the Guardian said.

''Do you?'' Lew said. He was seated in a comfortable armchair. The only complaint he had about his quarters was that they remained locked from the outside.

''What I believe doesn't concern you,'' Jistane said.

''I would have thought it does.''

''You think like an earthman.''

''I suppose I do,'' Lew said drily. ''What way is that?''

''Always looking on the surface of things,'' Jistane said. ''Never bothering to consider the long-term consequences of action—or belief for that matter.''

''I guess I'm just a cowboy,'' Lew said.

Jistane frowned, not understanding the reference. "We have known about the temple of truth for a long time," he said.

"Then you do believe me!" Lew said.

Jistane did not comment.

"Why haven't you investigated further? Don't you want to know who the Alethians are and where they came from?" Lew said.

"Maybe not," Jistane said in an uncharacteristic tone of voice. Then he proceeded to ask Lew about the tennis games.

"Virtual tennis," Lew said at one point.

"That doesn't matter," Jistane said. "We rarely play anymore. It's a shame. Another one of our great traditions that is fading. Our matches were legendary. We played in ancient times, when Europe consisted of wild forest tribes, before the Trojan War."

"Are *you* that old?" Lew said.

"No." Jistane got up and walked out without another word.

He looks like a tennis player, Lew thought.

"At this point we could just flip a coin," Selena said wearily.

"That is no way for a Guardian to talk," Jistane said. "This is our tradition. Since we failed to reach a decision, it will be decided arbitrarily. But the means should be elegant. That has always been the unwritten law. We don't toss coins for justice!"

The rest of the ten remained silent. Finally Selena spoke again. "And what do we do about the new prisoner?"

"Tennis," Jistane said.

"Tennis?"

"We could try him separately—"

"The *reasonable* thing to do," Selena interrupted him.

"Or," Jistane continued, "the contest could settle the matter of Lew Slack as well. I know he is accused of a very serious crime. But another trial would be long and tedious. Besides, I have interviewed him. The case is not so simple as it appears."

"Then you think he is innocent?" Selena said.

"I didn't say that," Jistane said. "But the matter of proving his guilt will take some time. What I propose is not unprecedented."

"So you want to play tennis with the earthling?" Selena said sarcastically.

"Exactly," Jistane said.

"All these years," Cliff said, "and I never really believed it until now." He was holding the grail, examining it in the subdued light of Phaedra's living room.

"The real is seeming," he continued, "but not for much longer."

"What do you mean?" Ira said.

"I mean that what we are about to do will finally make the real *real.*"

"Oh," Ira said. Phaedra was leaning against him on the couch. Her face was flushed with excitement. She kept rubbing against him, like an affectionate cat.

"So," Ira said, "we are supposed to take the grail to the sun? Why can't we just send it in a missile?"

"The book is very clear on that," Cliff said. "It must be delivered by one who is devoted."

"But you don't even believe that!" Ira protested. "This is ultimately about science, not religion. If I understand, the grail is made of a superdense substance that will trigger a chain reaction. It's physics! So all the rest of the mumbo jumbo is just superstition."

"That's one way to look at it," Cliff said. "But you must consider the result. We are about to create something totally new. The solar system will be transformed into a solar atom. We are going to unify matter, energy, and consciousness. After it is done, when you are a *virtual god*, then you might see it all differently—what looks like superstition now will become sacred."

"Just one thing," Ira said.

"Yes?"

"How do you know that we will exist at all—afterward?"

"The Eyes of Texas," he said.

"What?"

"It's more than a metaphor," Cliff said. "We have been watched over by the Eyes of Texas, and now we are about to merge with the Lone Star to become one with them, see what they see, and be as they are."

"Oh," Ira said. He could see that any further discussion would be useless.

Phaedra was murmuring in his ear, trying to get him to go to bed.

When he finally gave in, her passion was frightening in its intensity. She made love like a hurricane, and at times he feared he would be blown away.

Afterward she said, "Phoenix has the ship. You can leave tomorrow."

"Phoenix?" Ira said. "Is he going with us?"

"No," Phaedra said. "I didn't want to involve him since he really doesn't believe, but I had to."

"Why?"

"It was the only way. His father is a commander at the port. We needed his help."

"*Why* is he helping us?" Ira said.

"He's jealous," Phaedra said. "He wants me for himself. He thinks that you will be burned up in the sun."

"Oh," Ira said. As he looked at the shadows on her beautiful body in the half-light, his heart sank. He wanted to die in the fires of her love, be consumed by her.

"Umm," she sighed contentedly as he reached for her. "My Lone Star man."

39

The Last Day

"Aliens Send Message of Peace and Love," the headline read. Leslie had sold her story to the *National Moon*, a tabloid that graced the supermarket checkout stands in every state of the Union.

Millard and Helen Hatlestead were dismayed to find other tabloid journalists prowling around their fields.

Back in Austin, Drake just shook his head as he stared at the *National Moon* spread across his desk. It was going to be difficult to persuade the publishers to let her stay on in any capacity at the *Sun*. She would certainly be demoted from the plum, political beat.

In San Francisco she was getting some coverage. She went on a popular morning talk show, Michael Kresse's "Focus."

"Did you actually see these aliens?" Kresse asked.

"I met with one of them?" she said.

"Where?"

"In Austin."

"What did he look like?"

"He was tall and dark, appeared to be about fifty, but I think he is actually several hundred years old."

"So he was ordinary-looking. Human, I mean?"

"Yes," she said. "We had coffee—"

"Now wait a minute," Kresse said. "You had *coffee* with an extraterrestrial?"

"Why not?"

"Why not indeed, ladies and gentleman? This is 'Focus,' and I have with me a young woman, a reporter from the *Texas Sun*, who claims to have met with alien beings. She also has a message of great importance for the people of earth. Tell us more about the message."

"The time has come," Leslie said.

"What time?"

"The time for the final awakening. The time for truth. The new millennium is dawning. The old ways are passing. All will be made new, and we will see how to live in peace, love, and harmony."

"This sounds suspiciously like some things I heard back around 1966 in this fair city," Kresse said.

"It's different this time," she said.

"What makes it different?"

"This time it is real. This time there is a messiah."

"A messiah? Who?"

"Have you heard the new hit song?" Leslie said, changing the subject. "The one by the Resonators?"

"You mean 'What is Truth?' "

"Yes, that's it. Listen to that song. It's no coincidence that it's suddenly a hit. This is a cosmic synchronicity. That song is the herald. It is making the path straight for the one who brings the new good news."

"Who is that?" Kresse said.

"Me."

The switchboard began to light up as every self-proclaimed San Francisco guru dialed in. Kresse sighed. It was going to be a long morning.

"You can't be serious," Lew said to Jistane.

"You are in no position to dictate what is and is not to be taken seriously," Jistane said.

"As usual," Lew said.

"What?" Lew's sardonic humor caught Jistane by surprise, momentarily confusing him.

"Nothing," Lew said. "But I can't agree to it."

"Why not?"

"You want me to play you in a tennis match. That's fine. I like tennis. In fact, I bet I could kick your ass."

Jistane frowned.

"But," Lew continued, "tennis is just a game. You want to put the entire fate of my world in the balance. It's ludicrous."

"If you are so confident that you can win—" Jistane began.

"That's beside the point!" Lew said. "You can't even judge a single human life on the basis of a tennis match! And you're talking about billions of lives."

"How do you judge a human life—a *single* human life?"

"I don't think this is the time to talk philosophy," Lew said.

"Then what *exactly* are we discussing?" Jistane said.

"We are discussing your insane system of justice," Lew said.

"Would you rather stand trial?" Jistane said.

"What do you mean?"

"I'm offering you a chance to save yourself. If you stand trial, you are almost certain to be convicted, and for you that means execution, *death*."

"Death is something I would rather avoid," Lew said.

"A sensible judgment," Jistane said. In spite of himself, he was starting to like the earthman a little. "This is your only real chance to do that."

"What about my world?" Lew said. "How do I justify risking the lives of billions just to save my skin?"

"*Now* we are talking philosophy," Jistane said.

"I suppose we are." Lew smiled tightly.

"Here's how you can justify it. Selena wants to settle the issue of earth, and *Tana*, by a complicated calculation."

"What calculation is that?"

"We will measure the rate of growth of a recent sunspot in one twenty-four-hour period. That derivative computation will be carried out to twenty decimal places. If the number of odd integers in the decimal expansion is less than ten, the earth will be spared, otherwise—"

"You people are *insane*!" Lew said.

"I have already noted your *opinion* on the matter, Mr. Slack," Jistane said. "I remind you again that it is irrelevant."

"So," Lew said slowly, "it's tennis or sunspots, is that it?"

"More or less," Jistane said.

"If I understand the calculation you propose," Lew said, "the odds are about even."

"Correct."

"Then why don't you just flip a coin?"

"We could do that," Jistane said, "but computing the first derivative of the area of a particular sunspot, has a certain—I don't know if *elegance* is the right word—"

"I see what you mean," Lew said. "How's your tennis game?"

Jistane smiled. "Care for a game?"

"This one's just for fun, right?"

"Fun?"

"I mean, we aren't playing for the high stakes—if we play now?"

"No."

"Alright."

Jistane took Lew to a long-abandoned court outside the Palace of the Sun. It was a beautiful setting, in a shallow dale surrounded by gently sloping terrain. Large trees gave the place an additional secluded quality.

The court was covered with leaves. It was cracked in several places, and near the center the surface buckled from the pressure of a giant root from a magnificent tree.

The net, however was new. Jistane had installed it himself. Leaning against the tree were two beautifully crafted wooden rackets.

"Nice," Lew said, testing the grip on one.

"They are hundreds of years old," Jistane said. "I had them restrung."

"With what?" Lew asked, bouncing the sweet spot off his palm.

"We use a vegetable fiber. It's a freshwater weed that grows in Lake Telamon. Remarkable strength and elasticity."

They were both dressed in classic Atlantean tennis attire. This consisted of drawstring pants, loose at the hips and tight around the ankles, and tunic tops. The pants had pockets for balls. The shoes were constructed of a superlightweight fabric on top. The soles were made from the inner lining of a tree bark that was both spongy and firm. The tops of the shoes came up around the ankles, making them look like little boots.

"It wasn't easy to find two outfits in good condition," Jistane said.

"Not a popular sport anymore?" Lew said, brushing some of the leaves off the court with his feet.

"We seem to have forgotten it," Jistane admitted. "Like so much else," he added barely above a whisper.

"What?" Lew said from the other side of the court.

"Nothing. Let's play."

"Not until we sweep these leaves away," Lew said. "I'm not going to risk spraining my ankle." *The fate of a world depends on it,* he thought.

Jistane looked at him as if he knew what he was thinking and smiled.

When they started playing Lew thought, *I can beat this guy easily. He's old!*

Jistane's serve was erratic. In order to keep it in he had to let up. Lew nailed several returns with short backswings and long follow-throughs.

The man's forehand was better than Lew's. His form was flawless, the racket flowed up and around in an easy motion that put depth and topspin on the ball. And he could hit the crosscourt corner with such uncanny accuracy.

But Jistane was slower than Lew. He could only execute such shots when he had time to set up. Lew found he could rob him of that time by varying his strokes.

Even so, as the set progressed, Lew was forced to reassess his opponent. Lew still won, but it wasn't the easy time he had initially expected. The score was six–three, and Lew had been forced to use every shot he knew.

A few leaves crunched underneath his feet when they shook at the net. "That's quite a backhand you have," Jistane said.

"Thanks. My net game is still pretty shaky."

"Indeed," Jistane said. "So is mine. I prefer to stay back and work the corners."

"You certainly know how to find them," Lew said.

* * *

Alan was allowed to visit Lew that evening.

"I heard the same thing from Selena," Alan said. "She wants to decide the issue on some random, cosmic event."

"Sunspots," Lew said.

"Yeah, something like that. Can you believe these people? How can a culture that is otherwise reasonably rational—"

"But what's so irrational about it, really?" Lew said.

"What do tennis or sunspots have to do with—"

"But don't you see," Lew said. "Otherwise, these things are decided by judges and juries. That puts a semblance of reason on it, but doesn't it often boil to down to what the judge had for breakfast or how a particular juror is feeling?"

"I don't know, Lew," Alan said. "Maybe it does. There is nothing we can do about it now anyway."

"I can refuse to play him," Lew said. He described the sunspot calculation that Selena favored.

"That would give the earth and you a fifty-fifty chance," Alan said.

"Not me," Lew said. "The only way I get to throw my fate into the balance is if I play tennis. Otherwise, I stand trial separately."

"They'll kill you," Alan said.

"Probably."

"Then you have to do it, Lew!"

"Where is the logic there, Alan?" Lew said. "My life is not even comparable to the lives of billions. It would be selfish in the extreme to insist on playing just to save my skin, when losing could mean—"

"Alright!" Alan said. "But the other way is like flipping a coin. You said you played him."

"Yeah."

"Well?"

"What?"

"How good is he, dammit! Can you take him?"

"I think so. His ground strokes are good. I've never seen a forehand like that, but he's old and slow. If I can keep him moving and take the net once in a while.''

''Can you do that?''

''Yeah. At least I did.''

''Then you have no choice,'' Alan said. ''You have to do it for the people of earth, not just for yourself.''

''But—''

''You just said you have a better than even chance of beating him,'' Alan said.

''That was practice!'' Lew said. ''Things could be very different in an actual match—for such high stakes.''

''That's a risk you have to take,'' Alan said.

Lew remained silent.

''Lew,'' Alan prodded.

''Yeah.''

''You don't want to die here, do you?''

''No, I don't.''

''You're a better tennis player than he is, aren't you?''

''I think so.''

''I'll see you later then.'' Alan slowly got up and walked out, leaving Lew alone.

One image kept coming back to fill his mind—Jistane pulling his racket up and around, the racket head open with the confidence of experience behind it. *I can still beat him,* he thought, and his mind was made up.

Cliff loved the trip over Poseidon Pass. He and Ira were alone on horseback. ''This is a fine animal,'' Cliff said. ''I wish I could breed some of this stock in Texas. You sit a horse pretty good, Ira.''

''It's been a while, but I used to ride some.''

''Can you believe it?'' Cliff said. ''We're riding our last ride over the last mountain pass in the solar system. Soon it will all be over.''

''Over?''

''And then it can all begin,'' Cliff said. ''When I feel this horse, breathe this air, and look at that mountain, I can almost question whether or not we are doing the right thing.''

''Are we?''

''Of course we are. This world is beautiful, but it is

also full of pain. When the fields are unified all pain and suffering will be gone."

"How's that?" Ira said. His horse stumbled over a loose rock, pitching Ira forward so that he had to grab the big animal's neck.

"All will be one," Cliff said. "It's as simple as that. Everything interconnected."

"Isn't it already that way?"

"A little bit," Cliff said, "but that's just the point. Things are already tending toward universal harmony. We are just helping to speed the process along. Our system of sun, planets, and life will become the model for the rest of the Universe, a pulsating, blissful entity where all forces are one, and all life is eternal."

"How do you know it will be that way?"

Cliff's eyes narrowed and his face got dark. "I know because I have faith," he said. "I have the book—"

He was interrupted by a rumbling sound and a shaking of the earth. His horse reared up, nearly throwing him to the ground. "Whoa there," he said and, at the same time, reached out to grab the reins of Ira's horse.

"Thanks," Ira said. "I think she was about to bolt."

"The ground must be unstable around here," Cliff said.

Their departure was simple. Phoenix's father led them to a private air lock, where there were no guards, no people at all. "Phoenix told me what you were going to do," he said.

"And you approve?" Cliff said.

"I think you are fools, and it's a shame to waste a ship."

"Then why are you helping us?" Ira said.

"I'm hoping it will show the boy once and for all that he needs to grow up, forget about all that nonsense he says he believes," the man said.

"You don't understand your son," Cliff said as he climbed into the ship.

The parent looked stricken for a moment, as if hearing the truth were the most painful thing imaginable, and then he quickly regained a mask of composure. "All you have to do is plot a course visually on this map.'' He touched a pad and a map of the solar system was displayed. He demonstrated the simple way to program a course as a trajectory on the screen.

''Like a personal computer with a graphical user interface,'' Ira said.

The man ignored him. ''You can even come back here if you change your mind,'' he said, closing the hatch.

Within seconds they were back out among the stars. Cliff was busily plotting a course to the sun. ''I don't want to take the most direct route in,'' he said. ''With the levity drive's exemption from the normal speed constraints of relativity, we could finish it in a few hours, but I think we should spiral in, make it a deliberate, patient act. It demands a more stately pace.''

''So how long are you going to draw it out?''

''About twenty-four hours.''

''The last day,'' Ira said.

''Yeah.''

40

Practical Advice

The match had sparked some interest. Stands had been erected in the natural arena. Overnight crews had managed to smooth down the area of the court warped by the big root.

It had been difficult since the Atlanteans treated trees as nearly sacred. They would not hack away at it. Instead they managed to soak the earth underneath and press it down. Then they quickly resurfaced the court with more clay.

It was only a temporary solution since the root would

eventually bounce back, but when Lew arrived and examined it he was impressed. "Nice," he said, jumping on the springy red clay.

"This is a clay court," Alan said.

"Yeah."

"You didn't tell me that." Alan sounded worried.

"What's the problem, Alan?"

"You have never played on clay! You're a hard court player."

"Alan, shut up!" Lew said. "The last thing I need now is something else to worry about. The stuff I practiced on at Alethis wasn't clay, but it was springy—like this. Clay is a different sort of game than I'm used to, but I find it suits my style. In fact, if I ever get out of here, I'm going to get me a clay court to play on. That won't be too much to ask, will it—for saving the world?"

They were early. Only a few people were milling about. Alan hit a few balls with Lew to help him warm up. "You *have* improved!" Alan said, unable to return a deep backhand from Lew.

When Monica arrived, Lew was sweating. "You should save your strength," she said.

"It takes me a long time to warm up," Lew said. "If I don't hit for a solid hour now, I'll spend the first set just warming up. That's OK for recreational play, but I'd say we are past the fun stage here."

"I wouldn't say that." It was Jistane. He had just arrived. Lew thought he looked taller, more imposing, and, most disturbing, *younger*. "I intend to enjoy myself," Jistane said. "You should relax and do the same." He smiled at Lew.

In their practice match, Lew had almost come to like Jistane. He at least found some respect for the man. But as he looked at the white teeth and the imposing figure in front of him the thought pressed forward insistently into his mind, *Is this man evil? Is this the face of darkness itself?* He suddenly felt very cold.

"Hello, Jistane," Lew said, and offered his hand.

"Your hand is icy," Jistane said after they shook. "Are you well?"

"I'm fine," Lew said weakly. "Do you want to hit some balls?"

"No," Jistane said. "I never warm up. I need to save my energy." He turned abruptly and went to sit by some others in the stands.

"Come on, Lew," Alan said. "We need to keep hitting."

Alan was worried at the change in Lew's game. His ground strokes, which had been masterful, were suddenly mushy and shallow. And his serve had collapsed.

"Let's sit down," Alan said after a few minutes of play. He noted that Jistane was watching them with a thin smile on his lips.

"What happened, Lew? Man, you look terrible. Your face is actually pale green," Alan said as they sat down on the opposite side of the court from Jistane.

"I don't know," Lew said, "I feel cold, tired. My stomach is awful, I'm horribly nauseated."

"He's psyching you out, Lew! Don't even look at him. He's watching us like a bird of prey right now. You've got to get back into it—"

"Back into it!" Lew said. "It hasn't even started yet, and I'm beat."

"No, listen—where are you going?"

"I've got to go throw up," Lew said. He walked quickly behind the stands and disappeared into the trees.

He came back, no longer green, but still pale. "Feel better?" Alan said.

"Yeah," Lew said.

The stands lining the sloping green terrain were almost full. The sun was bright on one side of the courts; the other was bathed in dappled, tree-filtered light.

"Beautiful," Alan said. "Look at the way the red clay surface picks up the yellow light. And the green!"

"Yeah, I see it," Lew said.

"I'm just trying to help," Alan said.

"Thanks."

"Here's my advice," Alan said. "If you get distracted, try to focus on the aesthetics of the scene. The court, the reds and greens, the rhythm of the game."

"Tennis is beautiful." Selena had just arrived. She sat next to Alan.

"It's nice to see a game again, after so many years. They did a wonderful job with the courts. Are you alright?" she said to Lew.

"Yeah," Lew said.

"Because," she said, "you look a little pale."

"You were married once, weren't you?" Cliff said.

Ira blinked and stared at Cliff for a moment, as if he hadn't heard the question. "Yeah," he said finally.

"So was I," Cliff said. "Damn shame the way things fall apart."

"Yeah."

"No more. No more fragmentation, disintegration, dissolution. I think that's why I was drawn to politics."

"How's that?"

"The order of it. Ever since I was a little kid I was fascinated by the idea of a government. First it was kings. I wanted to be a king. Then, when I learned we had a big hall full of people, I imagined that as a kind of stately gathering. I wanted to be part of it. Hell, I wanted to be the whole thing, the entire assembly."

"You got your wish—more or less."

"Not really. The legislature ain't nothing like I pictured. It's a mess. You know that. Nobody does anything naturally. It's all finesse, money, and schmoozing."

"What did you think it would be?"

"You know"—Cliff pointed outside to the stars—"all elegance and light. People moving independently, but synchronized for the greater good."

"No," Ira said, "it's not like that."

"But," Cliff said, "when we get done it will be."

"What makes you think there will be any people left at all—afterward, I mean," Ira said.

"You worry too much," Cliff said. "There may not be you and me as we are right now, but our essences will remain. It's like in Plato, you know—the higher form of a thing. It's all the higher forms that will still be here."

"I thought everything was supposed to be fused together in the unified field, a giant atom,'' Ira said.

''That's right.''

''Then where's the room for individuals, higher forms or any of that stuff?''

''You can't think of it that way!''

''What way?'' Ira said.

''You just can't,'' Cliff said.

''Alright,'' Ira said. For the first time he detected a note of worry in Cliff's voice.

You had to win seven games to take the set in Atlantean tennis. The winner had to win by two games as on earth. But a set only went to a tiebreaker if it was tied at seven games to seven. Matches were the usual best of five sets.

The first set was a disaster for Lew. He was overwhelmed by Jistane. The man had lost ten years, or so it appeared to Lew. Not only was he hitting the baseline corners with both his backhand and forehand ground strokes, he was moving with fluid grace.

''He's dancing all over the court,'' Lew said to Alan when they changed sides after the third game.

''Attack his serve,'' Alan said.

The advice helped. Jistane's serve was not powerful. Lew moved in a few centimeters and went after his opponent's serves.

Jistane was forced back in the subsequent rallies and Lew almost won the game. But he was still feeling weak and could not find his groove. The game went back and forth at deuce for several points, but Lew lost again.

When it was over Jistane had won seven–love.

''You're looking much better now,'' Alan said, as Lew drank from a water bottle.

''I'm getting creamed,'' Lew said.

''You're starting to get your forehand back,'' Alan said. ''Remember to follow through. And don't turn it over.''

''Thou shall not turn over thy forehand,'' Lew said, recalling what their chemistry professor in college had told them. He was a tennis enthusiast and had insisted on giving them free lessons one summer.

"Ah yes," Alan said, "Dr. Madison. I wonder if he still plays?"

"He would have to be at least ninety by now," Lew said.

"So?" Alan said. "I bet he's still alive, and he's still playing."

"Never say die," Lew said.

"That's the spirit."

Lew lost the first two games of the second set.

In serving the first point of the third game he tossed the ball high and reached for it, stretching almost to a jump.

The explosive serve caught Jistane off guard. Not a confident net player, Lew forced himself to come in and volley Jistane's weak return.

It was an easy put away. Lew looked at Alan as he walked back to the baseline, and his friend nodded solemnly.

On the next point Lew hung back, where he was more comfortable, at the baseline. *Up around your ears*! He recalled what his Swedish tennis instructor at Golden Gate Park would say, trying to get him to finish his swing with a full follow-through.

He hit a forehand that was weak and shallow. Jistane nailed it, winning the point.

On the next point Lew had to run to get a deep shot. He forced himself to pull his racket up and around, finishing with the strings by his ears. The shot was perfect, a low crosscourt with great topspin that barely cleared the net, yet sailed all the way to the opposite corner before dropping precisely inside the baseline.

Jistane barely got his racket on it and the return was a high, shallow lob.

Lew moved in for the kill. Jistane turned away to avoid getting hit in the face by the overhead. The ball smacked into his back.

"Sorry," Lew said. Jistane glared back at him.

Lew won the second set seven–five. "Just remember," Alan said as Lew was gulping an energy drink, "the fate of the world is in your hands."

"What the hell did you have to say that for?" Lew said.

"It's a joke," Alan said. "I'm trying to get you to lighten up."

"A joke?"

"Yeah, sometimes the truth is the funniest thing of all. You just have to look at it the right way," Alan said.

"Is that the secret of levity then?" Lew said.

"Exactly! Now you're talking," Alan said. "Just stay loose."

Lew fairly floated over the court in the first game of the third set. He was whipping his racket up and around with a fluid quickness that sent the balls flying in deep diagonal trajectories. When it was over Lew had won seven–three.

"See what I mean?" Alan said. "You just need to win this set and it's over."

"Jistane's getting mad," Lew said.

"So what?"

Jistane was able to translate his anger into fierce forehands that put Lew back on his heels in the first game of the fourth set. Jistane took the set seven–four.

"OK, Lew," Alan said. "This is it, the final set. Do or die."

"The man is getting mean," Lew said. "I'm faster, but he is nailing me back there when he connects, which is too often."

"Think levity," Alan said.

"Levity and the humor of truth," Lew said. "Is that it?"

"Yeah. It's the source of all humor. It's the funniest thing in the Universe. The joke's on you, but you still get the last laugh."

"I see," Lew said.

"Do you really?"

"No," Lew said, toweling his forehead and flexing his right hand.

"Don't worry about it. We may never fully understand, but that doesn't mean we can't continue the work."

"The work?"

"Just win," Alan said.

In the fifth and final set, Lew was distracted by thoughts of Diotima. He couldn't get the image of her beautiful body, luxuriant fur, and penetrating eyes out of his mind. He lost the first three games.

He recovered his concentration in the fourth game and the set turned into ferocious battle. He had never hit the ball so well. He was swinging as hard as could, but with timing and form that kept the ball low and in the court.

Jistane, not as fast, was hitting even harder. Lew needed intense concentration to return the man's shots.

Lew was serving for the match at seven–six. He only needed one more point. He swung the racket up after a perfect toss, knowing if he could connect the ordeal would be over.

Just as he made contact with the ball his old wrist injury caused a momentary loss of grip. He barely got the ball over the net, and Jistane put it away with a big crosscourt. Lew went on to lose the game.

They were tied at seven–seven. The match would be decided by a tiebreaker. Atlantean custom dictated that they take an hour break before playing it.

"This is crazy," Lew said. The stands were emptying as the spectators went to take refreshments in the shade of the trees. "We will both be cold and stiff when we start playing again."

"Keep moving," Alan said.

"I was finally getting warmed up," Lew said.

"What happened on that serve?"

"The wrist," Lew said.

"Ah yes, the past," Alan said. "We can never quite escape from it, can we?"

"I suppose not," Lew said. "I can't believe it has come down to this though."

"Believe it or not, it's the truth. That's the defining feature of truth. It stands apart from our beliefs and desires."

"Pretty harsh," Lew said.

"That's one way to see it," Alan said, "but you can put another spin on it."

"What's that?"

"If we did not have assurance of anything outside of our beliefs or desires, we would be trapped in our own passions. That's a good definition of hell, by the way."

"Imprisoned by our desires?" Lew said.

"And their forms are legion," Alan said. "So truth must stand apart. You wanted to win that point, but your wrist failed. It served to remind you of the past, of things outside yourself. You see. In the truth is our only hope of freedom—ultimately."

"Do you have any practical advice?" Lew said.

"Yeah," Alan said. "His backhand is getting weak. Attack it."

41

Solar Reflex

Ira was beginning to feel the heat. "We'll suffocate in here," he said, wiping sweat from his brow.

"When I first came to the legislature they didn't have air-conditioning," Cliff said. "Man was it hot in there. They kept cold beer on hand. It was hell on the law, but those were the days!" He was exuberant.

"How much longer!" Ira said. "We could die!"

"Not long at all now," Cliff said. He picked up the grail.

"It looks different," Ira said. "It's radiating."

"The process is beginning," Cliff said. He passed his hand through the thin aura that was visible around the grail. "We are the messengers, and this is the message."

"What message?"

"The real is seeming, bright as any sun!"

"But what does that mean?"

"It means this is it! The Eyes of Texas are watching! We're gonna do it! You ever been to the state fair, Ira."

"In Dallas?"

"Of course Dallas! The greatest state fair in the country! Have you ever been inside the Hall of Texas?"

"Yeah, I think so."

"They got a big gold lone star on the wall in the back. On field trips to the fair, when the other kids were riding the roller coaster on the midway, I would sit and stare at that big gold star for hours. It gave me goose bumps. Now I know why."

"Why?"

"The lone star, man! What it symbolizes! It stands for the unified field! Don't you see! We are fulfilling the prophecy!"

"Prophecy? What prophecy? You can't mean that the founders of Texas were prophets. They were just land grabbers who took advantage of Mexico."

"Maybe they weren't fully aware of what they were doing. But who is?" Cliff said. "All history points to this moment. Any moment really. Haven't you ever glimpsed the truth of it, that the present is the full ripening of all that has gone before. But now! This moment is truly the final one. The lone star is the great symbol for the solar atom, which we are about to create, where all matter and spirit in the field of the sun will come together in a grand harmony more complex and more beautiful than anything before it."

"When?" Ira said. "How much longer?"

Cliff got very quiet. He was staring out the past the sun. His face was bathed in starlight and seemed to reflect the very void. Then he let out a great Texas whoop that made Ira shiver.

"Yeeehah!" He pushed a lever in the panel.

Ira felt the ship shudder, and the sun loomed even larger.

Jistane was serving for the match. He was up six–five in the tiebreaker.

Lew stood waiting, trying to keep from trembling. *That*

it should all come down to this! he thought.

"Come on Lew!" Alan shouted. "It ain't over yet!"

It was a powerful serve. Lew tried to put some topspin on the return but the ball only carried to midcourt. Jistane moved up and blasted a deep, down the line, forehand shot to Lew's backhand.

No way, Lew thought. He knew he couldn't get set in time to manage any sort of decent return. He was about to pull his racket up in a classic backhand motion, even while he felt the shot was doomed.

Suddenly his mind was filled with images of Diotima. Time seemed to slow down. Only dimly aware of the rapidly approaching ball, Lew was seeing the beautiful cat woman.

"Spank it," she said, flicking her tail in the direction of the ball. Then she wrapped her tail around in front of her chest and pulled the tip of it across her body. The motion was exactly that of a slice backhand shot.

Lew never ever used the slice backhand. He had never even practiced it. For him it existed only in theory. But as Diotima's image vanished he found himself mimicking her motion, pulling his racket across and slightly under the ball.

The shot was perfect. It was shallow, but the spin put Jistane totally off-balance. He missed it completely as it spun away from him. He stood for a moment and stared at Lew, as if he knew. Then he walked back to the baseline.

Lew won the next point. He was up eight–seven. *One more*, he thought, *and it's over.*

"The sun knows," Cliff said.

The grail's aura was brighter, and Ira thought he saw the solar sphere expanding. A gentle wave hit the ship.

"What was that?" Ira said.

"It begins," Cliff said. "That was the first in a series of waves that will get stronger as we merge with the sun. It's probably a levity wave." Suddenly Cliff's whole body shook, and he delivered a mighty sneeze.

"Photo sneeze reflex again?" Ira said.

"Yeah," Cliff said, "the fields will be unified from my nose on out." He didn't have time to laugh at his joke since he was seized by a violent series of sneezes. Another more powerful wave hit the ship.

His mind was filled with images of perfect harmony, all things in one, no more differentiation, no more crime, no more individuals, and no more newspapers. He didn't like it.

While Cliff was completely consumed by his sneezing, Ira reached for the control panel. He reversed the trajectory.

Cliff tried to stop him, but the man was paralyzed by his Texas-sized sneezing fit. "What are you doi—AaaaChoo!"

"I'm saving us all!" Ira said. "You, me, the legislature, and the *Texas Sun*. You are about to create a world with no spontaneity, one giant solar reflex!"

Cliff reached for Ira with his big arm. He would have done serious damage, but was again seized by a round of sneezing triggered by the powerful solar light. Ira took advantage of the moment. "This is for the Eyes of Texas," he said, and threw his fist into Cliff's jaw. The Speaker fell limply back in his chair.

Ira plotted a course back to Atlantis.

Jistane's serve had a wicked spin. Lew barely got it back. Jistane was unable to capitalize on the weak return, however, and the two began trading ground strokes, slugging it out.

It was the longest rally Lew had ever played. He couldn't remember seeing one as long. *This has to end*, he thought several times as he watched the ball sail over the net and land dangerously close to the baseline.

But he dared not ease up. Jistane was playing his best. Lew sensed that if he did not win the point, the man would regain momentum and finish the match quickly.

Lew hit a deep, down the line forehand. Jistane replied with a crosscourt backhand that sent Lew running to the other side of the court. He hit a good return, but he was forced into a vulnerable position.

Jistane took advantage of the situation and smacked one deep into the forehand court. Lew knew he couldn't run it down.

He was moving toward the impossible target when the first solar wave hit. It was a mild vibration that passed through everything with a fluid, thrilling ripple. It reminded Lew of something.

Levity, he thought. *The secret of gravity is humor.* He saw the earth destroyed, the solar system reduced to nothing or everything, and he didn't care. It was all so absurd. An all-consuming laughter began to well up in him from a place he had forgotten, but was, in truth, never very far from his experience.

He forced the laugh back down, sensing it was energy he could put to better use. His feet came a few millimeters off the court's surface. He was nearly weightless, and he pushed delicately with his toes and heels, dancing across the court.

To those watching it appeared that Lew was dancing sideways with miraculous speed. But he knew he was flying.

He got to the ball and was about to try a drop shot, which he felt certain would work, but he changed his mind. *No sense in going out that way,* he thought, and slammed a forehand with everything he had.

The ball shot over and deep. Jistane had no chance to get to it, but he cried that it was out.

It was close, so close that Lew held his breath and clenched his racket until his knuckles turned white.

But the judges were all in agreement. The ball had just caught the line.

"Yes!" Alan screamed.

Lew walked to the net. As they shook, he tried to read Jistane. The man looked at Lew with the most curious expression, as if he both feared and admired Lew. *He knows I flew*, Lew thought. *He knows it*!

Alan bounded onto the court and embraced Lew. "Well played!"

"Did you feel that?" Lew said to Alan.

"Of course," Alan said. Just then a larger wave hit.

This one was more threatening. Lew again felt the laughter rise from deep within, but he wasn't sure he could control it.

"The cosmic joke," Alan whispered.

"What do you mean?" Lew said.

"I mean that maybe Cliff wasn't as crazy as I wanted to believe. I know you felt it. I felt it, too."

"What is it?"

"Some say," Alan said, "that the Universe ends with the punch line to a vast joke. The story of your life, my life, all lives, all evolutionary processes, both biological and physical, come to a conclusion. And that conclusion reveals a cosmic sense of humor so strange and yet so obvious that we will all be swept away in the laughter."

"Swept into what?" Lew said.

"*That* is the question. Cliff thinks it's the unified field," Alan said.

"So the grail—"

"May actually be the catalyst he was looking for," Alan said. "I shouldn't have been so skeptical. Especially after what we have been through. I'll bet that grail of yours is made of superdense nous."

"Nouons," Lew said.

"Yeah," Alan said, "thought particles, arranged in a supersymmetry of metallic crystalline structure. No telling what such a substance would trigger if it were injected into the heart of the sun.

"Supersymmetry?" Lew echoed.

"Yeah," Alan said, "the vector space structure prefigures that found in ordinary atoms and molecules. But supersymmetry pales in comparison to what a solar fusion-triggered reaction could bring about."

"What?"

"*Perfect* symmetry," Alan said.

"Perfect symmetry?"

"No more individual structures of atoms, planets, minerals, no more you or me."

"What then?"

"We may be about to find out," Alan said.

The crowd had not moved since the second wave. All were waiting for something both longed for and dreaded. But nothing came, and the moment passed, becoming one among many, not the ultimate one at the end of all things.

That evening Lew and Alan dined with Monica and Selena in Selena's home. Lew was enchanted by the sparkling fountain and euphoric over his victory. "That last shot!" he said. "I've never hit the ball so hard. Did you see the way it came down, just catching the line? That's *topspin.*"

"I'm afraid I have some bad news," Monica said.

"What?" Lew said, as if such a thing were not possible.

"The waves we experienced earlier today triggered some small earthquakes in Mount Poseidon. It's the most unstable area of the continent. You know Tana is from Eidon?"

"Yeah," Lew said, slowly sipping his wine.

"We let her go back home while waiting for the verdict. Her parents have a vacation home in the foothills—"

"What happened?" Lew said, putting his glass down.

"A number of people were killed, Tana's family among them. Their house was buried."

"Tana's family," Lew said slowly. "What about her?"

"Her too," Monica said.

Lew stared at the fountain and the brightly colored birds and foliage. Then he turned to Alan. "And you thought she was evil," he said.

"I was wrong," Alan said. Lew got up angrily. "Please, Lew—" Alan said, but his friend was gone.

"Let him go," Selena said. "He needs to be alone for a while."

"Something else," Monica said.

"What's that?" Alan said.

"Tana was pregnant."

"So am I," Selena said, looking at Alan.

"And Phaedra," Monica said. "It is hardly a scientific, random sample, but I would say all the evidence points to an infertility problem with Atlantean males."

"So you may have some use for earthlings, after all," Alan said.

"Possibly," Selena said.

42

Stuff of Dreams

When the Guardians reconvened they voted unanimously to transport the four earthlings back to earth. Ira, much to his surprise, had successfully piloted the ship back to Atlantis. Cliff was sober and subdued when they arrived.

"You know," Jistane said to Alan before his final departure, "if you dabble again in levity, you risk bringing the entire matter back before the Guardians. And you may not fare so well if there is a next time."

"Don't worry," Alan said, as he followed Cliff and Ira into the Atlantean transport. "I have other things to work on now."

"Like what?" Jistane could not conceal his intense curiosity. Alan merely smiled and boarded the ship.

Lew was the last to enter. "You played well," Jistane said.

"Would you really have killed us all if I had lost?" Lew said. When he received no answer he said, "Maybe we'll play again someday."

"Maybe," Jistane replied. It was impossible to read the expression in his dark eyes.

The trip back was uneventful but beautiful. A few days later Ira was lounging with Cliff beside the Speaker's swimming pool under what seemed an impossibly ordinary Texas sun.

"I couldn't stay with her. I see that now," Ira said. The hill country was alive in a warm, mellow evening glow.

"Sounds like sour grapes to me," Cliff said. He was standing on the diving board. Ira noted that the man had lost weight and was more muscular. He actually resembled the image in the absurd painting that hung in his office. "The woman made it clear that she wouldn't have you."

"But she's going to have my baby," Ira sighed, sipping his beer.

"Space child, love child," Cliff said, and dived in.

Later, when they were eating barbecue on the patio, Ira said, "Are you sorry we didn't go through with it, Cliff?" The sun was now a bright orange on the rolling horizon.

"Not anymore," Cliff said, "and I'll tell you why. It comes to my mind these days that what happened was exactly what was supposed to happen. The unified field is not what I thought. If we had succeeded, there wouldn't be any Texas, no legislature, no *Sun*. Real unity has to preserve everything just like it is even while it brings it all together.

"Truth is resonance like the book says," he went on, "but the resonance we nearly created would not have done it justice. It would have been a wonder of the Universe, a nice picture. But the shape of truth has to be completely independent of what we imagine as right or beautiful. It is a resonance that can hold what is always right in front of you. Before we go trying to change the world into something we think we want we should try to understand it as it is. Not one of us can yet see what is trying to shine through in the most ordinary moment of the day. Do you follow me?"

"I guess," Ira said. "We saved Leslie's ass though. Those stories she wrote for the *National Moon* would have been enough to end her career, but when the solar waves hit, everyone went a little crazy for a while. Hell, even Drake started to take her seriously."

"But you got your job back, the political beat where you belong."

"And Leslie's back reporting murders. One thing

though,'' Ira added wistfully, staring into the sun as it dipped below the horizon.

''What's that?''

''It sure would be nice if I could tell this story, even part of it.''

''And lose your job for good,'' Cliff said.

''There is still the little matter of missing funds that have been tracked to the Speaker's office,'' Ira said.

''That's all taken care of,'' Cliff said.

''How so?''

''The comptroller has given me a clean bill of health. Ask him tomorrow. It seems that some of that funny money has shown up on the AG's books. *There's* a story for you.''

''How do you do it, Cliff?''

''It's politics man, just politics.''

Alan approached his hometown with a sense of dread. Grafton was such a normal place, but for him it had been the opposite. His father's work, which sometimes bordered on manic paranoia, still haunted him. Whatever he had seen out there in New Mexico, those many years ago, had stayed with him all his life. As a boy Alan had thought his father's eccentric passion interesting, and as a teenager he had found it ridiculous. Now he was beginning to suspect that his father had encountered a piece of the truth.

His mother had never understood. She simply smiled when she thought it appropriate, but mostly worked hard holding the family together on that crazy farm.

Alan was glad of the season. The sky was a brilliant blue, and the air fresh and warm. The evening would turn deliciously cool. The memory of North Dakota winters still made him shiver. Just thinking about it, he could almost feel the bone-chilling winds at forty degrees below zero.

He found the coffee shop. It had been one of his dad's favorite places to sit and talk many years ago. Talk that no longer seemed so wild and crazy.

Helen Hatlestead was there. She served him a cup of

coffee and a muffin. "Where you from?" she said.

"Texas."

"Where in Texas?"

"Austin."

"Really?" she said, "We had someone from there through here a little while ago."

"It's a happening place," Alan said, sipping his coffee.

"I'm surprised you didn't try to find an espresso bar. That Austin woman was pretty picky about her coffee."

"So am I," Alan said, "but I didn't come here for the coffee. I came here to see you."

"Not another reporter!" she said.

"No."

"Because that business is over and done with. When those strange vibrations hit everybody went a little nuts, too. People were talking about learning how to fly and migrating to the stars, the secret of gravity. It just made me laugh."

"It made a lot of people laugh," Alan said.

"Who are you?"

"Alan Fain," he said. "I used to live here."

"Well my, my, didn't you turn out to be a handsome specimen. Who would have thought it? That skinny little kid, the one who liked books more than girls."

"That's what they said?" Alan was clearly upset.

"Some people."

"It wasn't true."

"I can see that," she said.

On their way out to the Hatlestead farm Alan said, "Helen, no offense, but would you mind if we went by that espresso bar first? I'd like to get some decent coffee."

"Sure," Helen said. "Why not?"

Millard took Alan out to his barn. "Man!" Alan said. "This is quite a setup you have here."

"Not really," Millard said. "We monitor the sky, and I conduct my little experiments. Nothing fancy."

"But it is!" Alan said, examining the equipment. "I've never seen anything like this. Simple maybe, but elegant. Did you work with my father?"

"Not much," Millard said. "We talked. I guess he's

the one who sparked my interest initially. We were never colleagues. Your dad kept pretty much to himself, but so do a lot of folks out here."

Millard led Alan to the vault where he had stashed the charred remnants of Miranda. "I should warn you," he said. "She's pretty bad."

Alan watched with a terrible sense of irreversible doom as Millard slid the coffin out of the wall. He unclamped it and opened the lid.

The sight filled them with such horror that they both were speechless for a few moments. Finally Millard managed a weak, "Oh, my God."

Miranda was staring up at them. She was pitifully emaciated, little more than a skeleton covered with skin. Her burns were still severe, but they had started to heal. It was the haunted look in those eyes that had caused Millard to cry out. They had the look of a soul who has woken to eternal damnation in the depths of Dante's Inferno.

"Help me with her," Alan said finally, barely able to manage a whisper.

They took her to a couch and covered her with a blanket. Alan tried to give her some water, but she could not swallow. "Can you hear me?" he said.

She tried to speak but made a sound like sandpaper on dry wood. She blinked her eyes several times.

"You're going to be alright," Alan said. "I need to get some things to help you. I'll be back as soon as I can. OK?"

She blinked again.

"I had no idea," Millard said as they walked to the door. "She was burned so badly. I thought—"

"It's not your fault," Alan said. "She has great regenerative powers. Frankly I was surprised, too."

"Will she be alright?" Millard said.

"She is obviously alive, but whether or not she can recover anything like normal functionality is another question. The first thing to do is get some liquids in her. Where is the nearest pharmacy?"

Alan set up an IV drip. Within a few hours she could speak. "What happened?" she said weakly.

"You saved the world," Alan said.

"No, I mean out there."

"On Atlantis?"

"Yes."

"It's over," Alan said.

"Tell me," she said.

Alan described the end of the trial, the tennis match, and Tana's death.

"Poor girl," she said. "So Lew saved the world as well."

"Yeah," Alan said.

"What is it? Are you jealous?"

"Of Lew? No, it's not that."

"What then? Something's troubling you."

"You sound like my mother," Alan said.

She laughed. Her whole body shook. It was a shocking sight to see bones shaking underneath Helen's pajamas. The skin covering her lips cracked a little. She wiped away blood on her sleeve. "I'm alright," she said in response to Alan's look of horror. "Tell me what's wrong."

Alan described his romance with Selena.

"So you're going to be a father. Why didn't you stay with her?"

"She wouldn't have me," Alan said. "I actually wanted to. Or I thought I did."

"Not like you," Miranda said.

"No," he agreed. "But poor Ira." Alan described his affair with Phaedra.

"Sounds like he was more infatuated than you," she said.

"I wasn't infatuated!" Alan said.

"Sorry," she said.

"But you're right," Alan said. "He was. And she wouldn't have him either."

"Sounds like they need a few good earthmen up there. If they are going to survive."

"Maybe they don't want to survive."

"Maybe not."

"How do you feel?" Alan said.

"I'll be fine," she said, but Alan could see she was worried.

"Do you think you can walk a little yet?"

She shook her head, and a tear rolled down her cheek.

A few weeks later Alan bought a wheelchair. Miranda was strong enough to travel, and he wanted to get her back to his lab in Austin.

The Resonators were still getting a fair amount of airplay. "Isn't that Lew's band?" Miranda asked. She was sitting in her wheelchair, eating oatmeal and sipping orange juice, when the song came on the radio.

"Yeah," Alan said. He slouched a little in the booth; the red vinyl made a sour squeak in protest. "But that's not Lew on guitar."

"Surely—" she began.

"No," Alan interrupted. "Lew wrote the song, but all the copyrights, including the band's name are to the band as an entity. It's as if he never had anything to do with them." He bit into his burger. The big Texas 1015 onion slice made a giant crunch.

"But surely they want him back?"

"They feel he abandoned them," Alan said. "And besides, they like their new guitar player. He does have a more polished sound. Listen to that riff. Lew could never play that."

"But his sound had more soul," Miranda said.

"I know it."

They pulled into Alan's driveway late at night. Lew met them and helped Miranda into her wheelchair.

"Something arrived for you yesterday," Lew said when they were all inside.

"What?" Miranda said.

Lew handed her a letter. It was peculiar in that it had neither stamp nor postmark. The paper was heavy and coarse. The flap was sealed in green sealing wax. The imprint was of a serpent wrapped around a tree.

"Who delivered it?" she said.

"I don't know; I just found it in the mailbox."

Alan handed her a letter opener. She sliced through the paper and all three instantly smelled a fresh wild scent. It was gone in an instant, but it left little doubt about the letter's origin. After she read it she handed it to Lew. Her thin hand seemed heavy.

Lew read aloud,

Dear Miranda,

The strange shock waves hit yesterday. There were two of them, and they had the most remarkable effect. Arlandia is again reborn. All here is even more new and bristling with a deeper energy, a cosmic resonance.

We no longer need the sun. Our photosynthesis can now make energy from starlight—and something else, even more amazing. The life here has tapped into energy from structures that lie beneath the atomic nucleus. These may be the very essences of consciousness.

Or maybe not. But the time has come to move out. Today I begin the journey, leaving the solar system, going to I know not where, but I am sure this is only the beginning. We are prepared now to thrive in the spaces between the stars.

Maybe I will find Don out there. Maybe he needs me.

I regret that you are not here, but then maybe it is for the best. I think, after all, that you are still a little of the earth, and would need it.

Good-bye,
Raya

They went down to the lab, Alan and Lew both carrying Miranda. Alan tried to raise Arlandia on the nouancer, but got nothing.

"She's gone," Miranda said finally. "Give it up."

"You need to rest," Alan said.

"I still can't even move my legs," she said hollowly.

* * *

The next morning Lew and Alan met Ira and Cliff in the Speaker's office. The sun, reflecting off the capitol building's pink limestone outside, gave the chamber a subdued glow.

Cliff was particularly interested in Lew's adventures beneath the surface of the moon. "So the whole thing is an airtight, artificial world," Cliff said.

"What makes you think it's artificial?" Lew said.

"The moon is a spaceship," Cliff grinned. "Those Alethians came here before the dawn of recorded history from outside the solar system. That's their vehicle."

"Why?" Lew said.

"Don't know," Cliff said, "but it all makes sense. There are references to it in the *Secrets of the Golden Grail*, obscure and difficult to decipher, but they are there."

"Blake talks about them, too," Alan said.

"What?" Ira said. "Where?"

"He doesn't mention the Alethians by name, but he talks about an ancient race of giants and their relationship to the lost continent of Atlantis. It does all fit. The Alethians are humanoid, but alien. They came in their own interstellar vehicle, which is disguised as a small planet, the moon. Why they came is a mystery. But they are responsible for teaching the prehistoric hominids of earth the secrets of language and agriculture. The rest is history."

"What about Atlantis, though?" Lew said.

"The Alethians had a special relationship with the Atlanteans. Why is a mystery, but the culture of ancient Greece is our Atlantean legacy here on earth," Alan said.

"What happened to the Alethians?" Ira said.

"Indeed," Alan said.

"They may still be here," Cliff said.

"Where?" Lew said.

"Possibly they have transformed themselves genetically so as to blend in with the rest of us. They probably did this sometime after the ascension of Atlantis. When they lost their primary advocates down here, they decided to try and shape human history from within.''

''Interesting theory,'' Alan said. ''So who, in your opinion, are some of the Alethians we may have heard of?''

''Stephen F. Austin, Sam Houston.'' Cliff said the names of the Lone Star State's founders with only a trace of irony.

''George Washington or Abraham Lincoln?'' Ira said.

''Maybe.''

''What about Newton, Einstein?'' Alan said.

''I don't know. I'm not sure that science would have interested them as much as you might suppose.''

''John Lennnon?'' Lew said.

Cliff smiled. He was looking at the picture that still hung in its place across from his desk. The Golden Grail stood on an oak table beneath the frame. He got up, walked over to it, and picked it up. He passed it around.

None of them could any longer read the inscription. It was still there, but in a language ancient and indecipherable.

''What do you suppose it really is?'' Ira asked, handing it back to Cliff.

Cliff held it up to the window, where it caught the pink-and-yellow light. He popped a finger against it and the room was filled with a bright resonance. ''This, gentlemen,'' he said, setting it back down, ''is the stuff that dreams are made of.''

43

A Real Texas Night

"I can't believe that she wasn't real. She *felt* real and she killed Tantalyes," Lew said. Miranda was sleeping in the basement lab. They had just finished a delicious meal of curried shrimp that Alan had prepared.

"Think about it, Lew," Alan said. "The Alethians were obsessed with truth. If you wanted to discover the essence of truth, what would you do?"

"I don't know," Lew said.

"Their resonator, the one you found, is what powered their spaceship, the moon. It could produce a powerful levity drive. But it could also be used to manipulate the aether in other ways. It generates nouograms, images of consciousness.

"That made it the perfect instrument to investigate truth. If you could create the perfect illusion that seemed absolutely real, completely true, then—"

"Then what?" Lew asked.

"Don't you see? If you could create the perfect illusion, and then—if you could find the difference, discover how it is *not* the same as the real and the true, you would have it, the essence of truth."

"But did they find it?" Lew said.

"Now that's a really interesting question," Alan said, offering no answers.

After a long silence Lew finally asked the question that was on both their minds. "Will she be alright?"

"I'm worried," Alan said. "She has gained weight, and her burns are almost healed, but she still can't walk. I can't find any spinal fractures. I don't understand it."

"And once she could fly," Lew said.

"And may again," Alan said.

"But can't we help her?" Lew said.

"I'm doing all I can!" Alan snapped. "I'm sorry. I didn't mean to shout. It's just so awful—I'm so responsible I—"

"It's alright," Lew said. "I know you're trying. Let's not talk about it any more just now."

"Yeah." Alan sighed. He got very quiet for a few moments, and then said, "I'm sorry about your band, Lew. I guess if it weren't for me, you would be a famous rock star now."

"I guess so," Lew said.

"What are you going to do? Go back to San Francisco?"

"I've thought about it, but—"

"What?"

"Well, Cliff said he could get me a job."

"Doing what?" Alan said.

"The Texas secretary of state needs a data base person."

"But you can't!" Alan said. "You can't go back to being a computer programmer—"

"Software engineer," Lew interrupted. "And who are you to tell me what I can do?"

"OK," Alan said. "But I just thought that after all that's happened—"

"What?"

"I don't know." Alan sounded tired. "I'm thinking about looking for my dad," he said after several silent moments.

"You said he was dead," Lew said.

"He may be, but I don't know for certain. There is a lot I never told you about the past."

"Good luck," Lew said.

"Thanks."

About a month later, Lew got back from a hard day at the office. Alan had gone off to discover his past and had left the house to Lew and Miranda for as long as they wanted it.

It was a balmy October evening and Lew found Miranda sitting in her wheelchair on the front porch. She was smiling, which cheered Lew since he so seldom saw her smile anymore. She was back up to a normal weight. There were a few gray strands in her long black hair, and her skin was light and fair, no longer green. It looked to Lew as if the trauma had aged her about ten years, but this made her more, not less, attractive, in his opinion.

He sat in the deck chair beside her and they watched the sunset. He had not spoken of their recent adventures since Alan's leaving, but he felt compelled to say something.

"I never mentioned it, Miranda, but during the last point of the match, when I finally won, I flew."

"What did it feel like?" she said.

"It was like, all of a sudden, some ancient curse was lifted, and I just remembered, and it was the easiest thing in the world."

"I know," she said.

"It was that second solar wave, triggered by Cliff and Ira bringing the grail so close to the sun, that did it," Lew said.

"I felt it, too," she said. "It's what brought me back to consciousness inside that coffin in North Dakota."

"Maybe you will get it back," he said, "and fly again." He immediately regretted his words when he saw the look on her face.

"For now," she said, "I'm truly the woman who fell to earth."

"You know," he said, "you and I have something in common."

"How so?"

"Well, I never had the powers you did, but I flew in other ways."

"The Mind-Surfer episode, you mean?" she said.

"You could call it that," he smiled.

"Anyway, I had to come back to earth, and I'm finding these days that maybe it's not so bad after all."

"Me too," she said with a mysterious smile.

"What do you mean?" he said.

Slowly, with some obvious pain and stiffness, she got up from her chair and walked to the porch railing. She was wearing a cotton dress, and the white folds flowed around her legs.

"Fantastic!" Lew said as he got up to stand beside her. He hesitated a moment and then took her hand, pressing it gently.

"Hungry?" he said.

"Yeah,"

"Let's go celebrate. I'll take you out to Jeffrey's."

"But that's so expensive," she said.

"They're paying me pretty well," he said, "for a state job, anyway. Come on."

They went out into the warm Texas night.